THE **CUBS** AND THE *Kabbalist*

HOW A KABBALAH-MASTER HELPED THE CHICAGO CUBS WIN THEIR FIRST WORLD SERIES SINCE 1908

A NOVEL BY

BYRON L. SHERWIN

West Oak PRESS
Denton, Texas

West Oak Press
1004 West Oak Street
Denton, Texas 76201

www.westoakpress.com

Printed in the United States of America

09 08 07 06 05   010 1 2 3 4 5

This book is a work of fiction. Names, characters, places, organizations, and incidents are either products of the author's imagination or are used fictitiously. Any resemblance to actual events or locales or persons, living or dead, is entirely coincidental.

Cover illustration and book design by Crystal Wood

Library of Congress Control Number 2005922302

ISBN-13: 978-0-9764874-0-1
ISBN-10: 0-9764874-0-3

It breaks your heart.
It is designed to break your heart.
The game begins in the spring, when everything else begins again,
and it blossoms in the summer, and then as soon as the chill rains
come, it stops and leaves you to face the fall alone . . .
just . . . when you need it most, it stops.

A. Bartlett Giamatti
A Great and Glorious Game
President, Yale University 1978-1986;
Commissioner of Baseball, 1989.

Dedication

For my wife, Judith,
and her fellow Cubs fans,
who have hope despite experience,
and
for my friend, Neil Rosenberg, M.D.,
who implanted the seed of an idea
that became this book.

RABBI JAY LOEB WAS SURE THAT HIS WIFE, Tamara, was having an affair. What other explanation could there be? She would disappear for hours at a time; sometimes in the middle of the day, sometimes in the evening, and occasionally on weekends. In recent weeks, the other lawyers at Tamara's firm, her secretary, and her clients would call Loeb looking for the elusive Tamara. Her office phone, cellular phone and pager all produced recordings of Tamara's voice—but not the person to whom the voice belonged.

Maybe it's my fault, Loeb confided to himself. *Perhaps I'm no longer the companion, the lover, who can satisfy her needs. Life and work has changed us both over the years. Maybe each of us now lives with a stranger to whom we happen to be married.*

Who could it be? Loeb asked himself. *Maybe one of her partners, or one of those handsome young associates at the firm? Or someone she met by chance? Is there only one, or more than one?*

Her disappearances had begun in April, and now it was only May. *When did she have time for such a thing to develop? How can she have time for a lover? But, where there's a will, there's a way.* And strong-willed Tamara liked to get her own way.

Loeb sat at home in his book-lined study, his head in his hands. He could not concentrate on grading the exams stacked up in front of him. He had lost his appetite for studying the learned tomes that were crucial to his research. All he could think about was Tamara, and why she seemed to be dripping out of his life, like water through a sieve.

Meanwhile, on that morning in May, Tamara Loeb was in court awaiting the verdict in the biggest case in her legal career. The press had given extensive coverage to the trial. The *Chicago Daily News* had called her "the best Chicago trial lawyer since Clarence Darrow." The case was being discussed in law schools throughout the country. Though it was a *pro bono* case, which meant no huge tally of legal fees, it gave her law firm needed favorable publicity in the wake of the firm's recent string of highly publicized cases in defense of corrupt politicians and white-collar criminals.

The client in this case was not a large corporation, but an African-American man named Shawon White. A college honors student and star athlete, White had assaulted a Chicago policeman who had raped his fifteen-year-old sister. The policeman was never charged. Nor had DNA samples of semen been taken from White's sister when she was rushed to the hospital after she was beaten and raped. Nor had the policeman been tried for accepting bribes from local gangs for looking the other way while they peddled narcotics to children in the schoolyards of Chicago's west side. Suspended with pay, the officer still awaited trial on bribery charges after being caught red-handed by members of the Police Department's Internal Affairs division. Meanwhile, Shawon White languished in prison.

While in prison, White had ordered by mail some sexually explicit magazines. The prison guards refused to give them to him, claiming that they were pornographic. Believing that his constitutional rights had been violated, White asked for legal representation. The law firm of Farnsworth, McPherson, Blair, Lawless and Flaherty had pulled political strings to get the *pro bono* case assigned to them. In Chicago, even getting a case without fees had a price.

Having their top female litigator, Tamara Loeb, defend the constitutional rights of an African-American client incarcerated for defending the honor of his sister against a crooked cop was just what the Farnsworth firm needed to deal with its public image problem. Tamara led a legal team that—not surprisingly—included the firm's only African-American and only Hispanic-American attorneys.

Tamara knew that this could be a precedent-setting case that could potentially go to the U.S. Supreme Court. This was the kind of case she had been waiting for her entire career. During her years of practicing law, Tamara had become bored with writing and negotiating contracts, tired of corporate law. It was for a case like this that she had become a lawyer. But, practicing civil-rights law could not adequately supplement her husband's meager salary. So year after year, she sat in her office doing the kind of law that she had once promised herself never to practice.

Tamara's preparation for trial had been impeccable. The press and the legal community had followed it closely. Though Tamara was fast becoming a local legal celebrity, her husband had other concerns. "How will it look," he had asked her, "when the headlines read: RABBI'S WIFE MAKES AMERICA SAFE FOR PORNOGRAPHY?"

The courtroom was packed with journalists, civil rights activists, the top partners from Farnsworth, and the friends and family of Shawon White, including his still-traumatized sister, whom Tamara had strategically sat right in front of the judge's line of vision during the trial. Outside the courtroom were TV and radio crews, ready to broadcast the verdict as soon as it was announced. During the trial, Tamara could not comment to the press, but she knew that once the trial was over, the press would be all over her. She sat nervously, awaiting the judge and his verdict.

Usually, in a case like this, the judge would publish the verdict in writing. But Judge Nicholas Bowan decided to announce the verdict in his courtroom. Before being appointed a judge, he had been a famous trial lawyer who loved the limelight. Now, as a judge, he got little attention from the press. Bowan had the reputation of being tough, but fair. When he entered the courtroom and saw how many reporters were awaiting his verdict, he reveled at once more being the center of media attention. He savored the moment when his image and his words would be beamed across the country.

The bailiff called the courtroom to order. The judge, clad in his flowing black robes, entered with a dramatic flourish, and sat down in his imposing judicial chair. He shuffled some papers in front of him, ceremoniously put on his eyeglasses, ran his hand through his thick mane of silver hair, and affixed a serious expression on his face, posing for the courtroom artists from various national and local newspapers. He cleared his throat, poured himself some water, slowly sipped some, and spoke; softly at first, but then with the resonant voice of a seasoned actor.

Judge Bowan carefully reviewed the facts of the case and the legal precedents that related to it, summarized the arguments of both legal teams, and then, he leaned forward, looking right at Tamara, and said, "I couldn't have done a better job myself." Tamara blushed, and smiled. She knew she had won. Bowan announced the verdict in favor of Shawon White.

White would get his magazines in prison, where he was destined to stay for another four years. His sister would remain traumatized for the rest of her life. The police officer would never be tried for rape or bribery, but would be suspended from the Chicago Police force, only to become a sheriff in Louisiana some years later. The Farnsworth firm would pick up additional business because of this case. No doubt the judge would be promoted to a higher court. Tamara would be pleased when the decision would be affirmed on appeal. All in all, it was just another episode in the ongoing saga of American justice.

Out of the corner of her eye, Tamara saw the press corps moving toward her. She looked at her watch, turned to her colleagues and said, "Gotta go. You talk to the press."

Like a quarterback running for a touchdown, she wove her way through the crowd out into the hallway, and ran down the long hall into the ladies' room. Finding an empty stall, she entered and locked the door. She began to undress, and, like Clark Kent ducking into a phone booth to turn into Superman, she soon emerged in another outfit: Cubs jacket, Cubs hat, baseball pants, and her courtroom attire stuffed in a Cubs tote bag. She ran out of the bathroom, past the reporters who did not recognize her, out of the courthouse, into a taxi, and went to Wrigley Field for a 3:20 P.M. game. Aglow from her victory, she watched the Cubs suffer a humiliating defeat by their longtime nemesis, the New York Mets.

LIKE OTHER DEVOTED CHICAGO CUBS
fans, Tamara Loeb was an optimist against her better judgment. While
other Chicagoans gleefully anticipated the annual springtime relief from
the ravages of winter, Cubs fans, like Tamara, braced themselves each
springtime for another inevitable season of suffering. Being a fan of the
Chicago Cubs contradicted a fundamental dogma of Chicago politics:
"Don't back no losers." For almost a century, the Chicago Cubs had
been engaged in a "rebuilding effort." The old millennium had come
and gone, and a new one had dawned. How long could one be expected
to wait for a victory? Yet a World Championship became each year's
ephemeral dream, as the season moved from a springtime of hope to a
fall of disappointment and despair.

The "Friendly Confines" of Wrigley Field had not been friendly to
the faithful fans who continued to make their pilgrimages to its precincts
year after year, generation after generation. Wrigley Field, which had
opened during the First World War, had yet to host a World Series victory
for its home team. In its early years, veterans of the Civil War, who

remembered when the Cubs had won the first National League pennant in 1876, came to Wrigley Field with their grandchildren, hoping to see the Cubs again become World Champions as they had been in 1907 and 1908. Their stories of the days when the Cubs had dominated baseball fell upon their descendents' ears like antiquated legends about knights and ladies-in-waiting. For generations of fans, the story of the Cubs was one of hope despite experience. Despite the resilience of their fans, the Cubs seemed to labor under a perpetual curse placed upon them by a wicked wizard long ago.

In 1876, as America celebrated its centennial, and before there was a World Series, Cubs manager Albert Spaulding led his team to victory in the first National League pennant race, winning fifty-two games and losing only fourteen, a .788 percentage of victory. A century later, as America celebrated its bicentennial, the Cubs finished fourth with a percentage of wins that hovered well below .500.

In the early years of the twentieth century, the Cubs were the winningest team in professional baseball. The best five-year team record of any major league baseball team is still that of the Chicago Cubs of 1906-1910: .693. Yet, the Cubs ended the twentieth century with more losses than any team in the history of baseball. For the second half of the twentieth century, from 1946 through 1999, the Chicago Cubs were 592 games below .500. Of the sixteen teams that existed in 1949, all have since won league championships—all but the Cubs. Also to the Chicago Cubs goes the dubious distinction of being the first team to finish in tenth place, behind even the "expansion" teams.

In 1906, the Cubs won more games in a season than any team in the history of baseball: 116, with a winning average of .763. In 1966, sixty years later, their winning average was 400 points lower, with 103 losses. In 1908, the Cubs were the baseball champions of the world. Yet, forty years later, in 1948, Cubs management felt obliged to take out ads in the local newspapers apologizing for the team's consistently embarrassing performance on the field. Forty years after that, in a 1988 attempt to modernize, lights were finally installed in Wrigley Field. It was Cubs management's way of saying that they had not given up on the possibility of World Series play at Wrigley Field. Yet, consistent with their fate, the Cubs' first night game at home was cancelled midway because of torrential rains.

Until the advent of cable TV, Cubmania had been largely quarantined in the north side of Chicago. Then it spread throughout the country and beyond, like the devastating influenza epidemic of 1918; a year in which the Cubs had won the National League pennant, only to be mowed down in the World Series by a young upstart hurler for the Boston Red Sox named Babe Ruth.

It was to this legacy of losers, this incarnation of ineptitude, that Tamara Loeb—a poster-girl for grace under pressure—had plighted her troth.

Once, when she was making love to her husband, Tamara began to moan, "Oh Sammy, Sammy." Loeb thought that she had a lover named Sam. But, out of the corner of her eye, Tamara was watching then-Cubs slugger Sammy Sosa hammer a home run over the left field fence at Wrigley Field on the muted television in their bedroom.

JAY LOEB AND HIS SEVENTEEN-YEAR-
old son, Joshua, sat at the dining room table staring at their uneaten dinner.
They were waiting to hear how Tamara's "big day" in court had gone.

"Maybe Mom's out celebrating," Joshua said, breaking the long
silence.

"It's not like her not even to call," Jay replied. "With all of her gizmos,
I would think she could at least manage a telephone call."

Loeb taught at a small Jewish seminary in Chicago that trained rabbis
and religious educators. He had published many books on obscure
academic subjects that were read only by members of a small,
international fraternity of recondite scholars. Most of his life was like a
séance, in which he communed through study, with the great minds and
souls of the past.

Besides his rabbinic ordination, Loeb also had earned degrees in
history and philosophy from Princeton and Cambridge universities. Over
the years, he had been offered academic positions at many top
universities, but had declined them, preferring to remain at a Jewish

institution. Behind his back, his rabbinic colleagues readily acknowledged that only in pre-World War II Eastern Europe had there been Jewish scholars of his caliber, but in America, they confided, rabbis like him were a superfluous anachronism. People didn't want scholarly rabbis, but "pastoral" rabbis with good "interpersonal skills" and fund-raising abilities. Jay Loeb had clearly been born in the wrong century. He often comforted himself with the words of the French writer, Valery: "We are fated to live in the times into which we have been born."

The phone rang, and Loeb quickly picked it up, sure that it must be Tamara.

"Hi, sweetheart, how did it go?"

It was Charles Flaherty, one of Tamara's senior partners.

"Gee, Jay, I didn't know you felt that way about me," Flaherty chuckled. "Why aren't you two out celebrating? Tamara blew them away. We won. Is she OK? She ran out of the courtroom after the verdict like a bat out of hell, right into the ladies' room. Nerves, maybe?"

"I don't know where she is. Haven't heard from her. Thought she was still at the office—either celebrating or preparing for an appeal. Now, I'm really starting to worry. You have any idea where she is?"

"Maybe. But not sure enough to risk telling something."

Jay sighed. "Well, Chuck, congratulations on the verdict."

"No, Jay, the congratulations should go to Tamara. You should be proud of your little lady. Good night, Jay."

"Good night, Chuck."

An hour later, Tamara entered the house, dressed in her best business suit, which looked like it had been slept in.

Though relieved beyond measure to see her, Jay stated tersely, "Chuck called. Congratulations on your great victory. I bet you'll be in the paper tomorrow."

"Could be," Tamara said curtly. "I've had a tough day. I'm going to bed."

"Don't you want to celebrate?"

"No, Jay. Go to your books. They'll provide better company than I would right now."

"Joshua is in his room. He's very proud of you. I'll bet he's waiting up for you."

"I'll see him in the morning. Right now, I don't want to talk to anyone. One of those headaches."

Tamara undressed and lay down in bed, cursing under her breath, and soon, out of exhaustion—more from the Cubs defeat than from her courtroom victory—she fell asleep.

A few weeks later, Flaherty called again, this time to speak to Loeb.

"Jay, we've got to talk. Can we meet tomorrow for lunch at the Chicago Club? It's about Tamara. I've ordered kosher food for you, so don't worry. Noon, OK?"

"Don't you want to tell me what this is all about?" asked Jay, hiding the trepidation in his voice.

"We'll talk tomorrow."

"You lawyers are all so tight-lipped; you should all work for the CIA."

"Some of us do."

Loeb couldn't tell whether Flaherty was joking. "I'll be there, at noon. See you then."

Loeb entered the elegant, mahogany-paneled lobby of the Chicago Club at 11:45, and sat down in one of the luxurious chairs scattered throughout the lobby. He took out a book no bigger than a matchbox and he began to read the Psalms. Within a few minutes, he was deep in prayer, so much so that he did not realize that Flaherty was standing in front of him—with three other senior partners from the firm.

"Hi, Jay. You know Bob, Bill and Mike."

Loeb jolted, as if having been awakened from a deep sleep. He stood up and shook hands with each member of the somber-looking entourage. He wasn't sure whether they looked upset because they had something bad to tell him, or because they knew that the time they would spend with him were not "billable hours."

They walked to the elevator, went to the fourth floor, and entered a small private dining room. A lunch of steak, lobster and potatoes au gratin was served to the law partners. Loeb's kosher lunch, wrapped with many layers of tinfoil, was ceremoniously placed before him by a tall waiter in a tuxedo, who spoke with a phony French accent. As the others ate, talking about sports and the weather, Loeb, like an archaeologist moving through levels of time, unpeeled the layers of aluminum foil, below which, he hoped, a lunch was to be found. After the ritual of small talk had concluded, and after coffee and dessert had been served, the waiters vacated the room. Bill Farnsworth looked at Loeb and began to speak. Farnsworth, whose grandfather was one of the founders of the firm, spoke softly, almost inaudibly,

"We're worried about Tamara, and we wanted to share our concern with you. Despite her victory in court, her work has been suffering lately—I mean her real work, the kind that generates fees."

Loeb sat, his head perched on his hand, his eyes half closed, his lips faintly moving, as if he were talking to himself.

Farnsworth continued, "We wanted to talk to you before we take steps. We have assigned some of her clients to other attorneys, but they want her, not someone else. We know you must suspect this, too, Jay, so this shouldn't come as too big a shock: She has an addiction, like alcoholism, like substance abuse. She's hooked—on the Cubs. I'm sure it's causing problems for you and your boy, but that's your business. Our business is the firm, and we have to protect our interests. We're worried about losing business. We're worried about not generating enough new business. We're worried about exposure to malpractice actions, reports to the Attorney Registration and Disciplinary Commission. Tamara is part of a team, and she's not pulling her load for five to six months a year. It's having a negative effect on the other lawyers and the staff. The rest of the time she's a great asset, a wonderful colleague. But each year, this problem gets worse, and we've got to do something. We've got to take action, immediately if not sooner. I'm sorry, but the firm comes first." Loeb seemed oblivious to what Farnsworth had said.

"We're asking for your help, which is clearly in your own self-interest. You people have a reputation for being smart, for being good at business, for cleaning up your own problems. Christ, the Cardinal himself told me what a friggin' genius you are. How you got that medal from the Pope— like Michael Corleone."

Farnsworth suddenly realized that Loeb might take his comments about "you people" as an antisemitic insult. He thought that Loeb's silence was a sign of his having been offended. Farnsworth then continued his monologue and made matters worse by talking about "some of my best friends who are Jews," and about the Bar Mitzvahs, Jewish weddings and Anti-Defamation League dinners that he had attended. Yet, Loeb remained silent, except for the soft incomprehensible sounds his lips emitted. His eyelids were slightly drooped, as if he were in some kind of trance.

"Listen, Jay," Flaherty interjected, "What Bill is trying to say is that we want a win-win situation as far as Tamara's work at the firm is concerned. But this Cubs thing is making that impossible. Unless, or until, this problem starts to move toward a solution, her future with the firm is at risk."

"We cannot discuss our specific strategies for handling this matter," Farnsworth continued, "and, it wouldn't hurt for you to get some legal counsel of your own. All we want to tell you now is that the situation is becoming serious, that we have to take action. We felt it only fair to give you some time to see if you can come up with some strategy of your own on how to deal with this problem. Maybe get Tamara into therapy, on some pills. Maybe there's a 'Cubs Anonymous.' There must be other people around Chicago who have the same problem."

There was a long silence. Finally, Loeb opened his eyes widely, as if he had just awakened from a nap. He took his hand from under his chin and sat up, looking refreshed and alert.

"Sorry, gentlemen," he said. "I've been reciting the Grace after Meals prayer. I know you've been talking about something, but I really wasn't listening. Did I miss anything important?"

Used to having people listen to their every word, each of the four men looked like a baby forced to eat spinach for the first time. Clients, paying $450 an hour for their time, hung on their every word, like patients at an oncologist's office waiting for a life-or-death verdict.

Bob Smith, the firm's managing partner, then summarized in concise terms what had been said while Loeb was enwrapped in the cocoon of his prayers. As Smith spoke, a huge grin flashed across Loeb's face.

"You mean, she's not having an affair? That's what I thought it was. So, it's only that she's—er—hooked on the Cubs? Thank God."

Loeb thought for a few seconds and said, "I understand. Believe me, I understand. You're right, something must be done. Not for the firm's sake, but for Tamara's. Thanks. I appreciate your concern. I'll do something. I have to. I know she's always been a big Cubs fan—we've had season tickets for years. But now it seems like Tamara's become a follower of some strange religious cult. She must be freed from this spell."

Loeb continued to speak, more to himself than to the others. Farnsworth looked at his watch, and then he stood up; the others followed.

"Good luck, Jay," he said, extended his hand.

Loeb shook his hand, and the hands of the others. As they were about to walk out the door, Loeb said, "If you don't mind my asking, I have one question."

Farnsworth looked at his watch again, and said, "What is it, Jay?"

"Have you told Tamara any of what you've just explained to me?"

"Our hope," Flaherty said, "is that we wouldn't have to. But, we will, at the appropriate time. The ball's now in your court, Jay."

Loeb said, "You know, there are two expressions you use a lot that I don't understand: 'immediately, if not sooner' and 'at the appropriate time.'"

Farnsworth shrugged. He had done his duty, but he had no time for discussions of semantics. As they entered the elevator, the lawyers mumbled quietly to each other.

After they had left, Loeb sat alone at the table, his head in his hands, processing information that he had accumulated during a lifetime of learning, in order to see whether any of it could be applied to the problem at hand.

Loeb returned home, went to his study, and made a series of phone calls. The first was to Rick Nicklesen, a reporter he knew at the *Chicago Tribune*. He had met Rick when he was the *Trib*'s religion editor. In a career move that had pleased Rick but dismayed Jay, Rick was now assigned to the Chicago sports-beat.

"Hi, Rick, it's Rabbi Loeb. How are you?"

"Not bad, Rabbi, how are you doing?"

"Fine, Rick. Thank God, fine. I need a small favor. Some information. About sports. About the Cubs."

"Isn't that a little out of your line, Rabbi?"

"Yeah, but, it'll help me help someone."

"I understand, Rabbi. What do you want to know?"

Years earlier, Loeb had met a young Catholic priest, Father Hood, at a conference on bioethics at Notre Dame. They had kept in touch over the years when Hood was teaching philosophy at Holy Cross College in Iowa. They remained in constant contact after Hood was unexpectedly appointed the bishop of the small, out-of-the-way diocese of Belleville,

Illinois. Hood saw it as a punishment, but unbeknown to him, the Vatican had plans for him.

When Hood, to everyone's surprise, including his own, was appointed the new archbishop of Chicago, the first person he called was Loeb. When he came to town, Loeb arranged for Nicklesen to get the first interview with the new Archbishop. In Chicago, the Archbishop is always big news. Nicklesen knew it, and he never forgot what Loeb had done for him.

"What do you want to know about the Cubs, Rabbi?," Nicklesen asked.

"Many things, but specifically, why they can't seem to win. I understand they haven't won a World Series since 1908, and they haven't won the National League pennant since 1945."

"Yep, Rabbi, that's true—lamentably true. Still, the fans remain loyal, and the more the Cubs lose, the more loyal the fans get. And since the Cubs games have been on cable TV, the phenomenon has spread beyond Chicago to the rest of the country, and even beyond. Like a virus, spreading though the miracle of TV. Maybe people like an underdog. I don't really know."

"So there are two mysteries," said Loeb. "Why they lose, and why the fans remain loyal."

"Yep, they're mysteries, all right. When the Bulls won, everyone was a Bulls fan. Now that they don't consistently win the NBA title, the fan base has fallen off. When the Bears won the Superbowl, everyone was a Bears fan; now that they are lousy, few people care. The White Sox have some loyal fans, but nothing like the Cubs. Cubs fans remain loyal, no matter what. I guess baseball's like a religion, and Cubs fans are like members of a religious cult. It's something you take or leave. Not something you fully understand."

"I never thought of it that way," Loeb said. "But now that you mention it, it's true. It has rituals, rules . . ."

"And, if you'll pardon me, Rabbi—also, superstitions."

"Superstitions?" Loeb asked.

"Oh, yeah, a lot of superstitions. Some players will only play if they wear certain socks, if they use a particular bat or glove, if they eat chicken before a game. Some wear certain good-luck underwear under their uniforms. Lots of superstitions. You know what the seventh inning stretch is?"

"Sure."

"But do you know how it started?"

"No, how?"

"Years ago, President Taft was at a baseball game. He was a real fat guy—over 300 pounds. He was uncomfortable in his seat, and so he got up. Out of respect for the president, the game stopped and the crowd stood up until the president returned to his seat. Only when he sat down, did they sit down. At that point in the game, the home team had been losing. But, after that intermission, they rallied to win. The inning the president stood up in was the seventh. Since then, for good luck for the home team, people get up in the seventh inning. That's the seventh inning stretch."

"And the Cubs," asked Loeb, "they also have superstitions?"

"Sure. All teams have them. Listen, Rabbi, the sports writers explain the Cubs annual screw-ups with all kinds of sophisticated analysis: bad middle relief, ineffective manager, not enough strength in this position or that position, so-and-so's in a slump. And they may be right, for one season or another, for a few weeks at a time—but that doesn't account for so many years of failure, for consistent perennial loss. That's why some sports writers and a lot of the fans believe in the Billy Goat curse. You've heard of it, right? Everybody in Chicago has."

"Everyone, I guess, except me."

"Well, Rabbi, here it is in a nutshell. In 1945, when the Cubs last won the pennant, the owner of the Billy Goat Tavern, Bill Sianis, came to Wrigley with a goat to act as the mascot for the Cubs during the World Series. He had bought a ticket for the goat, whose name was

'Murphy.' Sianis believed Murphy would bring the Cubs luck and victory, as he had brought him luck in his business. But Sianis and his goat were thrown out of the ballpark. In anger, Sianis put a curse on the Cubs and on Wrigley Field. 'They not gonna win no more,' said Sianis. In a telegram to Wrigley, Sianis stated that the Cubs were never going to win the World Series, let alone the National League championship. From that day onward, the Chicago Cubs have won neither a pennant nor a World Series. They've had good teams and bad, good managers and bad. But they don't win the big ones. Other teams have problems too. Some have had luck. The Cubs also have luck—consistently lousy luck. And many believe it's because of the curse."

"Do you believe in the curse?"

"Look, Rabbi. I only report the news. In the short run, week to week, month to month, season to season, there are many reasonable explanations for why they don't win. But, over the long run, nobody knows. The curse is as good of an explanation as any—and better than most. Who knows? Maybe there are other curses on them as well. After all, Sianis cursed the Cubs in 1945, but they haven't won a World Series since 1908. In the early years of baseball, they won a lot—but not recently.

"Remember when they played their own farm team—and lost? They're pathetic, jinxed, cursed. All of the above. Case closed. And, since the Red Sox won the World Series in 2004, the Cubs remain the only team in baseball that still labors under a curse. The curse on the Sox seems to have been lifted, but not the curse on the Cubs. The curse on the Sox lasted eighty-six years, but the Cubs have been cursed for much longer, long before Sianis and his goat."

"Thank you for telling me all this, Rick. One more question and I'll let you go."

"Sure, Rabbi, fire away."

"These fanatical Cubs fans. You compared them to members of a religious cult. I've worked with kids, getting them out of cults, deprogramming them. There are substance abuse programs to help people fight addictions to narcotics, Alcoholics Anonymous to help alcoholics, behavior modification programs to stop people from smoking. Do you know of any programs or support groups for people hooked on the Cubs?"

"Nope, sorry I don't—though it might be a good idea to start one!"

"OK, Rick. Thanks. Sorry to have taken so much of your time."

"Hope I've been of help."

"You have, Rick. You have. I just don't yet know how. 'Bye."

"Have a nice day, Rabbi, and take care."

No sooner than Loeb had hung up the phone, he picked it up again to call Dr. Harold Chernowitz of the Department of Psychiatry at Northwestern University's medical school. He had met Chernowitz some years before through one of the donors to his seminary, who also had given a large financial gift to Northwestern to establish a center to study and treat compulsive behavorial disorders. Chernowitz had helped raise the money from their common donor, and, to no one's surprise, he had been named director of the Center. Jay mistrusted shrinks as a general rule and had made no secret of his feelings to Chernowitz. Even so, Chernowitz had been the donor's family shrink for three generations.

"Hi, Harold. It's Jay Loeb. Are you in a session now? Got a few minutes?"

"If I were in a session, you think I'd answer the phone? What's up? This a social call or a professional visit?"

"The latter."

"Should I bill you for it?"

"You can if you want, but you can well afford not to."

"Sorry, Jay. What's up? Read about some dream of one of your crazy kabbalists that you want me to interpret for you? Had one yourself?"

"Nothing that profound, Harold. But, something equally mysterious. Have you ever treated addicted Cubs fans? How do you explain their fixation on a team that always loses? Is there a recognized syndrome these people have? Who treats such people? Is there a cure?"

"Hey, Jay, slow down. What's this all about? Asking for a friend?"

"Harold, you know very well that I can tell you about as much about the people I try to help as you can tell me about the ones you try to help. The only difference between us is that you bill for it."

"Ouch! You still have that hostile attitude towards shrinks? Why don't you come in and we'll talk about it? You might find out something interesting about yourself."

"I can neither afford my time nor your fees."

"All right. Calm down. I'll try to answer some of your questions. No, there's no official psychoanalytic designation for a syndrome related to an obsession with the Cubs, but it might be subsumed under some established compulsive disorder. No, I've never treated anyone like that, and I don't know anyone who has—but I could find out. Backing losers can simply mean that a person sees himself as a failure—and misery likes company. Or, specifically in the case of the Cubs, a person might be comforted by the fact that these young, well-paid, popular, and athletic guys screw up—yet everyone loves them—so he can be loved too, and can make a lot of money, even if he screws up. If I had some more time, I could probably come up with something else."

"Do you believe that a person or a group of persons like the Cubs could be cursed?"

"I'm a scientist, Jay, not a voodoo doctor. No, I don't believe in those superstitions. But it's not what I believe that's relevant here. If a person believes that a curse is real, then it's real—to him. Then it has power over him. Convince that person not to believe in the power of the curse, and the curse will have no power over him. It's that simple. Why, Jay, someone put an 'evil eye' on you?"

"Thanks, Harold, you've been more helpful than you know."

"Aren't I always? Bye, Jay."

Loeb quickly went to the next call on his list, Lewis Kalinsky, an elderly lawyer and friend who had done legal work for him, long before he even had met Tamara. Though Kalinsky had practiced law for more than fifty years, his real passion was writing poetry.

"Lou, hi, it's Jay. How are you?"

"Aging faster than I'd like. Losing the battle against galloping decreptitude. Don't ask how I am, or I'll have to recite the entire *Merck Manual.*"

"So, nothing's changed since we spoke last?"

Kalinsky chuckled.

"Something wrong, Jay? You don't sound so hot yourself."

"It's Tamara. She's in trouble. I need your advice."

"After her big porno victory, it's hard to imagine that she'd need any help from me. In all my years of practicing law, I never got as far as she's already gotten. She must have tons of job offers, lecture invitations, big law schools after her to teach, radio and TV interviews. Front page news coverage. An enviable situation from where I sit."

"Don't knock yourself, Lou. For all she's accomplished, she couldn't write one line of poetry the way you can. Besides, she's in trouble at the firm."

"So, she'll go to another one. Listen, I know big-firm politics. If you do good, they're jealous and resentful. If you do bad, they get rid of you. One minute you're a hero—if you bring in enough billable hours. The next minute, if you falter, you're out on your ass, and in ten minutes some kid right out of law school is sitting in your office, picking his pimples, trying to figure out where the courthouse is, and collecting a salary bigger than yours. Been there, done that."

"I wish it were so simple, Lou. Tamara's got a problem. You know she's always been crazy about the Cubs. You've been to the house when the game is on. Well, it's getting worse—a lot worse. It's affecting her work, her relationship with me, Joshua, her partners, everyone. The longer the season goes on, the worse it gets. I just found out how deep this obsession is for her. But, in one sense, I'm relieved. I thought she was having an affair. Yet, in another sense, I'm concerned. She could destroy her career, just when she's getting near the top.

"Last week, she was watching the game on TV and something happened—I don't know what. She yelled and cursed like a crazy person and threw one of our best antique chairs across the room and broke it. It's bad. Real bad. Getting worse. The senior partners in her firm met with me and talked about some kind of 'plan' they had to deal with her. Said I should talk to my lawyer."

After a brief pause, Kalinsky said, "I don't know what to tell you about how to deal with Tamara, Jay. But, I can guess at what her partners are talking about. They're probably talking like caring partners, but in the meantime they're plotting how to rid themselves of Tamara with limited legal exposure. They've apparently come to the calculated conclusion that Tamara either is more of a liability than an asset to the firm, or, that she may soon become one. So, they want her out—unless, of course, she can shape up fast. Or, after her big porno victory, they don't need her anymore. They got what they wanted and needed—good publicity. So, maybe the whole business about the Cubs is just a ploy."

"It might be a ploy for them, but I see what it's doing to Tamara," said Loeb.

"I'm sure Tamara's partners have 'built a file' on her, and have documented every time she's acted out, been late, been away from work, etc., because of her fixation on the Cubs," Kalinsky continued. "I'm sure they've estimated or even fabricated figures on how much money and business they've lost as a result. They may have even gotten affidavits from her colleagues and staff. These are not nice guys. Don't doubt it, Jay, those lawyer jokes aren't jokes; they're true.

"My guess is that they'll soon start their little dirty work to get rid of her. Probably, those bastards are only holding off for a few weeks because they're trying to get Tamara a job at another firm, so they can avoid any confrontation or exposure, each of which would be costly and time-consuming. But any firm they try to palm her off to will be suspicious. Why does a firm for which she won such a big victory want to get rid of her? In fact, if they try discreetly to get her another job, the result will be that if she really wants to leave, it will be harder for her to find one.

"My advice to you is this: don't make their work easy for them. If you play your cards right, you will see her in a new and better-paying job, and getting a big settlement from her current firm. If they offer a settlement, just keep asking for more and more outrageous things in the settlement agreement, and stop when you think you've gotten enough."

"Thanks, Lou," said Loeb. "Now I understand better what's going on. But, right now, my main concern is not Tamara's job; it's Tamara. I'll take things one step at a time. Take care, Lou."

"Any time, Jay. Good luck. I know you'll think of something. It'll be good for you to put your incredible mind on something practical for a change, instead of your Talmudic dialectics and kabbalistic fantasies."

Loeb hung up the phone, sat at his desk and thought about what he had learned that afternoon. Though he had no solution, at least now he had a better understanding of the problem. Loeb closed his eyes and began to intone a kabbalistic chant.

In his studies of Kabbalah—the Jewish mystical tradition—Loeb had concentrated on its intellectual and moral insights rather than on its magical side. He was more interested in what Kabbalah had to say about the big problems, like the meaning of life, the challenge of leading a moral life, how to attain communion with God, how to decipher the hidden meaning of the Torah. He was less concerned with things like how to write and how to use amulets, how to exorcise a person who had become possessed, how to battle evil spirits, how to cure spiritual illnesses, how to read palms and minds. Though he had studied these things, he never thought of practicing them. For him, they were simply matters of historical interest. But, when Loeb had completed his meditations and opened his eyes, the first thing he saw was the Hebrew Bible that he always kept on his desk, and the long forgotten magical ritual of bibliomancy came to mind. He had not thought about it in years, and never had actually tried it.

Loeb recalled that bibliomancy was used when a person had a difficult problem for which he was seeking an elusive solution. It was believed that Scripture has the answers to all human problems, but we don't always know how to access its wisdom. In bibliomancy, a person thinks deeply about the problem that vexes him, closes his eyes, and then randomly opens a Bible to any page, and, with his eyes still closed, places his finger down on the page. Then, he opens his eyes and reads the verse that his finger is pointing to. That verse, or phrase, it was believed, would have an answer to the problem.

"*If not now, when?*" he said to himself, quoting the Talmud.

Loeb followed the ritual, and looked down at his finger. He had opened to the book of Jonah, where it read, "on whose account this misfortune has come upon us?"

Loeb thought about it for a few minutes. "What does it mean? How does it address to my problem?" He let his mind wander. The first thing that popped into his head was what Nicklesen had told him about the curse. That was the answer! The place to begin was "on whose account this misfortune has come upon us?" It was not Tamara, nor her partners, not even the Cubs—but the Billy Goat curse, and perhaps other curses that had been put on the Cubs and on Wrigley Field over the years. If he could remove all those curses, he might cure Tamara. The Cubs wouldn't always be losers and her problems would disappear. But, how to do it? Loeb mulled this question over in his mind, and soon a plan began to take shape.

It was late in the afternoon. Tamara and Joshua would soon be home. Loeb reached for the phone and called David Levy, the president of Hang Me, Inc., the largest manufacturer of clothes hangers in the United States. A few years before, Levy had come to Loeb to seek his help. Levy had built up a huge company from scratch to leave to his only child. But, one day, his son had come home from college and announced that upon graduation, he would not be entering the family business, but would be seeking admission to a monastery of Trappist monks. Levy's rabbi had recommended that Levy ask Loeb for help. Levy pleaded with Loeb to try to talk his son out of becoming a Catholic monk, living under vows of silence, poverty, obedience and chastity. Loeb succeeded, and convinced the boy to enter a kabbalistic yeshivah in the Old City of Jerusalem. Five years later, the boy emerged as a learned and committed Jew. Though he still refused to take over the family business, he did take over the family's charitable foundation—a compromise that his father could accept. At the time, Levy had promised Loeb, "Anytime you need a favor, just ask. Anything you want." Loeb never believed him; nor had he asked for anything. Until now.

After being passed through a long line of administrative assistants, Loeb finally got to Levy's executive secretary. When she told Levy who was on the phone, Levy immediately picked it up.

"Rabbi, what an unexpected and pleasant surprise."

Loeb listened, picturing Levy making facial expressions that indicated that he was about as happy to be hearing from Loeb as he would be to learn that he needed a root canal.

"How is your son?"

"Oh, he's great. I'm terrific. I work all my days making money and he spends his days giving it away—except of course for the time he spends studying those books you keep sending him. But I guess, it's better than him being a monk. At least this way, I have him around, have grandchildren, and I have a family to leave my money to. How are you doing, Rabbi? I read about your wife's big victory for pornography."

"Thank God, I'm fine, Mr. Levy. I am calling to ask a small favor."

"Sure! Want a donation to go somewhere? Just call the boy, and he'll take care of it for you—especially, for you."

"No, Mr. Levy, not a donation; something else."

Levy's voice echoed a note of anxious caution.

"Then what can I do for you, Rabbi?"

"Doesn't your company have one of those private sky boxes at Wrigley Field?"

"Sure, one of the best. Want it sometime; it's yours."

Levy now sounded relieved. *If that's all he wants, now I'm finally off the hook with him*, Levy said to himself.

"I need it very soon, but for a night game. The whole box."

"Sure, Rabbi, I'll messenger the tickets over to you tomorrow for the next night game. I'll just throw out whoever I promised it to. It's all yours. Want catering? I can even order you kosher catering. Just let us know for how many."

"Thanks, but the tickets alone would be fine. I don't need any catering. Please, just be sure the game is not on the Sabbath. Thanks. I'll look forward to getting the tickets—but please—for a night game only."

"You got it. Take care."

"Thank you Mr. Levy. You are most generous. God bless you. Goodbye."

The following day, passes to the Hang Me, Inc. sky box for a night game the following Thursday against Atlanta were delivered to Loeb by messenger. Loeb already had begun to prepare for his encounter with the curse of the Billy Goat and with the power of other curses that might be obsessing the ballpark. The only thing for which he could not prepare, was a chance encounter with Tamara at Wrigley Field.

ON THE MORNING OF THE GAME, LOEB pretended to be asleep until Tamara and Joshua had left the house. He then arose and went to the bathroom, after which he exited to recite the blessing one says after going to the bathroom—a blessing thanking God for the miracle of a successful venture there. He re-entered the bathroom, showered and shaved, and then he dressed. Taking his prayer shawl and phylacteries, Loeb took a taxi down to the seminary, and locked himself in the seminary's synagogue to recite the morning prayers. He prayed softly, and with intense devotion, concentrating on every word, felt each syllable bind him closer to his Creator. Loeb concluded his prayers with the Psalm designated for Thursday, Psalm 81. When he came to the words, "In distress you called and I rescued you," he thought of Tamara and of what he would try to do for her that night, and tears came to his eyes.

Loeb removed his prayer shawl and phylacteries, kissed them, and replaced them in the velvet pouch that was their home. He opened the Holy Ark, kissed the Torah scrolls, and left the synagogue. Leaving the seminary, he hailed a cab, and went to the *mikvah*, the ritual bath, to purify his body for the ordeal yet ahead.

Loeb undressed in the small dressing room, showered in the adjacent bathroom, and then opened the door to the small square-shaped pool of water that constituted the men's section of the *mikvah*. He descended the seven steps into the lukewarm water, covered his head with his hand, and recited various blessings and kabbalistic meditations. He then completely immersed himself in the water three times. Naked, and feeling both vulnerable and pure, he climbed the steps, dressed, and took a taxi home. Loeb entered his study, and turned off the phone. He reviewed the kabbalistic texts and prepared the amulets that he would use that evening.

At 4 P.M., Loeb went to the kosher butcher, where two live chickens in a box made with wooden slats were handed to him. At Loeb's request, the butcher gave him a bag of grain that had been treated with sedatives, so that the chickens would not make too much noise. Loeb covered the box with a large kerchief that he had brought from home—one of Tamara's best designer scarves—and with the chickens in one hand and his briefcase in the other, he set out for Wrigley Field.

The walk was a few miles, and the day was unseasonably warm. In compliance with the ritual he was about to perform, Loeb was fasting, which meant no food or drink. He arrived at Wrigley just as the gates were opening. He showed his passes and was directed to the sky box.

It was a huge room, with a marvelous view of the field, right above home plate. Fortunately, the room was air-conditioned. It had a private bathroom, a large closet, and even a small kitchen. He fed the chickens, put them in the closet, and recited the afternoon and evening prayers.

Loeb had recited these prayers almost every day of his life. But when he came to the words "Remove Satan from in front of us and behind us. Shelter us in Your presence, for You are our guardian and deliverer," Loeb began to shiver.

Soon after Loeb had finished his prayers, waiters began to come into the box, in what seemed like every few minutes, to offer him food and drinks, which he declined. Loeb locked the door to the sky box and began to study one of the kabbalistic books that he had brought with him to keep him company during the long night.

At 7:30 P.M., Loeb heard the singing of "The Star-Spangled Banner," and he realized that the game was about to begin. He searched the stands with his binoculars, looking for Tamara. There she sat, with Joshua, in a seat along the third base line, dressed in her Cubs outfit, a beer in her hand, her mouth wide open emitting a yell he could not hear.

Loeb knew a little about baseball, but it was of small consequence in his life. He knew that in baseball, as in life, things could radically change from minute to minute. As the Talmudic rabbis had put it, "Life is like a wheel. One moment you can be on the top, and the next minute the wheel spins and you are at the bottom—and vice-versa." So, he sat in the sky box and returned to his reading, and when he sensed the game's end was coming closer, he closed his book and looked down at the field.

Loeb had not been in Wrigley Field for years. When he started to date Tamara, he often would go with her, usually bringing along a book to read, which embarrassed her—so she no longer asked him to come. He remembered how Tamara had brought Joshua to the ballpark when he was still an infant, like the biblical Hannah bringing her son Samuel to the Temple to be consecrated there to God's service.

There were no night games yet at Wrigley in those years, so Loeb never had been to a night game there before. The beauty of the park, with its green vines incandescent under the lights, gave him a strange feeling of confidence and tranquility.

It was the top of the ninth inning. The Cubs were winning 14-12. The Cubs' "closer" was brought in to wrap up the game. The fans held their breath with every pitch, as if their lives depended upon its outcome. Many were on their feet, yelling and gesturing, waving banners, eating, and drinking Coke and beer—Tamara among them. It did not take long until the game was tied. Tamara was standing, yelling like a banshee, and cursing like a truck-driver. Joshua tried to pretend he did not know the loud-mouthed woman standing next to him. A new Cubs pitcher was brought in.

The first pitch was a strike on the inside corner that jammed the batter. The fans roared their approval. But the next pitch hit the batter. The catcher and the pitching coach came out to confer with the pitcher. The third pitch was a split-finger fast-ball that fell down and away from the batter, who tripped over his own feet as he lunged to hit it. On the next pitch, the batter couldn't pull back fast enough from checking his swing, and a ground ball rolled slowly toward the second baseman, who charged the ball, slipped on the grass, and fell. The runners were all going on the pitch. Another run crossed the plate. The Braves were ahead, 15-14.

No one booed. No one seemed surprised. Things like this happened all the time at Wrigley Field. Loeb saw Tamara yelling and throwing things on the ground and into the now empty seats in front of her. Joshua had sunk back into his seat, already surrendering to defeat.

In the bottom of the ninth, the top of the Cubs batting order came to the plate. But it was a quick three up, three down. Just another defeat in a long litany of defeats. The fans left the ballpark like mourners leaving a church at the end of a funeral. By 10:30, Wrigley Field was empty, except for the grounds crew, who cleaned up the stands, and took care of the playing field.

Loeb peeked out the door of the sky box and saw the maintenance staff exit the men's room after cleaning it. Loeb then left his sky box, figuring that they would soon come there to clean. He took his stuffed briefcase and his chickens and hid in the men's room, waiting for the midnight hour. In kabbalistic tradition, midnight was the most desirable time for prayers of petition, for it is then, the mystics believe, that we have the most direct access to God.

At 11:50, Wrigley Field was pitch dark. Loeb took his chickens and his briefcase, and with a flashlight to illumine his way, he descended the stairs to the box seats behind the Cubs dugout. He crept across the roof of the dugout, to which he affixed a small rope ladder that he had brought, and carefully lowered first the chickens and then himself onto the field. When he arrived at the pitcher's mound, Loeb put down his briefcase and his chickens, and prepared for the age-old ritual of removing curses from places that had been cursed.

Already in ancient times, wonder-working rabbis would draw a circle on the ground to protect themselves from evil spirits that might attack them as they performed these rituals. Loeb did not have to draw such a circle, because one already existed on the field—the pitcher's mound. He stood on the rubber at the center of the mound and placed around his neck an amulet that he had prepared. On it were written secret names of God and verses from the Bible that were known to have protective powers against evil spirits, and that were supposed to be effective in the removal of curses.

From his briefcase, Loeb took out some rope. He recited to himself from memory a section of the medieval mystical treatise, *The Book of the Pious*: "Measure off the spot from north, south, east and west. Mark it with rope. While doing this recite the priestly benediction from the Book of Numbers and the Psalm designated to protect you from curses and evil spirits. When this has been done, one should then say the prescribed formulae to remove curses and evil spirits from places they have obsessed."

Loeb made a square of rope around the perimeters of the pitcher's mound. He intoned the Hebrew blessing that the Bible prescibed for the ancient priests to use to bless the people: "*Yivarekhakhah ha-shem ve'yishmarekha*—May the Lord bless you and keep you. *Ya-air hashem panav aylekha vi-huneka*—May the Lord allow his presence to shine upon you, and be gracious unto you. *Yisah hashem panav aylekha, ve-yaseim lekha shalom*—May God turn His face towards you, and grant you peace."

Loeb then recited Psalm 91, which had been used for centuries to combat the effects of curses and to overcome the forces of evil: "Oh you who dwell in the shelter of the Most High, and abide in the protection of the Almighty—I say of the Lord, my refuge and stronghold, my God whom I trust that He will save you from the fowler's trap, from the destructive plague. He will cover you with refuge under His wings. His fidelity is an encircling shield. You need not fear the terror by night . . ."

Loeb kept repeating the priestly benediction and the psalm until he had placed his strings in the prescribed configuration.

In keeping with the tradition that evil spirits are afraid of light, he took from his briefcase a number of small candles, each in a small jar, lit them, and placed them along the circumference of the pitcher's mound, until he was surrounded by a ring of fire.

Loeb recalled how his father used to make fun of his grandfather's superstitious practice of spitting three times to keep away malevolent spirits and bad luck. Loeb now linked this memory to one of the texts that he had read that described the spit of a fasting person as a substance that was guaranteed to chase away bad luck, curses, and bad spirits. So, he spat three times in each of the four directions: north, south, east and west. Now that he had taken the prescribed steps to protect himself from any malevolent spirits that might inhabit Wrigley Field, Loeb prepared himself to cast them out of that place forever.

Loeb took the chickens out of the box, holding one in each hand. He swung the one in his right hand around his head seven times in a counter-clockwise motion, and then the one in his left hand in a clockwise motion, while still reciting the priestly blessing and the Ninety-First Psalm. The sounds of the frightened chickens echoed through the ballpark.

After he had completed that part of the ritual, Loeb said, "May all curses that have been put on this place now be placed into these creatures. May the curses upon this place now be removed." Gently, he returned the chickens to the box where they desperately flapped their clipped wings, trying to fly away.

In a loud bass voice that echoed throughout the field, Loeb intoned, *"Abra cadabra, cadabra, dabra, bra, ra, a"* and then he kept silent for a few seconds. The idea was that just as the words of this formula dissipate down to silence, so would the evil powers that he was battling likewise dissipate into silence and nothingness. Loeb was well aware that non-Jewish magicians had appropriated the words "Abra cadabra" from an old Jewish formula in Aramaic that meant, "I create as I speak."

Loeb then recited the formula that he had read in *The Book of the Pious* the requisite seven times: "With the consent of the Almighty, and with the consent of those that guard and protect this place, may it now be forbidden for any demon, male or female, to dwell in this place. May all curses and maledictions placed upon this place, from all times past and present, now be removed and banished, never to return. Amen."

Loeb then reached into his briefcase and took out a *shofar*, a ram's horn. He blew seven short staccato notes, three longer wailing notes, and repeated this litany seven times. He then blew the "great blast"—a long, high shrill note that sliced the still night air like a scalpel. When Loeb finished, he was out of breath, but taking in one large gulp of air, Loeb exhaled, quickly reciting the Aramaic phrase: *K'ra Satan*—"Satan be gone"—until he had repeated it seven times.

Unsure of whether his nocturnal activities would have any affect, Loeb began to gather up his things and prepared to leave when he heard a voice calling to him, "Hey, Jew."

A MAN IN A UNIFORM WALKED TOWARD Loeb. He wore a badge. In his left hand he held a flashlight with a powerful beam that shined in Loeb's face, obscuring his vision. In the other hand, he held something that Loeb thought might be a gun. Instinctively, Loeb raised his arms. It looked like he and his chickens would be spending the night in jail. *Perhaps it is good to have a lawyer as a wife after all*, Loeb thought.

"What da hell jew doin' here?" the man said.

As he came closer, Loeb realized that the man was not carrying a gun, and so Loeb lowered his arms. As the man approached, Loeb saw that he was wearing the uniform of a security guard. The man had Mexican features, and Loeb realized that because of his accent, he pronounced "you" as "jew." Trying to recall his high school Spanish, Loeb shouted, *"No esta una problema aquí. Por favor, yo quiero salir."*

Loeb reached into his pocket to take out the ticket stubs to the sky box, hoping that upon seeing them the guard would think that somehow, Loeb had been locked in the stadium after the game. But, when the guard heard the chickens cackling, Loeb knew that his attempted ruse would not work.

"*Que pasa aquí, hombre?*" the guard asked.

Hoping that the guard spoke English, Loeb said slowly,

"I am a rabbi—a Jewish rabbi. I came here to do a ritual to remove the curse from the Cubs. My name is Rabbi Jay Loeb. I live here in Chicago. I attended the game in a sky box. Here are the tickets. Now I want to leave, but I do not know how to get out. Can you help me?"

The guard shined the flashlight right into Loeb's face, thinking about whether to believe him and considering what to do. Calling the police would be a hassle. But, letting Loeb go free might cause even worse problems.

The guard began to stare at Loeb as if he recognized him, but couldn't remember from where. Suddenly, a wide grin appeared on his face,

"You dat rabbi—da buddy of *el Cardinal, sí?*"

"Yes," said Loeb, "I am Rabbi Loeb, Rabbi Jay Loeb, the friend of Cardinal Hood."

"*Con mucho gusto*," said the guard, extending his hand to Loeb. "*Me llamo Jorge Matalón.*"

Loeb shook his hand, and unable to think of anything else to say, replied, "*Gracias, muchas gracias.*"

"I 'ope you take out dat curse, *señor rabino. Pero*, why chickens?"

"It's a long story. Please, do not tell anyone I was here. Please help me to leave."

"OK, seence jew da Cardinal's friend, I 'elp jew. Follow me. I take jew out."

The guard led Loeb through the dugout to a hallway that passed by the dressing rooms to a door that led to the street. The guard made the sign of the cross of his chest, kissed his fingers, unlocked the door, and motioned for Loeb to leave.

"*Vaya con Dios*," said the guard.

As he left, Loeb recited a Hebrew blessing and thanked the guard, who crossed himself again.

Loeb went out into the damp Chicago summer night air, carrying his briefcase and his chickens, and recited a Hebrew prayer said on occasions when one escapes harm after having been in a dangerous situation. A little dizzy from his fasting and parched with thirst, yet exhilarated by the night's adventures, Loeb walked toward Sheridan Road, his chickens and his briefcase firmly in hand.

Reaching Sheridan Road, Loeb felt safe for the first time that evening. There were still people walking on the street, returning from a late evening out. Traffic was flowing on Lake Shore Drive. Loeb walked south toward Lincoln Park, contemplating the fate of his chickens.

There was a variety of customs as to what to do with chickens into which a curse has been transferred. One custom was to kill them, and give their meat to the poor. But Loeb did not have the heart to do that to his companions for that unusual evening. Soon Loeb came to Lincoln Park, and he remembered the Children's Zoo to which he often had brought Joshua when he was a little boy. He went there, and placed the chickens within the yard that housed chickens during the day. The chickens seemed delighted with their freedom, and immediately started pecking on the ground to find some of the kernels of grain that were scattered there. Loeb left, hoping that in the morning they would be found and made part of the family of chickens that populated the Children's Zoo. "Better to give joy to children, than to provide someone with a Sabbath dinner. After all, the curse is not contagious," he said to himself, convinced that he had made the right decision.

Loeb remembered that there was an all-night pancake house not far from the zoo. He used to take Joshua there when he was a little boy because they made "smiley face" pancakes with whipped cream and chocolate chips that Joshua liked. He went there, ordered orange juice, coffee, two bagels and cream cheese, and went to the men's room to wash up and to relieve himself. After reciting the blessing for going to the bathroom, he sat down to his breakfast, saying the requisite blessings over the food. When he was done, he felt better. After he recited the Grace after Meals, Loeb paid the bill, leaving a generous tip, left, and took a taxi home, where he found Tamara and Joshua peacefully asleep. Before he could recite the prayer said before going to sleep, Loeb had fallen asleep.

IT WAS A FRIDAY MORNING, AND TAMARA woke up at her usual 6:30 to get ready to go to work and to drop Joshua at school on the way. She knew that her husband had come to bed in the early morning hours, so she tried not to wake him. He often spent all of Thursday night studying and writing, so she didn't give a second thought to his coming to bed so late. She kissed him on the cheek, shook her head in disapproval as she listened to him snore loudly, and left the room. About a half-hour later, Joshua came in, and, as he did every morning before leaving for school, yelled, "See ya, Dad," and he and Tamara left the house. Loeb slept past noon, not even stirring to the sound of the telephone.

Loeb awoke refreshed, wondering about the outcome of his nocturnal activities. He showered, shaved, and sat a long time on the toilet contemplating what he had done. The Talmudic adage, "He who prolongs his stay in the privy, extends the years of his life," popped into his mind. He dressed, and because of the time of day, he recited both the morning and afternoon prayers, and made himself some eggs, toast and coffee. At 3 P.M., the housekeeper arrived, having already shopped for the groceries, and began to prepare the Sabbath meal. When Loeb saw her preparing chicken soup and roasted chicken, he lost his appetite, thinking of the chickens with which he had spent the previous evening. By now, the chickens should have become part of their newly adopted family, safe from the butcher's knife.

Loeb went to his desk and opened the mail. "Only bills—no checks," he muttered to himself. He called the office at the seminary to see if he had received any calls, but the seminary had already closed for the day, since the Sabbath was only hours away. Looking into his wallet, where he had placed the instructions for accessing his voice mail, Loeb followed the procedures, and listened to a litany of messages, each of which concluded with a request to return the call to a number recited so quickly that he had to listen to each message four or five times to be able to write down the phone number. Some messages were from colleagues with questions, others from students about their assignments, a few lecture invitations, and one message from a literary agent telling him that there was no real market for his scholarly writings and that perhaps he should write a "popular" book about kabbalistic magic.

Loeb was a technophobe, distrustful of machines, always afraid he would inadvertently break them—which he often did. Having successfully retrieved his voice mail messages, Loeb decided that he should try his hand at his computer.

Joshua had taught him how to surf the web—though in a fashion correlative with his father's skills. Joshua also had taught him how to send and retrieve e-mails, though it took Loeb a few lessons until he caught on. To his surprise, Loeb found that he had over twenty e-mail messages, mostly from his colleagues in Europe and Israel, and by the time he had finished responding to them, Tamara and Joshua were home.

"You were up late again last night?" Tamara asked.

Loeb knew that living with a lawyer meant that you were constantly like a witness on the stand being cross-examined. He knew that lawyers were argumentative, both by training and by disposition, so he usually ignored Tamara's polemical approach to just about anything he might say, including "Hello."

"Uh-huh," Loeb answered noncommittally. "See you at dinner? 6:30?"

Tamara grunted what he presumed was a "yes." Loeb shut down his computer for its Sabbath rest, and recited the prayers welcoming the Sabbath. As he saw the sun descend, Loeb looked at his watch and realized that dinner would soon be served.

The Friday night Sabbath meal was Loeb's favorite time of the week. It was the only time the family was together, without the intrusions of work, school or the telephone, which was not used on the Sabbath. It was a time in which the Loeb family could re-establish the intimacy that had slipped away during the preceeding week.

Tamara lit the Sabbath candles, after which she kissed and hugged Loeb and Joshua, wishing each of them a Good Sabbath—*Shabbat Shalom*. They joined hands to sing the age-old tune welcoming the Sabbath angels, the angels of peace, into their home. Following custom, Loeb then sang the verses from the Proverbs about the "Woman of Valor" to Tamara, who winced as each verse escaped his lips, hoping for a speedy conclusion to the monotone chanting of his expression of love and admiration for her.

Placing his hands on Joshua's head, Loeb blessed his son with the ancient blessing with which the biblical patriarch Jacob had instructed his descendants to bless their children from generation to generation. Loeb gently kissed Joshua on the forehead, silently thanking God for the blessing that had illumined his life, the blessing that was Joshua.

Each washed their hands in the manner prescribed by ritual—filling a cup, and then pouring the water over one hand, and then the other. They went to the table where the blessings over the wine and bread were recited. Since Joshua's Bar Mitzvah, Loeb had assigned the recitation of these blessings to him. Joshua only complied with his father's wishes because he knew how much it pleased his father to hear him chant the age-old blessings that had been recited each Sabbath, for so many generations before them.

Still thinking about his chickens, Loeb refused to have either the soup or the roasted chicken set out before him. Claiming that he was starting a new diet, Loeb restricted himself to salad and gefilte fish. Turning to his son, Loeb began the conversation the same way he did every Friday night.

"Tell me about your week."

Loeb knew that this particular week, unlike other weeks, there were things about his own activities that he had to keep a secret from his family. It was ironic, because this week—unlike most weeks—what he had to tell them would be of real interest for them to hear.

Joshua talked about his schoolwork, going systematically from subject to subject and reviewing his progress in school that week. He reported on each of the tests he had taken, on each of the grades he had received, being sure to explain that on the tests on which he thought he should have had a better grade, the other students had not done well either. He talked about his friends, his school baseball team, on which he played shortstop, and occasionally pitcher. He announced that he had a date that Saturday night, but offered no information about with whom, or where he planned to go. Then, as he did every week, Joshua made an excuse for why he wanted to be permitted to leave the table. This time, it was to study for SATs. Loeb let him go, and for the first time all week, he and Tamara were alone—a portent of things to come when Joshua would go off to college.

"So, what's happening at the firm? Any repercussions from the trial?" Loeb asked.

"I'd rather not discuss it now, Jay. I've had a tough week. I'm tired. I'm going into my study to read a little. You understand, don't you?"

Loeb had been alone most of the week, and he cherished the time he had with Tamara, especially at the Sabbath dinner table. But he looked at his watch, and let her go. It was almost 8:00, and he knew that the Cubs game must already have started.

Tamara went into her study, closed the door, lay down on the couch in her room, put on earphones and listened to the Cubs game on the radio while she watched it on the television that she had preset before the Sabbath to the right channel. It took all of her self-control not to yell and scream as she watched. Loeb did not approve of watching television on the Sabbath.

At the end of the game, Tamara emerged happily from her room. The Cubs had shut out the Braves, 7-0, with a no-hitter by the rookie Cubs pitcher against the veteran Braves hurler. She went into the bedroom, where she found Loeb in bed, still dressed, with a Hebrew book in his hand. He apparently had been waiting for her, but had fallen asleep. She crawled into bed, and soon was asleep, with a joyous grin on her face.

The next day, Sabbath morning, Jay Loeb awoke early, and seemed surprised to find himself still dressed from the night before. The sun had begun to rise. Tamara slept soundly. Loeb went into Joshua's room to look in on him, and found him tossing and talking in his restless sleep. Loeb washed, and tried to decide whether he would go to the synagogue that morning. After reviewing in his mind the various synagogues nearby to which he could go, he decided to pray alone, at home. He had no patience to sit though the three-hour-long service, to listen to people gossip when they should be praying, and to a rabbi deliver a sermon that he had downloaded from a sermon service on the internet the day before.

Loeb went into his study, enveloped himself in his huge prayer shawl, and began to intone the Sabbath morning liturgy. When he was done, he reviewed the Scriptural readings designated for that week and he studied some of the commentaries on it. Loeb folded up his prayer shawl, kissed it, and put in back in the large velvet bag from which he had taken it.

Finding himself unusually energetic, Loeb felt like a long walk. Returning to the bedroom, he changed into shorts and a tee shirt, and left the house.

Not paying much attention to the direction he had taken, Loeb found himself on the way to Lincoln Park. The walk took over an hour, but it was worth it when he saw his chickens clucking away happily in their new home, instead of constituting someone's Sabbath lunch.

Loeb walked through the underpass near North Avenue that took him under Lake Shore Drive and onto the shore where sunbathers carpeted the beach. An animated volleyball game was well underway. Children played in the sand. Couples fondled one another under the blankets that covered them. Barely dressed young men and women looked one another over, as if they were window-shopping on Michigan Avenue's "Magnificent Mile." On the walk nearby, joggers puffed along, roller-bladers sped by, and older people slowly shuffled past, recalling the stamina they once had.

Loeb lay down on a patch of grass, and looked up at the sky. He heard the waves of the lake gently caressing the shore. He listened to the laughter of children, and he thought of the verse in the Psalms, "How marvelous are Thy works, O Lord. You have made them all in wisdom. The entire world is Your dominion." When Loeb next looked at his watch, some hours had passed. He had fallen asleep.

Loeb went to a water fountain, washed his hands and face, sprinkled some water on his neck, and began the long trek home. He wished it were not the Sabbath when riding in a car and using money are forbidden; otherwise, he would have walked back to Sheridan Road, and taken a cab home.

Loeb walked northward along the lake. The sailboats were out in force, punctuating the bright blue water with dots of white from their sails. As Loeb approached Belmont Harbor, he noticed that traffic had thickened. "There must be a game—maybe a double-header at Wrigley today," he said to himself, as he continued his way home.

When Loeb arrived home, he found the house empty. Drenched with sweat from his long walk in the humid heat, Loeb washed himself off, changed his clothes, drank a bottle of mineral water, and made himself a late lunch. He picked up a book and started to read, but soon he fell asleep and dreamed that he was making love to Tamara on a deserted North Avenue Beach, early in the morning, before the joggers came out to run. The sound of the front door slamming abruptly awakened him. It was Joshua.

The sun was setting, and the Sabbath would soon come to an end. Joshua went to prepare for his date. Loeb went into his study and said the afternoon and evening prayers, bringing the Sabbath to an end. Before Joshua left, he and Loeb "made *havdalah*"—the ritual separating the Sabbath from the other days of the week, the holy from the mundane. Joshua held the braided candle as his father sang the plaintive chant, sorrowfully bidding the Sabbath "goodbye" for another week. They each smelled the spices—meant to revive one's soul after its having to part with the "extra soul," granted for each Sabbath day. Together, they sang the song of Elijah the prophet, who, according to tradition, wanders the earth in a variety of disguises, and who, one day, will announce the coming of messianic redemption. After he and Joshua had drunk the sanctified wine, Loeb put out the candle in the remaining wine, as was the custom. He wished his son "a good week," and kissed him on the forehead. Soon after, Joshua left and Loeb was alone once more in his study, with his books—his constant companions and faithful friends. But not for long.

About an hour later, Tamara bounded through the front door. She had been at the Cubs game—a double-header, a double victory for the Cubs. "Three in a row," Tamara said to Loeb, greeting him with a big kiss on the lips. *The chickens have done their duty*, Loeb thought to himself, and he turned to go into his study. But Tamara pulled him back.

"Aren't you tired from walking back and forth from Wrigley, and from being outside all day in the sun?" he asked her.

"No. I went to my friend Becky's after the game, and she drove me home. Sabbath was already about over by then. Let's go out tonight. I feel like dancing."

"How would dinner do?"

"OK. My treat."

They went to a restaurant near the house, and Tamara ordered a cocktail because the restaurant did not carry kosher champagne.

"Are we finally celebrating your triumph this week in court?"

"No, we're celebrating the Cubs' three-game winning streak. It's been a long time since the last one."

The menu had little on it that they could eat, given their observance of *kashrut*—the Jewish dietary laws. But Loeb didn't mind. He was pleased to see Tamara so happy.

"Since the trial, I've been offered a contract to write a textbook on the First Amendment. DePaul University Law School has offered me a visiting professorship for the next semester. Lecture invitations from law schools have been coming in. And the Cubs won three games in a row. What a week!"

"Are you going to accept any of those offers?"

"What do you think I should do, Jay? It's all coming so fast."

Since she had passed the bar, Tamara rarely had asked her husband's opinion about anything having to do with her legal career. That she asked now caught him by surprise.

"I have to go to the bathroom. Don't get 'picked up' while I'm away."

Loeb returned a few minutes later. He really did not have to go to the bathroom, but he needed a few minutes to think. Loeb reviewed in his mind what Kalinsky had told him, and he realized that he should urge Tamara to take the offers.

Loeb returned to the table, sat down, and said, "I think that the first thing on Monday, you should ask the firm for a leave, and take the offers. They may never come again. And when the leave is up, you can always go back to the firm; or, perhaps, go somewhere else."

"I do have other offers, you know?"

"From other men, or other firms?"

"From both. You're still jealous after all these years?"

A serious look came over Loeb's face. He took Tamara's hand in his and kissed it.

"I don't usually give you advice about your work, primarily because you don't seem to want it. But, since you asked, I think you should take a leave, write your book, teach the classes, give the lectures, and ask for a nice big severance package from the firm—I think they'll offer it, if you ask. And go somewhere else. Your partners are not your friends. Believe me."

Tamara was stunned by the intensity of Loeb's gaze as he spoke. Not knowing how to respond, all she could say was, "I'll sleep on it—after we sleep together. Get the check and let's go home. I'll give you 'dessert in bed'—just the way you like it."

Jay and Tamara walked home like new lovers, hand in hand, staring at one another. When they got through the door, they began to kiss and to undress one another. During the hour that followed, they left no erotic stone unturned.

Loeb staggered naked into the bedroom. Tamara picked up their clothes and followed, wearing only her shoes.

"I'll wait up for Joshua. You go to sleep," she said.

"I don't hope that he had as good a time tonight as his father did," Loeb said, as he shut the bedroom door. He put on some underwear, but forgot to say the prayer before retiring for the night. His last thought before falling asleep was, "That was even better than my dream. Thank you, chickens. Thank you, God."

THOUGH THE FOLLOWING DAY WAS A day off for most people, Sunday was a regular work day for Loeb. Sunday morning was when he usually went to his office at the seminary to work on his correspondence and to meet with his students. In the afternoon and into the early evening, Loeb taught his seminars: one in medieval Jewish philosophy, and the other in Talmud. Meanwhile, Joshua stayed home, practicing the piano and doing his homework. Tamara headed out for the last game of the Cubs homestand.

As a season ticketholder, Tamara sat in the same seat every time she attended a game. Loeb referred to her seat as her "endowed chair" because of all the money she spent on Cubs tickets. Her fantasy was to be sitting in her reserved seat during a World Series between the Cubs and the Yankees. Loeb always told her that the Messiah would probably come first.

Tamara bought a beer and went to her seat. She was wearing her Cubs hat, shorts with the Cubs logo, and a halter top. Her ample breasts strained the tight orange top of the garment. Her legs were the envy of many of her female friends. Her jet-black hair had only the slightest hint of gray. Her eyes were a sparkling green. Though in her mid-forties, she looked as if she were only in her mid-thirties. As had happened so many other times when she had attended the games alone, both men and women tried to pick her up. But Tamara was oblivious to their initiatives. Her attention was completely focused on her beloved "Cubbies."

After the national anthem had been sung, the Cubs took the field. A wave of cheers from the crowd greeted them, as if they were coming out of the dugout to start the first game of the World Series. Tamara joined in the mantra-like chant, "Let's go Cubs. Let's go Cubs." It was the top of the first inning, and the top of the St. Louis batting order came up to bat.

Each time Tamara saw the Cardinals, she remembered how excited Joshua had been when Loeb had invited him to meet his friend, the newly-appointed Cardinal of Chicago. Joshua thought that Loeb was taking him to meet one of the St. Louis Cardinals. So, when Joshua was introduced to a tall man in a black suit, wearing a clerical collar and a pectoral cross, the boy was clearly disappointed.

The Cubs pitcher, Hank Hornsberry, who had recently been called up from the minors, looked like a lanky farm-hand. He had long, dirty-blond, stringy hair, a pock-marked face, and a decidedly sinister gaze, aimed at intimidating the batter. He also had a ninety-eight-mile-an-hour fast ball, and a wickedly effective slider.

This was not Hornsberry's first appearance at Wrigley Field. The previous season he had pitched there in an exhibition game between the Cubs and their AAA farm club. Because of the long string of Cubs losses during that season, Cubs management had decided to demonstrate that the Cubs could beat someone with no trouble—their own farm team. But the Cubs ended up losing even to them. Hornsberry had been the pitcher for the minor league club, and because of the interest he had sparked among the fans, he was brought up to the majors.

When Hornsberry walked the first batter, the deafening cheers of the crowd that had jammed the ball park turned into a deep sigh that sounded like air escaping from a balloon. But, when each of the next three batters struck out, the screams of the crowd carried over the "Friendly Confines" of Wrigley Field into the surrounding Wrigleyville neighborhood. The chain of strikeouts reminded Tamara of the time she had taken one of Loeb's European colleagues to a baseball game, and had tried to explain to him the rules of baseball.

Jan Bjorklund taught biblical studies at Sweden's University of Lund. He had been in Chicago to serve as a visiting professor at the King Gustavus Adolphus Lutheran Seminary of Chicago. Some years before, he had met Jay Loeb at a conference in Warsaw at The Academy for Catholic Theology, and they became friends—meeting occasionally at conferences throughout the world, reading each other's books and articles, and regularly corresponding with one another. Unlike Loeb, Bjorklund was an avid sports fan. He had visited the United States many times, but could not understand the American fascination with baseball. Like most Europeans, he found it a tedious and slow-moving game when compared with basketball, soccer or hockey. Yet, he thought that if he could attend a game and have it explained to him, he might develop an appreciation for this peculiar American "national pastime."

Bjorklund could not understand why baseball, unlike so many other sports, had no time limit. For example, a basketball game was divided into four quarters of equal duration, but baseball was divided into nine innings of no pre-determined duration. And, if the game were tied at the end of nine innings, it could extend indefinitely until someone triumphed. In other sports, there were penalties for fouls, but in baseball a foul was not necessarily a bad thing, but usually a do-over, and stealing was a good thing. In other sports, like rugby, the goal is to strike the ball. But, in baseball, a strike could mean that the ball was not struck at all. Indeed, one could receive a strike without even trying to strike the ball. The more Tamara tried to explain the rules of baseball to him, the more confused and befuddled Bjorklund became.

Loeb had explained to Bjorklund that a baseball game was like the study of a complicated text. It had many levels of understanding, and the more a person knew of the game, the more he or she understood all of the subtle nuances of each play. On the surface, it seemed very simple: a man stands with a piece of wood, and tries to hit a ball thrown at him at high velocity. If he hits it, someone on the opposing team tries to catch it, preferably before it hits the ground; or, if not, to catch it and throw it to his teammate who must step on a pillow-like square object before the person who hit the ball arrives there. On deeper levels, however, Loeb explained, there were the subtleties of each pitch, the mysterious signals given by the manager and coaches to the players and by the catcher to the pitcher, constant shifts of fielders' positions, the ongoing cat-and-mouse game between the pitcher and the hitter, and so much more. Loeb suggested to Bjorklund that he think of baseball as if it were a chess game, replete with complex strategies and attempts to anticipate the opponent's next move. Loeb had given articles to Bjorklund explaining why the hardest thing to do in any sport was to successfully hit a baseball.

After the game, when they had returned to Loeb's home for dinner, Bjorklund confessed that he could decipher the most abstruse texts in ancient languages no longer spoken, like Phoenician and Ugaritic, but he doubted whether he would ever be able to get any more than a very fundamental grasp of the game of baseball.

But Tamara understood every nuance of the game, every idiosyncrasy of each player. She knew the tactics of each manager, and more often than not, predicted his next move, even before he had decided to make it. When she listened to the games on the radio or on TV, she would often offer the same observations—usually to herself—that the sports commentators would eventually provide. She might not be able to explain the game to a European—but which American could? Nor could she explain, even to Loeb, why baseball evoked such a strong passion in her and in so many millions of others. For Tamara, baseball was more than entertainment, more than a diversion. It was like a religion, a way of life, based on faith, hope and commitment. And that was why Tamara resented her husband's lack of interest in what was of paramount importance to her. Tamara was jealous that Loeb had the opportunity as a boy to play baseball in Little League and in school, while she had been restricted to "girls' sports." When Joshua was born, she made sure that baseball was a big part of his life. She took him to games, coached his Little League team, and even hired a personal coach to train him. Often it seemed that Joshua was caught in a tug of war between his father's religion and his mother's. To Loeb's dismay, it often seemed that Tamara's religion was winning, capturing his son's allegiance.

Joshua was no superstar, yet he was the mainstay of his high school baseball team. Though his fastball hovered in the seventy-mile-an-hour range, Joshua had learned how to pitch with his head. He was not fast, but smart. He would psych out the batter, often getting him to strike out or to ground out. He wasn't much of a batter, though. He had to work hard at it. As in so many other things he did, Joshua made up for what he lacked in natural abilities with perseverance. He took very seriously the quote from Thomas Alva Edison that Loeb had told him when he was a little boy: "Genius is one percent inspiration, and ninety-nine percent perspiration."

Loeb's apathy for the game of baseball, indeed, for all sports, was not because of a lack of exposure to them. His father had been a champion athlete in high school, college, and later in the army. Until well into his seventies, he played full-court basketball every week at the Jewish Community Center gymnasium.

As a child growing up in New York in the 1950s, Loeb had seen some of baseball's greatest players: Mantle, Mays, Snyder and others of that vintage. Throughout his childhood, he listened to his father's stories of how he had seen the great Ruth and Gehrig play. Loeb had heard again and again his father's story of how once, when he was hitching a ride to a game at Yankee Stadium, Babe Ruth's limo picked him up on the Grand Concourse, and he met "the Babe," who gave him an autographed ball that remained his prize possession. However, Loeb never saw the ball; his father always claimed that it was locked up in a safe-deposit box at a downtown bank.

Every Father's Day during his childhood, Loeb would accompany his father and his grandfather to Yankee Stadium to watch the champion Yankees play. Loeb's father encouraged him to be athletic, especially to play baseball. To please his father, he made an effort. Many times, Tamara told Loeb, "Some men marry their mothers, but you married your father," to which Loeb would always reply, "My father never looked like you."

Loeb's grandfather—his mother's father—was a Jewish immigrant from the Ukraine. His name was Sammy Shane (*né* Shmuel Yashonofsky of Kiev). Loeb always believed that his grandfather's love of baseball was simply his way of proving to himself that, despite his thick accent and East European mannerisms, he had finally become a "real" American. In contrast, Loeb's father considered baseball as a way of demonstrating one's manhood, as a rite of male passage. However, Tamara's motivation for being obsessed with the game completely eluded Loeb. Rather than being preoccupied with sports, Loeb was obsessed with learning and study. There was so much he wanted to know; so much to understand, and so little time to do it. Life, after all, as the prayer book put it, was "like a fleeting breath, like a withering wind"—somewhat like hopes for the Cubs to win the pennant.

As a child, Loeb had learned many things from his grandparents, but none so important for his later life as how to give complete and unconditional love. From his father, Loeb also had learned many things, such as always to see things from a broad, long-run perspective, rather than to react immediately, and often too emotionally, to the exigencies of the moment. But, despite everything his father had tried to teach him, baseball was, for his father, the most important thing he had to teach his son. Loeb was attentive to his father's lessons in how to play baseball, not out of interest, but out of a desire not to disappoint his father. Other Jewish fathers wanted their sons to be doctors, lawyers, businessmen. But Stanley Loeb wanted his son to be a professional athlete.

Except when he was with his grandfather, Loeb never chose to watch baseball on TV. But he cherished every minute he had with his doting grandfather. Some of his friends had already experienced the deaths of their grandparents, and the young Loeb instinctively knew that later on in life, he would regret those precious and irretrievable moments he had with his grandfather. He especially treasured those few minutes during the commercial breaks that punctuated the baseball games on TV, when his grandmother would come into the living room, bringing milk and sponge cake, and he would listen to his grandparents reminisce about the "Old Country," or about how they spent their honeymoon on a fire-escape in Jewish Harlem.

Loeb's "Grandpa Sammy" would sit in his favorite chair in front of the TV, sipping tea through a sugar cube he had placed between his front teeth. He had assigned Yiddish names to almost all of the Yankee players. It was not until Loeb began school and traded baseball cards with his friends that he knew their real names. Mickey Mantle was Moshele Mendel. Phil Rizzutto was Faivele Ruski. Yogi Berra was Yossele Babka. Ken Boyer was Ketzele Boyarsky, and so forth.

To make his father happy, Loeb joined the Little League when he was about nine years old. To his father's surprise, Jay Loeb, though catastrophic in the field, emerged as one of the best hitters on the team. Once, Loeb was asked to pinch-hit in a playoff game. There were runners on second and third with two out, in the last of the ninth. The score was 9-7, with the other team ahead. Loeb missed the first two pitches. Though the third pitch was high and outside, he lunged at it, sending it into the outfield for a double. Two runs scored. The game was tied. The next batter nervously approached the plate, aware that everything depended upon him. But, before he stepped into the batter's box, Loeb called "time." The coach went out to second base to see what he wanted. Loeb asked that a pinch runner be put in for him. Everyone thought this was a clever move because Loeb was a chubby boy, and running was not his forte. But Loeb had another reason for his request. When he went into the dugout, he took out a book from his tote bag, and began to read. He had done what he knew his father had wanted him to do by getting a hit. Now, he could do what *he* wanted to do, which was to study.

THE CUBS CAME UP TO BAT IN THE bottom of the first. As each player stepped into the batter's box, he was welcomed by the fans as if he were a war hero returning home. As often happened at Wrigley, the wind was blowing in. Each batter launched a high rocket into the outfield, only to watch it hit a wall of wind, and be blown back over the field and caught. Yet, even this was cheered by the fans, who yelled, "At least, we're hittin' 'em."

During the top of the next inning, when the Cubs took the field, Tamara screamed instructions to the Cubs manager, coaches and players, and during the bottom of the inning, she yelled her orders at the Cubs batters. When a Cubs hitter got on base, she told him when to steal, and when he was in danger of being picked off. Her efforts at playing phantom manager went unheeded; yet, by the fifth inning, the Cubs were leading 7-4. By the seventh inning stretch, when the crowd got up to sing, "Take Me Out to the Ball Game," Tamara was so hoarse that she did not recognize her own voice.

In the eighth inning, the Cubs' veteran "closer" was brought in.

Even though he was having his worst year in the majors, the fans greeted him with a roar of acclaim. Fifteen pitches later, the stunned fans rose to cheer. The Cubs had won. They had won more consecutive games at home during this homestand than they had won in the past six years. Tamara jumped up and down, cheering so hard that she failed to notice that her breasts had popped out of her halter. Luckily, she felt it happen and replaced them before the WGN cameraman had embarrassed her in front of the Chicagoland viewing public. She thought of the headline that might have been: "Rabbi's Wife, Porno Defender, Becomes TV Porno Queen."

When Tamara arrived home, she heard Joshua practicing on the piano. Loeb was still at work. She undressed, showered, changed her clothes, and went to the kitchen to do something she rarely did—prepare dinner. Soon after Joshua was born, she hired a housekeeper to be sure that her "boys" were fed, especially when she was working late at the office, which was increasingly frequent as Joshua got older. During the early years of their marriage, Loeb did all of the cooking. He was an unusually fine cook, but he always left the kitchen a mess. When their first housekeeper arrived, Loeb's career as the family cook came to an abrupt end.

Tamara had made a concerted effort to learn how to cook, but with limited success. However, she had progressed significantly since she and Loeb were first married. On their first Saturday at home together after their honeymoon, Loeb prepared the Sabbath meals for Friday night and Saturday lunch. After lunch, she provided the first of many of what she called "our desserts at home." Then they slept the "Sabbath rest," that somehow always seemed more satisfying than any other period of sleep during the week. When Loeb awoke that first Sabbath at home, she offered to make a light supper when the Sabbath had come to a close.

They made their first *havdalah* together, and kissed deeply. Tamara asked Loeb what he wanted for supper. Knowing that Tamara was then "culinarily challenged," Loeb tried to make it simple: "A tuna salad would be fine."

"Piece of cake," said Tamara. "I'll call you when it's ready." Loeb retreated into his study to await her call. For the next hour, all he heard was banging in the kitchen, the noise of various kitchen appliances, and the sound of Tamara cursing. About an hour and a half later, Tamara called him in for supper. On his plate was a piece of lettuce, a sliced tomato and a puddle of some grayish substance.

"What is this?" Loeb asked.

"Tuna salad," she answered defensively. "That's what you asked for."

"Yeah, but I never saw it like this before."

"I innovated."

"How?"

"I made it in the blender."

Loeb drank his tuna salad, and from then until Joshua was born, Loeb became the resident chef.

It was now twenty years since then, and Tamara had learned how to make certain things well. One was hamburgers. By the time Loeb had returned home, a dinner of hamburgers, mashed potatoes and asparagus was set out on the candle-lit table. Loeb and Joshua ate, while Tamara provided a play-by-play description of the Cubs game.

The following morning, Tamara took Joshua to school while Loeb stayed home to prepare for his classes that evening. As was often the case, the seminary was having financial difficulties. And, as usual, this meant that there would be a faculty meeting to discuss the situation before classes began. Meanwhile, Tamara arrived at her office, and attacked her work with gusto. The Cubs had that day off as a "travel day," so she knew she could work straight through the day, trying to catch up with her work. The housekeeper would give Joshua dinner.

Tamara ploughed through her work with efficiency and speed, alternately dictating letters and memos, returning phone calls, reading her mail, dealing with her e-mail and visiting her colleagues for updates about progress on this or that legal matter.

At about 12:15, Chuck Flaherty knocked on her door, and walked in before she had a chance to react.

"Lunch, fifteen minutes? Meet you at the receptionist's desk?"

Not waiting for a response, he left. Tamara looked at her watch, completed dictating the memo she had begun, handed a minicassette to her secretary, went to the ladies' room, and left to meet Flaherty. Though he often prided himself on being "fashionably late"—more a matter of a power game than of fashion—Flaherty was waiting for Tamara when she arrived. They took the elevator down while he talked about the surprising stream of Cubs victories. They went to a restaurant less than a block from the office where Flaherty had reserved a corner booth, discreetly distanced from the closest table. Tamara began to become suspicious, and she remembered what Loeb had told her about her partners.

Flaherty continued to talk about the Cubs as they reviewed the menu and ordered lunch. Tamara had the distinct impression that he was trying to bait her, and not just to make polite conversation. She remembered one of the quotes from the Talmud that Loeb liked to cite: "The gate to wisdom—silence." As Flaherty spoke, she occasionally nodded, but kept silent. She could see that her strategy was working on Flaherty, and that he was aware that his own strategy, whatever it was, had begun to fail. She knew that he had an agenda, possibly not a pleasant one, so she just waited until he was ready to reveal it. But Flaherty knew that if he revealed his hand too soon and too overtly, he would not get what he wanted.

Tamara also knew that Flaherty was attracted to her, and that he had had a string of young mistresses. His strict Catholic upbringing made divorce an impossible option for him to consider, so he preferred to live with his dalliances and his guilt. Tamara was not sure whether he was about to try to seduce her, to request her resignation from the firm, or to offer her a promotion from income partner to capital partner.

Flaherty rarely said what he had on his mind. Even when he said something that he knew was unpleasant, he said it in a way that sounded like he was doing the other person a favor. Tamara had once seen him fire an associate at the firm by telling the young lawyer that his being "separated from the firm" was actually "a great opportunity for career advancement."

"What's been the fallout from your verdict?" Flaherty asked.

"Besides embarrassing Jay, not much."

"What's not much—no offers?"

"Well, yes. An offer from Binder Books to write a textbook on the First Amendment. An invitation to teach at DePaul Law School. About thirty lecture invitations—each with a hefty honorarium—mostly out of town. Magazines, radio and TV asking for interviews. The usual stuff—so far."

"No offers from other firms?"

"Would I tell you if there were?" Tamara asked rhetorically.

Flaherty downed his second Scotch while the entree was served, and he thought about his next move.

"Going to take anything?"

Tamara knew as well as Flaherty that it's easier to catch a bear with honey. So, she heaved her breasts, put her hands in back of her neck and stretched, thereby diverting Flaherty's attention from the issue at hand. She sighed seductively, and said, "I've been thinking about it. Got any suggestions? You know, I always value your advice."

Pretending to be both gallant and caring, Flaherty said, "I think you should take the offers. It may be a once in a lifetime opportunity. If you like, I'll talk to the firm's executive committee, and push through a leave of absence for you."

"You know, that's just what Jay said you'd say when I discussed this with him."

Flaherty thought to himself, *The jewboy's as smart as everyone says he is. After all, look at what he's got in the sack every night.*

Flaherty winked and said, "And, after I arrange all this for you, I'm sure you'll find an appropriate way of thanking me."

Tamara smiled coyly and shot back, "You're teetering on the brink of sexual harassment, Chucky."

Flaherty had a reputation for having verbally and physically abused some of the female members of the firm's support staff. A few of them had come to Tamara to discuss it, and she urged them to file formal charges. But, afraid of jeopardizing their jobs, none ever did.

Flaherty thought that he had won round one. By giving Tamara a leave of absence to write her books, teach and lecture, he had taken the first step toward pushing her out of the firm, without encumbering the firm with any legal exposures. By the smirk on his face, Tamara knew that he thought he had achieved his goal, whatever it was, and that he would now begin a careful and calculated campaign to try to seduce her. Tamara's years of courtroom experience had taught her how to read a jury made up of strangers. Certainly, she knew how to read a man with whom she had worked for the past seven years.

"How does a six month leave sound to you, Chuck? But with my usual monthly draw and with benefits," Tamara added before he had the chance to respond.

"OK," said Flaherty reluctantly, suddenly aware that he had just lost that round.

Flaherty called over the waiter to pay the check, and gulped down the remaining coffee in his cup. The waiter came over to take the check and Flaherty's credit card. Tamara knew that Flaherty was her captive for at least a few more minutes. She folded her hands on the table, leaned forward and said, "And, besides my draw, Chuck, I want a nice fat severance offer from the firm, if you don't want me back after my leave."

Before Flaherty had a chance to respond, Tamara got up and walked toward the ladies' room, but as she approached the ladies' room, she waved "goodbye" to Flaherty and left the restaurant, hailed a taxi, and went home.

Loeb was still at the seminary, and Joshua was still at school when Tamara arrived at home. The housekeeper was straightening up the house, doing the laundry and beginning to prepare dinner. The phone rang, and the caller-ID indicated that it was the office—probably Flaherty. She didn't answer.

Tamara went into her study and began to compose drafts of letters responding to the offers she had received to lecture, teach, write, and to be interviewed by the media. She started to work on an outline for her textbook. For the first time in years, Tamara felt free. And her Cubbies had just had a winning streak. Life was beautiful. But, in baseball as in life, things change quickly.

Loeb came home rattled. The faculty meeting had been tense. He quoted the Talmudic adage, "When the wheat in the kitchen jar is diminished, tension increases in the household." The president of the seminary had underplayed the financial problems. In fact, they were worse than Loeb had imagined. There would be salary cuts, and an increased teaching load. There were pressures to compromise the institution's academic integrity by admitting underqualified students. The trustees wanted to interfere with the curriculum. Over the objection of the faculty, they had instituted a new degree program in computer science and business administration, primarily as a way of boosting tuition revenues. Things had never been good financially at the seminary, but now they were going from bad to worse.

Loeb had refused academic appointments at prestigious universities to stay at the seminary. He now began to feel that his sacrifices had been for naught. He sounded like Tamara often did after the Cubs had suffered a disastrous defeat.

Tamara knew that unless she diverted Loeb's attention from his immediate problems, he would fall deeper and deeper into despair. These problems were ongoing at the seminary. They would pass, and he would bounce back, like he had so many times before. She had to change the subject.

"Well, sweetheart," she said, "we may be unemployed together. I told Flaherty that I was taking the lecturing and writing offers, that I wanted a six-month leave, and that I want them to make me an offer I can't refuse if they want me out."

Joshua entered the room.

"Not now," Tamara said.

Nervously, Joshua asked, "Everything OK?"

"Dad's having some problems at work. Don't worry. Go inside."

"Again?" Joshua asked.

"Still," Loeb responded.

Tamara took Loeb's hand, led him into the bedroom, turned up the radio, and locked the door.

"Maybe some dessert before dinner will make you feel better?"

It didn't take long until he did.

In the weeks that followed, the Cubs lost almost every game on the road. City after city was littered with Cubs defeats. Tamara's mood turned ugly. Ironically, that expedited the firm's executive committee to move faster. Three weeks after her luncheon with Flaherty, she had in her hands a written agreement setting out everything she had asked for. At Jay's suggestion, she went to see Kalinsky, who would represent her in her dealings with the firm. In his negotiations, Kalinsky got her more than she was initially offered. He urged her to sign the agreement. The deal was sealed, but Tamara was nervous. "What happens later? I haven't gotten any offers from other firms. What if I don't? What if other firms don't want me?" Kalinsky simply smiled and recited an expression he had learned from Loeb: "God will provide."

The Cubs returned to Chicago, and to everyone's surprise, except Loeb's, they won almost all of their home games. But, when they went back on the road, they struggled for each rare win. In the past few weeks, a pattern of home victories and on-the-road defeats had clearly emerged. Sports writers around the country were perplexed, and they conjured up all kinds of theories to account for it. The Cubs players and management were even more confused. They played just as hard on the road as at home, but the results were markedly different. No one seemed able to explain what was happening. The All-Star break was days away. Perhaps, during the latter part of the season, things would straighten out.

"MINNIE" SOTA HAD LEFT HIS NATIVE CUBA for America just before Battista's regime collapsed, and Castro had come to power. He had played professional baseball in Cuba, and thought that he would auction off his services to the highest bidder when he arrived in America. But, in those days, there were few Hispanics in the major leagues, especially black Hispanics like him. Sota was a decent player, but he was no Roberto Clemente. After a year of banging around in the minors, Bill Veeck invited him to join the Chicago White Sox. Sota played as a utility infielder and as a pinch hitter for the Sox for many years, attracting a considerable following among the Chicago fans. By the time he retired from active play, the color lines had dropped in the major leagues, and he was hired by the Cubs as a batting coach—more for his local popularity than for anything else. Sota was liked by everyone. Cheerful and upbeat, he was always accessible to sign autographs and talk to whoever wanted to talk to him. It was not surprising, therefore, when one of the security guards at Wrigley Field came up to him after a home night game, pulled him into a remote corner of the locker room, and began speaking to him in a rapid, agitated Spanish.

Jorge Matalón was well aware of the recent pattern of Cubs victories and losses. He didn't know whether what he had seen after midnight some weeks before at Wrigley Field, could explain it. But he felt obliged to tell someone what he knew. Though he had wrestled with his conscience because of the promise he had made to the rabbi not to reveal what had happened, his Catholic upbringing compelled him to confess. Rather than speaking to a priest, he decided to talk to Sota.

Sota listened patiently, wondering about Matalón's motivation as well as his mental stability. *Is he trying to cover his ass? Is he looking for a raise, a promotion? Is he making it all up? But who could make up such a story?* After Matalón had completed his rapid-fire monologue, Sota said, "All right, what's the name of this mysterious rabbi who walks around in the middle of the night carrying chickens?"

Matalón had forgotten Loeb's name, but reminding himself that the rabbi was a friend of the Cardinal, he told this to Sota. Sota thanked Matalón for coming forward with this information, and assured him that he would not lose his job for allowing a person on the field after hours. In fact, he assured Matalón that if the information he had provided could help the Cubs address their problem, there might be a raise or a promotion in it for him.

Sota couldn't sleep the entire night because he did not know what to do with what Matalón had told him. Early the next morning, he decided to call Bob Wriggles, the Cubs manager, to share his acquired information. At 8 A.M., Sota called Wriggles, who listened to the whole story without interrupting once, which was unusual. When Sota finished, Wriggles said, "I have three questions. Who is this crazy rabbi? Why did he do it? And did it work?"

"I can't give you an answer to any of those questions," Sota said. "But, I thought you should at least know what the guard told me."

"Well," said Wriggles, "it's a screwy story, but so far, it's the best explanation I've got for our pattern of wins and losses. Let's follow through on it. I'll call the GM and see what he wants to do."

At 9:05, Wriggles put through a call to the Tribune Tower Building on Michigan Avenue where the Cubs General Manager's office was located. Since the Wrigley family had sold the Cubs in a bargain-basement sale to the *Tribune*, the General Manager was no longer a baseball person, but a corporate-MBA-type, who reported to the *Trib*'s Board of Directors. Because the Cubs were playing no better—and actually worse—under *Trib* management than they had under Wrigley management, GMs regularly came and went. The current GM was Roger Post.

After listening to Wriggles' somewhat distorted version of what Matalón had told Sota, Post said, "Let's stop playing the telephone game. Get the guard, yourself and Sota up here ASAP." Within an hour, the four men were huddled around the conference table in Post's large, top-floor office at the Tribune Tower, with its marvelous bird's-eye view of Lake Michigan.

Post asked the visibly nervous Matalón to tell his story slowly, leaving nothing out, and he asked Sota to translate sentence by sentence. Matalón told his story, adding a few things he had not mentioned to Sota, like the description of the rabbi: tall, a little overweight, balding, brown hair, a mostly gray beard, dressed in a dark suit, and wearing a white skull cap— like the one the Pope wears, early fifties. Post took notes. Wriggles, who had enough trouble trying to follow the conversation, remained silent. When Matalón had completed his report, Post asked, "But how much of this magical ritual did you actually see? What did he do with those chickens?"

"I saw nothing. Nothing of the ritual. Nothing with the chickens. They were in the box when I got there. But I heard the strangest noise. Like the trumpets they blow in the Viking movies when they call the soldiers to war. That's what I heard, and that's why I went to the field to see what was going on." Sota translated almost as fast as Matalón spoke.

"And, this rabbi's name. What was the rabbi's name?"

"I can't remember. Believe me, I tried. I know he told it to me. He introduced himself, and we shook hands. I recognized him from the newspaper as the Cardinal's Jewish friend—the rabbi who got some medal from the Pope because of some book he found. I've tried, but I just can't remember his name."

"Was it a Jewish name, like Cohen, Levy, Schwartz, Horowitz, Lansky?"

"No, nothing like that. Short. Both his first and last name was short. One syllable, like 'law,' like 'day,'" said Matalón, inserting a few English words into his Spanish response.

"And, do you have any idea of why he did it? What his motivation could have been? Is he a fan?"

"I don't know, Mr. Post. Please don't fire me. All I can tell you is that he had sky box tickets, that he had been at the game that night, and somehow he stayed in the park until after midnight. It was after 1 a.m. when I let him out of the park. I looked at my watch."

"And why did you decide to report this now and not earlier?"

"I was afraid. Afraid of losing my job. Afraid of breaking my promise to the rabbi. Afraid of not telling someone. May I please go to the bathroom?"

Matalón shuffled the short distance to the private bathroom adjacent to Post's office. The tension had given him a nervous stomach. Meanwhile, Post reviewed his notes, asking questions as he read them, "What do you know about this guard? How long has he worked for us? How's his work record been? Any problem with alcohol or drugs?"

Wriggles had brought Matalón's employee file with him. "None that I can see. No problems. He's been with us two years. Seems to be OK." Wriggles handed the file to Post, who reviewed it for himself.

Post called his secretary to come in. An elderly woman carrying a steno pad entered the room within seconds. She looked like Jane Hathaway from the old TV show, "The Beverly Hillbillies." Post spoke.

She wrote. "Get me the head of maintenance at Wrigley—find him if you have to, and then get me the religion editor at the *Trib*—find him, too."

She left the office, gently closing the door. Within seconds the phone rang. Post answered.

"This is Post, who's this?"

"Tom Pawlikowski, head of maintenance at Wrigley."

"Listen, Tom, don't ask questions. Just do what I tell you. Over two months ago, a tall middle-aged man, bit overweight, brown hair, white beard, dark suit, was in a sky box at a night game. He might have been wearing a white beanie on his head. Ask your nighttime clean-up crew—the ones that handle the sky boxes—if they saw some such guy, and get back to me ASAP."

"Sure, boss. Did he steal something?"

"No. Just get back to me—no later than tomorrow morning. Call in your staff now, or talk to them on the phone. I need this info fast. 'Bye."

Seconds after Post had hung up the phone, it rang again. Post answered.

"Roger Post. Who's this?"

"Larry Ray, *Trib* religion editor. Sure you don't want the sports editor?"

"After what that son-of-a-bitch's been writing about us lately, the only thing I want with him is to cut off his nuts. No. I want you. What do you know about some rabbi who's friendly with the Cardinal?"

"Look, Mr. Post. I've only had the religion beat for a few months. I've been with the *Trib* thirty-two years, and they needed somewhere to put me until I retire, so they put me in religion. The person you might talk to is Nicklesen, Rick Nicklesen. He used to handle religion. Now he's on the sport's beat. He's the guy whose—um, who you want to castrate."

"I'll hold on. Get him to the phone."

Post pressed a button on the phone, activating the speaker. The toilet flushed in his bathroom, and a few seconds later, out came Matalón. Sota put his finger over his mouth, gesturing at Matalón to be quiet. Matalón tip-toed out of the bathroom, and he sat down. Suddenly, a booming voice issued from the speaker, "Nicklesen here. Well, the way the Cubs have been playing, maybe it's *your* nuts that should be excised."

"Listen, Nicklesen. Don't get your bowels in an uproar. I'm not calling to ask you to compromise your journalistic integrity, or any crap like that. We have a situation here. I can't get into details, but I'm looking for a rabbi."

"I didn't know you were Jewish," Nicklesen interrupted.

"Not for me. I told you I can't go into details. I need your help. Is there some rabbi in town who is a friend of the Cardinal, and who got some kind of medal from the Pope? Tall—"

Nicklesen interrupted again, "Only one person fits your description, Rabbi Doctor Jay Loeb, scholar extraordinaire."

"Dat's eet," Matalón exclaimed in a high pitched voice, forgetting that he was supposed to be quiet.

"Who was that? Some guy whose balls you already cut off?" Nicklesen asked.

"You know this guy? This Loeb?"

"Sure do. Nice guy. Cute wife."

"Heard from him lately?"

"Not for awhile." Nicklesen paused. "But, now that you mention it, it's strange. The last call I had from him was about the Cubs, about why they can't seem to win the pennant. Stuff like that."

"That's not strange. A lot of people want to know that. Including me," Post said, hurling an unpleasant look in Wriggles's direction.

"Believe me, Roger. From a guy like Loeb, who's always got his head in a book, it's strange. And, the other thing he asked was even more strange. He asked if there was anything like Alcoholics Anonymous for addicted Cubs fans. Maybe one of his 'flock' has problems like this. I didn't ask, because he wouldn't tell me anyway. Oh, yeah, and he was extremely interested in hearing about the Billy Goat curse."

"Where's this rabbi's synagogue?" Post inquired.

"Doesn't have one. He's a scholar, a teacher, a professor at—wait, I'm checking my Rolodex—at The Jewish Theological Seminary of Chicago on La Salle. Want his phone number?"

"No, thanks. Be back to you—probably in the next few days. Thanks. 'Bye."

Post had his secretary get the head of the *Trib*'s research department on the phone.

"John Murray here."

"Hi, John. This is Roger Post. I have a request. Please don't ask questions."

"My job is answers, not questions. What's up? Want to know what we've been writing about the Cubs lately?"

Post restrained himself and responded, "No. Thanks anyway. I need everything—and I mean everything—you can get for me on a rabbi in Chicago named Jay Loeb. Teaches at The Jewish Theological Seminary of Chicago. Is friendly with the Cardinal. Got some medal from the Pope. How long would it take?"

"I'll have a packet sent over to you by the end of the day. If you need more than I send, I'll get you more."

"Thanks, John. Thanks. I owe you."

Post grabbed a Cubs employee directory on his desk and punched in a number.

"Hi, this is Roger Post, the GM. Is this the ticket office?"

"Yep, Marv Basta here. What can I do for you, sir? Need some tickets for a friend?"

"No, Marv. Information. I want you to check all your records and tell me if anyone this year has ordered tickets with the last name of Loeb. I know you can't check purchases at the gate, but you can check purchases by mail and . . ."

"Don't have to check, boss. Know who it is. A lady, two seats on the third base line—season tickets for many years. One of the first orders every season to get the same seats. Hold on. I'll get her full name and address . . . Yeah, here it is, boss, Tamara Loeb at Farnsworth, McPherson, Blair, Lawless and Flaherty—sounds like a law firm, 100 North La Salle. That it, boss?"

"Yeah. Thanks. Thanks a lot."

"Anytime, boss. We goin' to win a few again at home this time?"

"Hope so. Thanks again. 'Bye."

Post's secretary entered the room, waited for him to hang up the phone and said,"I have the head of maintenance on hold. Want to talk to him?"

"Yeah, and call Murray at the *Trib*. Research department. Tell him I also want info on a lawyer, Tamara Loeb."

Post picked up the phone.

"Yeah, got something?"

"Yep, Mr. Post, sir. Some of our clean-up people and one of our waiters remember this guy. Mostly because he was all alone in the sky box. Most of the time, a whole group comes to the sky boxes. They think it was the Hang Me company box, but they're not sure. Hope it's not a problem."

"Thanks. You did good."

"Thank you, sir. Anything else I can do for you?"

"No, not now. 'Bye."

Post hung up the phone once more, turned to Wriggles and Sota, and said, "You be here tomorrow at 9 A.M. I want to see what info I've got on this Loeb guy by then, and we'll decide where to go from there. Seems Matalón, you were right, he was identified as having been in a sky box. You just got yourself a twenty-five percent raise, my friend."

Matalón smiled, relieved.

"And, seems his wife's a season ticket holder. By the time you get here tomorrow morning, we'll know a lot more. See you then."

Wriggles and Sota headed for the door. Post stopped Matalón and shook his hand vigorously.

"*Muchas gracias*," Post said, and he closed the door behind them as they left his office.

At 4:45 that afternoon, a messenger arrived from the *Tribune* with a thick envelope in hand. It contained more things about Jay and Tamara Loeb's lives than either of them would have been able to remember. Post shoved it into his briefcase to take home to read.

THE FOLLOWING MORNING, WRIGGLES
and Sota were in the waiting room outside of Post's office when he
arrived at 8:45. They entered the office. Wriggles nervously asked, "Got
anything, boss?"

"The Trib sent over a bunch of info. Read it last night. Began as a
big puzzle. But, now the pieces are startin' to fit together. Here's what I
got so far: Loeb's a rabbi, a professor at a Jewish seminary here in
Chicago—tiny place over on La Salle. But, he's a big shot scholar—
heavyweight class. More degrees than a thermometer. Wrote lots of stuff,
in various languages. In fifteen *Who's Whos*. He and the Cardinal go way
back, from when the Cardinal was a college teacher. Got medals from
the Czech and Polish governments. One from the Pope, too. Seems he
discovered some old book that sheds light on the early Church—some
big find. Grew up in New York. He's lived a long time in Chicago—
over twenty-five years. Solid citizen type. No criminal record. Wife's a
hotshot trial lawyer. Won that big porno case, few months back. She's a
season ticket holder for a long time at Wrigley—two seats, third base

line. Good lookin'. A son, seventeen. According to maintenance, this Loeb guy was probably at Wrigley the night Matalón saw him—guest in the Hang Me sky box. That's about it."

"We know why he did it?" Sota asked.

"No clue."

"Is the other seat at Wrigley for him?" asked Sota.

"No clue."

"Wait a minute, boss," Wriggles said. "I know who that broad is. Comes to almost every game. Bitch is always yelling orders at me. A real piece of ass, and a real pain in the ass. Wears a Cubs hat."

"He come with her?"

"Don't think so."

"What about the kid?," Sota asked. "Interested in baseball?"

"Plays on his high school team. All we know."

"Maybe we can get the rabbi in to talk to us," said Wriggles.

"Little chance," said Post. "Not a fan from what the guy at the Trib tells me."

"Maybe we can get him in through his wife or kid. Don't know how, but worth a shot," said Sota.

"Not a bad idea. Let me work on it," Post said. "Be back to you when I've got something. Good luck at the game today. Giants can be tough."

"We know, boss. 'Bye."

A few minutes later, Post left the office and went to the University Club for a swim. He often found doing laps the best time to think. By the time he emerged from the pool, a plan was coming together in his head. He lowered himself into the whirlpool, and within a few minutes, it all came together. If only it would work.

From the locker room, Post called Tom Couch, the Chairman of the Trib's Board of Directors, and asked him to lean on his editors for a favor. Couch was hesitant when Post informed him that he couldn't tell him the reason. He simply said, "You know, Rog, you're putting your job on the line with this?"

Post swallowed hard, hesitated, and said, "Yep. I know, Tom. But, if I'm right, it'll be worth it—for all of us."

"And, if you're not right?"

Post's hands began to shake. "Thank you, sir."

"I'll set it all up for you. It'll be done by noon today. 'Bye, Rog, and good luck."

Post showered and dressed, and headed back to his office. At 11:35 his phone rang. It was Nicklesen.

"You've got low friends in high places. But, I've been ordered, from the very top, to cooperate with you in every way possible. I just hope my journalistic integrity's intact when this is all over. What do you want me to do?"

"First, you can meet me for lunch. My office. One hour. OK?"

"We'll have to stop meeting like this. See you soon. Your place."

Post's secretary spread a linen tablecloth with the Cubs logo on the conference table in Post's office. On top of the tablecloth she placed fine china, crystal and engraved silverware. Moments after Nicklesen arrived, she served lunch and left.

Post did not speak much over lunch, just some small talk, trying to break the ice with Nicklesen who, as a seasoned reporter, knew how to read people pretty well.

"This mean you're not going to cut off my balls?" asked Nickelsen.

Post finished his coffee, went into his bathroom to wash his hands, leaving the door open, returned to the table, sat down, and said,

"Look, Nicklesen. I'm putting my job on the line with this. You know how many GMs have been in and out of here since the Trib took over the Cubs. First, I need your word that this is all confidential, 'off the record'— as you guys would say. I need your help. The Cubs need your help. Need it real bad. Sorry if this sounds weird. But here's where we're at."

As Post began to outline his plan, his voice shifted from a plaintive tone to a bureaucratic one. Nicklesen took out a pad and pencil, ready to take notes.

"Ya know the Cubs suck this year?" Post began.

"Is the Pope Catholic?" Nicklesen responded.

"And, ya know that recently things have changed, at least at home?"

"And the $64,000 question is, why? Do you know?"

"I think I know," said Post, "and it has to do with your rabbi friend. This Jay Loeb. Just before the Cubs started winning at home, he was at a night game. The maintenance staff at Wrigley confirmed it. That night, after the game, around midnight, he was on the field—on the pitcher's mound, performing some kind of magical ritual, presumably aimed at removing the Billy Goat curse. One of our guards caught him, just as he was wrapping things up. Identified him. No question about it—it was him. Since then, the Cubs have been winning at home, but not on the road. Sounds strange, but we can't explain it in any other way. Must be because of what he did. Seems that whatever he did, works only at Wrigley. We've got to find out what it was and why he did it. Got to see if he's got some magic that also works on the road. Worth a try. Got nothing to lose. A lot to gain."

Nicklesen jotted down some notes, and pulled some rumpled papers from his pocket.

"These are my notes from my last talk with Loeb. I make notes on all my calls—never know when you need them. I reviewed them on the way over here. What you say fits together with what I've got. I don't know how much you've found out about Loeb, but he's into Kabbalah—Jewish mysticism. Lots of magical stuff there, I hear. Other stuff, too. But Loeb's no baseball fan. Why did he do it? Probably to help out someone. Not you, not the Cubs—someone else, but I don't know who. From what he told me, probably someone who's a fanatical fan. This guy's got integrity. Rare today."

"I know about his character," Post said. "Checked him out pretty good. Know you can't play 'let's make a deal' with guys like this. That's why I need your help. He knows you. You know him. You met his wife. Maybe he'll trust you."

"Listen, Post. Loeb helped me out when he didn't have to. He got me the first exclusive interview with the Cardinal when he came to town. I'm not goin' to screw this guy. Even for you."

"Not asking you to do that. Wouldn't."

"Bullshit. You're a desperate guy. Your career's on the line. Desperate people do desperate things. I've seen it before."

"Here's my plan, Nicklesen. It's a little sneaky, but neither illegal, immoral nor fattening—and, I'll lean on you to cooperate if I have to. Just listen. I only want to set up a way of meeting and talking to this guy. That's it. But I need your help."

"I'm all ears. Let's hear it."

"You will announce in your column that you're starting a series of interviews with season ticketholders who are professional women, to get their views on the Cubs' performance this season. A few days after it appears, have someone from your office call Loeb's wife at work. They'll tell her that she's been chosen for the first interview. If she doesn't agree, tell them to sweeten the pot. Have them tell her that if an interview appears, the interviewee can co-manage a spring training game next year—travel and lodging expenses paid for the person and their family. That, if they have a kid, the kid can be a bat boy or bat girl at a game at Wrigley this season. Free season tickets, next year. Whatever you want. Only have your people get her to agree to the interview. And, after she's agreed, have them let her know that the deal is only good if the interviewee's family attends the interview at the Trib—in case, for added color commentary, there are questions to be asked of family members. Have them tell her that you're doing the interview. She'll be less suspicious that way. Put it all in writing, and have it messengered over to her office after she takes the bait. After all, she's a lawyer. That's it. Then, when they come in for the interview, I'll get to meet this Loeb guy. We'll go from there. Don't worry. We'll keep our part of the deal. She'll be able to manage a game at spring training in Mesa, and the boy will be a bat boy, and you can publish the interview—and keep your precious journalistic virginity intact. Only for now, you can't write anything about the rabbi and his voodoo, or whatever he does. That's it."

Nicklesen finished scribbling on his steno pad and said, "All right. I'll do it. Though I don't really like it. Maybe he did it all for his wife. Maybe she's the Cubs 'freak' he had in mind when he called me. But if the Cubs only win at home because of him, he's got to finish the job. I bet he knows it by now, and is trying to figure out how. I'll do what you ask to help him, to help her. OK, you've got a deal, but you better not screw me, or him; or, you wouldn't like what you'll read about yourself in my column. Because I'll do in print to your balls what you wanted to do to mine."

To seal the deal, Nicklesen extended his hand, and Post shook it limply. Nicklesen left, and set the plan into motion.

Tamara's secretary was used to getting telemarketing calls at the office. Tamara had given her strict instructions not to let any through to her. So, when the Trib called, thinking it was a telemarketer, Tamara's secretary simply hung up—each of the five times they called. Nicklesen then went to "Plan B." He wrote up the deal in memo form, signed his name, and faxed it to Tamara's office. Unbeknown to him, the office staff that received faxes were under orders to deliver faxes to the addressee immediately. Within minutes, the fax was on Tamara's desk.

Tamara stopped working on the legal brief she was writing, read the fax, and began shouting, "Yippee!" as if she had won the lottery. Her secretary paid no attention to the sounds coming from Tamara's office. She knew that the Cubs were playing that day at Wrigley, was surprised Tamara wasn't there, and assumed that Tamara was watching the game on TV and that the Cubs had done something good. Tamara signed the document, and called in her secretary, asking her to have it immediately messengered back to the *Tribune*. Tamara thought that many people must have received similar agreements, and she didn't want to lose her chance at the interview or the "goodies" that would come with it. She knew that Joshua would be elated, but that her husband would see it as a waste of his time.

That evening at dinner, Tamara told Joshua and Jay what had happened. Joshua was overjoyed, but Jay was even more resistant than she had expected. Yet, Tamara had in mind a strategy that she knew couldn't fail. She would get Joshua to work on him. Loeb could resist temptations that most other people would cave into in a minute. But, the one thing he could not resist was the pleadings of his son. Joshua was so excited about the possibility of being a bat boy, and at actually meeting the members of the Cubs team. He knew that tears were his trump card with his Dad. It had never failed before. Since he was a little boy, Joshua knew that Loeb could not bear to see his son cry. It took four days of Joshua's arguments, pleadings, and occasional tears, but Loeb finally agreed. Loeb was suspicious, but learning that Nicklesen was doing the interview, rather than Joshua's "crocodile tears," was what actually had convinced him to go.

Nicklesen had guessed correctly. Loeb believed that he had been responsible for the Cubs' victories at home, but not on the road. He was wondering about what to do next. In fact, Loeb was at wit's end. Tamara's violent mood swings from euphoria when the Cubs played at home, to constant outbursts of violent irritability when they lost when out of town, were like a text-book case of manic depression. In trying to make things better, Loeb believed, he had actually made things worse. Something needed to be done, but what?

THE FOLLOWING TUESDAY AFTERNOON,
the Loeb family arrived at the Tribune Tower lobby at 4 P.M. Nicklesen
met them there, greeted them warmly, and escorted them upstairs to
the GM's suite of offices. He led them into a small conference room,
and conducted the interview in a serious and professional manner,
focusing on Tamara, and occasionally directing questions at Jay and at
Joshua. Loeb read most of the time, barely looking up when he had to
respond to a question.

In an adjoining room, Post stood with Matalón and Sota, looking
through a two-way mirror.

"Is that the guy?," Post asked. Sota translated.

"*Sí*," said Matalón, nodding his head.

"And, you're absolutely sure?"

"Yes, Mr. Post. I am sure," Matalón said in Spanish, nodding his
head again.

Post did not wait for Sota's translation, but went into his office where
Wriggles and some of the Cubs pitchers and best hitters were waiting.

"In a few minutes, I want you guys to go into the room down the hall. Some very important people are there, and I want you to charm them," Post said to his players. "There's a seventeen-year-old kid and his parents. The kid plays on his high school baseball team. Talk to him. Give him some pointers. Talk to his mother. She's a big fan. Leave the father to me."

Post went back to the room with the two-way mirror, and when he saw that the interview seemed to be ending, he opened the door and introduced himself.

"Hi. I'm Roger Post, Cubs GM, and I have here some people who are anxious to meet you. He went into his office and escorted Wriggles and the Cubs players into the conference room. Tamara's eyes lit up. Loeb continued to read. Joshua took a ball out of his back pack and asked for autographs.

"I hear you're a pitcher for your high school team," Hornsberry asked Joshua, who was trying to restrain his excitement.

"Yes," said Joshua. "Maybe one day, I'll be as good as you."

"Give me the ball. I'll show you how to throw a few trick pitches."

Tamara watched Hornsberry patiently instructing her son on the art of pitching, and tears came to her eyes. *I guess Hornsberry's not as mean as he looks on the mound,* she said to herself.

And, as if he were reading her mind, Hornsberry said to Joshua, "Listen, kid, part of being a good pitcher is how you throw. The other part is psyching out the batter. You do it not only with what you throw him, but at how you look at him." Hornsberry made some mean-looking facial gestures that got Joshua and Tamara to break out laughing.

Meanwhile, Loeb continued to read his book, unaware that an additional person had entered the room—Matalón. Sota led Matalón toward where Loeb was sitting, and when Loeb heard someone say, "*Buenos tardes, el Rabino Loeb.*" Loeb looked up, saw Matalón, dropped his book on the floor, bent down to pick it up, kissed it, put his head in his hands, and began to rock back and forth in his chair, muttering to himself in Yiddish. Suddenly, the room was silent. Tamara went over to her husband, whom she had rarely seen like this before, hugged him hysterically, and said, "Jay, Jay. What? What's the matter?"

Joshua rushed over to his father, not knowing precisely what to do. "I did it for you, my love, for you. I just couldn't take it any more. To see you like that. I had to do something. You were falling apart. I saw it. Your partners saw it. Joshua saw it. I had to do something before you destroyed everything. Us. Your career. Your health. Everything."

Nicklesen saw that Loeb was "losing it," and so, he interceded,

"What your husband is trying to tell you, Ms. Loeb, is that he was worried about you. About your addiction to the Cubs. I don't know the details, but he decided to do something about it. He snuck into Wrigley one night and did some kind of kabbalistic ritual aimed at removing the Billy Goat curse from the Cubs. From the recent Cubs record of home games, seems he succeeded. But, he seems to have removed curses against the Cubs at Wrigley, but not elsewhere. He exorcised Wrigley, but not the team. That, it appears, is why they win at home, but not on the road."

The icy exterior that Tamara was known for in the courtroom suddenly dissolved into an onrush of tears. Joshua's eyes were as big as the baseball that dropped from his hand to the floor.

"You did that, Dad? You did that? Gee, I didn't know you could do things like that," said Joshua, showing a rare expression of admiration for his father's knowledge and abilities.

"I did it for you, my love. I did it for you. And, now I've made a big mess of things. The holy books warn us not to dabble in these things. Maybe they're right. Maybe I did wrong. Maybe I should have left things alone."

Post handed Tamara a box of tissues he had retrieved from his secretary. He poured Loeb a glass of water and handed it to him. Loeb took it and emptied the glass.

"Listen, Rabbi. You did good," Post said. "Good for your wife. Good for the team. Now, at least, they know they can play. They know they're not jinxed—at least at home."

Post turned to Tamara. "Don't worry, Ms. Loeb. We won't press charges against your husband. We'll keep our promise. You get to manage in Mesa. The boy gets to be bat boy. You get free season tickets. Better tickets for next season. And, Nicklesen will print the interview with you and your son. Your husband's name wouldn't even appear. All we want is to make a deal with your husband. It's all written up. You can check it over. Think about it. I believe the fate of the Cubs this year's in your husband's hands. Not Wriggles's, not mine. And, listen, ma'am, let me be frank about this—my job and Wriggles's, too, is on the line. In your husband's hands. We've got no better explanation but to believe he did something at Wrigley that night that worked. We need him. Hell, we need him more than we need good middle relief."

Loeb cleared his throat, took a few deep breaths to help restore his composure, looked at Tamara, then at Joshua, and finally at Post, and said, "Mr. Post, I did something that I did not expect to be able to do. I don't know if I can do anything else like it. But, I'm listening. What do you want of me?"

Post handed a document to Tamara, sat down facing Loeb, and said, "All we want, Rabbi, is for you to try. No obligations. No guarantees. We want you to come with us on the road, and to attend games at home. We want you to provide spiritual guidance to the players and the coaches. To perform any rituals you see fit. Till the end of the season. That's it."

"Can I come, too? After school's over, I mean," Joshua asked.

Joshua's question shattered the tension that had built up in the room. Everyone began to chuckle—except Jay and Tamara.

"I've got my responsibilities at the Seminary. My teaching and research. What about the Sabbath? I can't do such things on the Sabbath."

Tamara stood up, smoothed out her skirt, and asked to use the ladies' room. Post escorted her to the private bathroom next to his office. Joshua began, once more, to speak to the players and to Wriggles. Loeb thought,

"The gate to wisdom—silence," and he said no more. A few minutes later Tamara returned. She had washed her face, redone her make up, brushed her hair, and had on her "lawyer look."

"We'll consider everything you've said. I'll review the agreement you propose and will speak to my husband about it. Frankly, I don't know whether to be angry at your deception or grateful for it. But, as for now, this conversation is over. Joshua, we're leaving now. Shake hands with everyone; let's go."

Tamara took her husband's hand, and led him from the room to the elevator, down to the lobby, and outside into a taxi. A half-hour later, the Loeb family was at home. Loeb retreated into his study and Tamara into hers. Joshua got on the phone to call his teammates, knowing that he could only relate part of what had happened to him that afternoon. At 6:30, as usual, the housekeeper called everyone in to dinner. They ate in silence, and after dinner, while the housekeeper cleaned up, Loeb and Tamara went into their bedroom and closed the door.

"I really don't want to talk about it, Tamara. Not now. I've had enough for today."

"I understand. Sweetheart, believe me. I understand. But, I read the contract Post gave me, and I want to talk to you about it. Not as your wife, but as your lawyer."

Loeb shot back, "You're not my lawyer. Kalinsky is."

"All right. Not as your lawyer. But, as a lawyer. And, as your friend."

Tamara didn't wait for a response from Loeb, but continued, speaking as she would to a client. "Look at it this way. This deal solves your current problems at the Seminary. The Cubs are offering you $5000 a week to be their 'spiritual advisor.' No specific duties are given. You are only obliged to attend all games that do not interfere with your religious observances, and to offer spiritual guidance in any way you see fit. Most things are at your discretion. I've also checked the Faculty Manual from the Seminary, and it says clearly that any full-time faculty member, upon his or her petition, can be granted a leave of absence without pay at any time."

"That's their way of trying to save money. To encourage us to take leaves by teaching elsewhere so they don't have to pay us."

"No matter. This time, you can use their rules to your advantage."

Tamara put on her glasses, picked the contract off the dresser where she had placed it, and said, "Listen to this." She began to read, "'Loeb may resign from his position with the Chicago National League Baseball team at any time before the end of the regular season. He will be paid $5000 per week for services rendered during that time. This amount will be prorated should he resign in the middle of any said week. In addition, should the Chicago National League Baseball team advance into the first round of the playoffs, he will receive, in addition to his weekly salary, a single time bonus payment of $250,000. Should the team advance to the second round of the playoffs for the National League pennant, Loeb would receive a single bonus payment of $500,000. Should the team win the National League pennant, Loeb would receive a single bonus payment of $1,000,000. Furthermore, should the team win the World Series while Loeb is under its employ, he will receive a single bonus payment of $2,500,000 in addition to all and any other compensation he has already received from the team.'"

Tamara took off her glasses, looked at Loeb and said, "They've made you an offer, you can't refuse."

Loeb responded, "'We don't rely on miracles,' the Talmud teaches. I'll think about it. I'll even talk to Kalinsky about it. But, right now, I'm going to bed. I have classes and meetings tomorrow at school."

Loeb stripped down to his shorts and teashirt, climbed into bed, turned out the light, puffed up the pillow beneath him, said a prayer, and went to sleep.

The next morning, as usual, Loeb slept as Joshua and Tamara prepared to leave. However, that particular morning, Tamara and Joshua, each kissed Loeb before leaving. "Thanks, dear," Tamara said as she leaned over to kiss him. "Cool, Dad," Joshua said as he did likewise.

LOEB FELL BACK TO SLEEP, AND DREAMED of establishing his own seminary. He awoke about 10 A.M., spent some time in the bathroom, dressed, and went into his study to pray. Loeb donned his prayer shawl and phylacteries and began to recite the liturgy, but found trouble concentrating. So he stopped praying, sat down and began to do kabbalistic meditations aimed at focusing his thoughts. When he found himself no longer distracted by the events of the previous day, he returned to his prayers. Afterwards, he called Kalinsky, and set up an appointment with him at 2 P.M. He studied some Talmud, reciting and explaining the text to himself in the sing-song melody he had learned years ago in the yeshivah. Then, he prepared his classes for that evening, ate brunch, looked at his watch, and realized it was time for him to leave to meet Kalinsky.

Usually, meetings between Kalinsky and Loeb began with a discussion of literature. Kalinsky had been especially anxious to talk to Loeb about Kafka, particularly about why, on his deathbed, Kafka had asked his friend Max Brod to burn all of his manuscripts. Kalinsky wanted to ask

Loeb what he thought about Kafka's request, and about Brod's refusal to fulfill it after Kafka had died. Kalinsky, who saw his own literary work as his legacy, could not understand why so gifted a writer as Kafka, who was also—like him—a lawyer, would want nothing of his literary creativity to survive his death.

But, Loeb was in no mood to talk about literature, especially about Kafka. He was beginning to see his own situation as if he were a character in one of Kafka's stories, and he wanted Kalinsky's advice to help him escape from that role.

Kalinsky knew about Tamara's problem with the Cubs. He had represented Tamara in her dealings with the firm. But, now Loeb told Kalinsky about his own activities that night at Wrigley, at what the results seemed to have been. He told him about the events of the previous day, about the situation at the seminary, about the offer he had received from Roger Post. Kalinsky listened carefully, made some notes, and when Loeb had completed his monologue, Kalinsky said, "Even Kafka couldn't dream up something like this. Did you bring the agreement you got from Post, and the Faculty Manual from the Seminary?" Loeb reached into his brief case and extracted both documents, handing them to Kalinsky.

"Give me a few minutes to read this," Kalinsky asked. While Kalinsky read, Loeb took a Hebrew book out of his brief case and began to study. About twenty minutes later, Kalinsky broke the silence. "Well, my friend. You hit the jackpot. I don't know about the Cubs, but you and Tamara have both hit it big. Want me to represent you on this deal with the Cubs? I can probably get a few more bucks out of them. Shall I proceed and finalize the deal?"

"Yes, please," said Loeb. "You know I trust you explicitly. Whatever you decide, is fine with me. I'll sign whatever you tell me to. Thanks. I wish I had more friends like you."

"OK, Jay. We'll discuss Kafka another time. Now, go along to school. If you have any trouble with President Schwartz of your seminary, just let me at him. I'll get back to you as soon as I can."

They shook hands, and Loeb left. He walked about a mile up La Salle Street to the old brownstone that housed the seminary. The meeting he had come to attend already had started. He looked at his watch, surprised that he was late. It was not like him.

President Harold Schwartz was presiding, as usual. Next to him sat Sol Kaplan, chairman of the seminary's board of trustees, a socially amiable but culturally primitive man, who, since the onset of the AIDS epidemic, had made a fortune in the manufacture of "designer condoms." Around the table sat the members of the faculty and a representative of the student body. With Kaplan's support evident, Schwartz was laying out his plan for how the seminary would weather its current economic crisis. Loeb's colleagues were relieved when he came in. In the past, Loeb had fought the board and the administration on their behalf. But, though Loeb was a heavyweight scholar, Schwartz considered him a threat, and Kaplan thought of him as just another troublesome employee who had to be put in his place periodically. This time, Loeb remained silent. Seeing this, Kaplan interrupted Schwartz, and turned to the oldest member of the faculty, Professor Mendel Poznansky, and asked for his opinion. Kaplan knew in advance what Poznansky would say.

"I think I speak for my colleagues when I say, Chairman Kaplan, President Schwartz, that we are grateful for all of your efforts on behalf of our wonderful institution. We know how hard working you always are on our behalf, and we trust that whatever you have decided, is in the best interests of all concerned."

Following Kaplan's lead, Schwartz then invited the representative of the student organization to speak. Sarah Cohen was a twenty-year-old education student who knew she would need Schwartz's help to find a job when she graduated, but who meanwhile needed good grades from the faculty to be able to graduate. She, therefore, didn't really know what to say. Nervously, she finally said, "I agree with everything Professor

Poznansky said."

Schwartz looked at his watch, put his hand on Kaplan's forearm, and said, "Mr. Kaplan and I have an important appointment with a prospective donor who potentially could solve all our problems, so we must leave you now. You are all free, of course, to continue the conversation."

A few of the faculty muttered under their breath. One mumbled something about how Kaplan could underwrite the entire budget of the school himself, just from what he had made that year from sale of banana-flavored condoms. Another suggested that if Schwartz paid himself what he paid the faculty, there would be no budget crisis. However, as Kaplan and Schwartz got up to meet a donor whom nobody at the table believed to really exist, Loeb said, "May I make one brief comment, before you leave?"

Kaplan and Schwartz bristled. Schwartz looked at his watch. "As long as it's short. Go ahead, Jay." Neither man reclaimed his seat. They remained standing, continuing to walk slowly toward the door.

"Consistent with the provisions laid out in the Faculty Manual," said Loeb, "I shall be taking a leave of absence, effective the end of this week when my teaching duties for the current semester will have ended. And, no later than November 1, I shall inform the board of whether I plan to return for the winter semester. My written request will be submitted before I leave here today."

Kaplan and Schwartz stood still, like deer paralyzed by the headlights of an oncoming truck. Loeb arose from his chair, pushed his way passed Kaplan and Schwartz, who stood near the door, said, "Excuse me," and left the now-silent room. Loeb breathed a sigh of relief, and went to his classroom to teach his class.

During the days that followed, Loeb dealt with numerous phone calls from Schwartz, Kaplan, his colleagues and students, urging him to change his mind. To his surprise, they even offered him a modest raise. But Loeb stayed his ground. After Kalinsky called to tell him that he had finalized the deal with Post, and had gotten his salary and bonuses with the Cubs substantially increased, Loeb refused to talk with anyone from the seminary. He had nothing to say to them—for now.

"How did you get them to agree to so much more money when they've already promised me a fortune if the Cubs win the pennant and/or the World Series?" Loeb asked Kalinsky.

"First of all, it's such a long-shot that they readily agreed. No one thinks it will happen, not even them. So, they agreed to be sure they'd clinch the deal. Second, if by some miracle it happens, they'll well be able to afford it from the extra revenues post-season play would generate."

"Going to be home for a while?" Kalinsky continued, "I'll messenger you the papers right now. Have the messenger wait. Sign three copies, keep one for your self, and give the others to the messenger to bring to me. Congratulations, Jay. 'Bye."

To the surprise of few, the Cubs won all of their games but one during their homestand against the Colorado Rockies, and then they left for New York. Predictably, they lost all of their games against the Mets but one. That Monday morning, Loeb reported to Roger Post for work, unsure of what he would be doing.

POST ESCORTED LOEB TO AN OFFICE THAT had been prepared for his use. Though it was lavishly furnished, with a breathtaking view of Lake Michigan, Loeb somehow felt out of place there, and soon realized why—it had no books. He couldn't imagine spending time in a room without books.

"What do I do first?" Loeb asked Post. "I'm kind of new at this corporate stuff."

"First do your R&D, prepare your strategic goals, and your action plan. Then submit them to me for review. If they're within parameters, we'll conference on how to accelerate the benchmarks," Post said.

"Please excuse me, Mr. Post," said Loeb. "I really didn't understand what you said."

"Sorry, Rabbi," said Post. "I guess I can't talk business without jargon. Let me put it another way: do your research and plan out what you want to do, set your goals, and figure out how you will achieve them. Then, discuss your plan with me, and if I approve, go and do it, as fast as you can. OK? Ms. Biondi's your secretary. Just call her if you need anything. Good luck."

"And when do you want all this, Mr. Post?"

"Immediately—if not sooner. Anything you need before I go?" Post asked.

"Yes. I need some books about baseball, so I can understand it better. And, I need information about the Cubs—history, current players—that kind of stuff. The more I understand about something, the better I deal with it."

"I'll send some data over to you. But for books, try the bookstore down the street. Buy as much as you want—on us. Also, try the internet. Never know what you'll find there. Maybe start with our web page, and go from there. Good luck, Rabbi. I look forward to seeing what you'll come up with."

Loeb went to the huge duplex bookstore down the street, and returned about an hour later with three shopping bags full of books and magazines about baseball. By the time he had returned to his office, four large cartons marked "Do not remove from premises" had arrived. They were filled with photos, personnel files, scouts' reports and all kinds of statistics. That's where Loeb started his research.

Loeb read the entire day, leaving his chair only to go to the bathroom and to pray the afternoon prayer. He was amazed at how much personal information the files contained about each individual player: shoe size, childhood diseases, sexual preferences; what kinds of flowers to send mothers, wives, girlfriends and grandmothers on Mother's Day and on anniversaries; information about child abuse, spousal abuse and substance abuse; detailed description of favorite bats used in games, idiosyncratic superstitions about the game; religious affiliations . . . and more. Each file also contained a copy of the player's contract. After Loeb had read a few contracts, he no longer felt guilty about working for wages and potential bonuses that he considered excessive. *Maybe Dad was right when he wanted me to become a professional baseball player*, Loeb thought. *After all of my studies, what do I have—aggravation and a lot of knowledge no one is interested in?* At 6:00 P.M., Loeb left the office, carrying his bags of books, thinking about what to do with what he had learned that day. Loeb arrived home just as dinner was being served.

"How was the first day at your new job?" Tamara asked.

"Different," said Loeb, who was still trying to assimilate all he had read that day. After dinner, he adjourned to his study where his real learning for the day began. He opened a volume of the Talmud, and was soon lost in his own sing-song melody of study until late into the night.

When he awoke the next morning, Loeb decided to work at home that day. Despite the luxury of his new office, he found it confining. Nor was he used to a workplace where people usually smiled and were polite. Loeb attacked the pile of books he had bought the day before, occasionally making notes. He alternated between reading his books and surfing the World Wide Web. By early afternoon, he had filled many pads of paper, but his mind was still a blank about what to do. Meanwhile, the Cubs were in Philadelphia, dropping a game to the Phillies. Loeb went into Tamara's study and turned on the TV to watch the game.

Loeb recognized each of the Cubs players from the personnel files he had read. As he watched the image of each man flash on the screen, Loeb recalled what he had read about him in his file. He analyzed each play of the game, as if he were deciphering some ancient text, layer by layer. He listened to the sports commentators, trying to see whether his interpretations agreed with theirs. Loeb tried to figure out why the Phillies were winning while the Cubs were losing. Statistically, they seemed well matched. It was a mystery that he felt compelled to penetrate, not unlike those of the many inscrutable kabbalistic texts that he had decoded throughout his scholarly career.

Loeb quoted to himself the Hebrew proverb: "*kol hathalot kashot*— all beginnings are difficult." As an author, he knew that the hardest part of a book to write was the beginning. That's why he often started writing a book in the middle, hoping that the beginning would eventually find its way onto the paper. He decided to work the same way here.

Loeb attacked his new job the same way he approached doing research for a new book. He would gorge himself with the subject—in this case, baseball—until, like a glutton ready to explode, something came out. Though he found this analogy to be crude, it was how things happened. He hoped it would happen that way here, too. Only, he didn't have much time. Loeb realized that he needed to give a little push to the spirit that would move him. He turned off the television, and recalled a saying of Yogi Berra: "We're lost, but we're making good time."

Loeb left the house and walked toward Lake Michigan. He thought of a story he had read about a scholar who wanted to learn how to swim. The scholar read everything he could about swimming. He then bought a bathing suit and went to a swimming pool, jumped in, and almost drowned. "Don't you know how to swim?" the lifeguard asked, as he hauled the scholar to safety. The scholar responded, "I don't know how to swim, but I understand swimming." Loeb felt like this scholar. He decided that instead of trying to master the game of baseball, he would focus on how he could use the knowledge he already possessed to help out the Cubs.

The following day, Loeb returned to his office and handed a one-page typed document to Roger Post. The more of the document Post read, the more disturbed he became. It read:

Ultimate Goal:

For the Cubs to win the World Series.

Penultimate Goals:

1. For the Cubs to win an adequate number of games so as to qualify for post-season play.

2. For the Cubs to win the pennant.

Immediate Goals:

1. For the Cubs to continue to maintain a high percentage of home game victories.

2. For the Cubs to initiate and to maintain a high percentage of victories in games on the road.

Methods of Achieving these Goals:

1. Remove the effects of curses, spells, sins and other factors that may be inhibiting Cubs victories.

2. Enhance the spiritual and moral standard of living among the Cubs players.

3. To immediately place Sandy Greenberg on the Cubs roster, but with the understanding that he will be available for post-season play only.

Practices to be introduced to bring about these goals:

1. Ritual immersion of all team members in *mikvah*.

2. Recitation of Psalms.

3. Prayer before and after games.

4. Encourage repentance and contrition over sins committed by Cubs players.

5. Increase Cubs players' donations to charity.

6. Remove curses and spells on team and individual players.

7. Distribution of amulets to team members.

8. Individual spiritual counseling of team members.

9. Increase cultivation of the moral virtues and the dispelling of the moral vices among the team members.

"With all due respect to you, Rabbi," said Post, "what the hell is this? I asked for a strategic plan, and you give me an agenda for a religious revival meeting. And, who the fuck—pardon my French—is Sandy Greenberg?"

"Look, Mr. Post," Loeb began calmly and confidently. "You know your business, and I know mine. And, in my best professional opinion, this is what the team needs right now in order to get them to where you want them to be. They need more than physical and athletic skill. They also need spiritual health and stability. That means two things: curing the spiritual maladies that afflict them and perpetuating spiritual well-being once they've been cured, or perhaps I should say 'exorcised,' of the evils that afflict them.

"Look at it in medical terms: the team is sick, spiritually sick. I want to help cure them of what ails them and to help them retain their spiritual health once they attain it. It's that simple. That's my plan. It's clear, precise, efficient and economical. And, I believe it will work. Isn't that what you business people like?"

Post was somewhat surprised at Loeb's forthright tenacity. His voice softened, and he asked, "And who is Sandy Greenberg? I never heard of him. I thought I knew all the current major league players, all the hot college and high school prospects. We have scouts, you know. Who is this guy? Why can he only play in post-season? And why should we put a player on the roster who can't join the team until then? And what makes you qualified to tell me who to put on my team? And how much money does he want?"

Loeb sat down at Post's conference table, placed his hands on the table and brought them together, almost as if he were about to pray. Loeb cleared his throat, searching for his "pastoral voice," a tone of speaking he had learned from his teachers when he was studying to become a rabbi that aims at instilling trust in the congregant while vesting authority in the cleryperson. Loeb slightly lowered his head, looked Post directly in the eye, and said, "This is what you asked for. This is my package. Take it or leave it. But, you have to take it all. This is what I believe will work. That's what you want, right—something that works? You trust me, don't you?"

Post was used to corporate spin-masters, and Loeb's sincerity and conviction was something that he wasn't accustomed to dealing with. So, the only thing he felt he could do was to nod his head in assent.

"As for Sandy Greenberg," Loeb said, "he can't be here just yet. I hope I can get him here in time, when he's really needed. But, if and when you see him play, I think you'll admit that he was brought into this world just to play baseball. He will be the best player you've ever seen. But, right now, our primary task is to get into the playoffs. Only then, will I be able to try to get him to come. It wouldn't be easy. I'm not exaggerating when I say that it will take a supernatural effort to get him here. And, as for money, he requires none. He'll be compensated out of my bonus when the time comes. I need him added to the roster now because of the rules. It is forbidden to add players to the rosters once a team is in post-season play."

Loeb was proud of himself for having become as conversant with "baseball law" as he was with Jewish law.

Post went to the small bar in his office, poured himself a Scotch, drank it down in a single gulp, and said, "OK, Jay. You got it. He's on the roster—here or not. You leave tomorrow to meet the team in Pittsburgh. I'll call ahead tonight to Wriggles and will bring him up to speed. Good luck."

"All I can promise is to do my best. I hope it'll be good enough," Loeb said. The two shook hands, and Loeb returned home to pack for his flight the next morning for Pittsburgh. That night, when he made love to Tamara, he felt a new sense of vitality surging through his entire body. That night, "dessert" was on him.

A car met Loeb at the airport in Pittsburgh and took him to the ballpark. The team had been briefed by Wriggles and Sota, and they were both anxious and apprehensive about meeting the mysterious rabbi about whom they had heard so much. It was two hours to game time, and the team was gathered in their locker room preparing to meet their new "spiritual advisor."

Loeb knew that he would face a group of hopeful skeptics when he entered the locker room, but he had faced skeptics in his classroom every day for many years. He knew that some of the players might resent him because he was a rabbi. But, he also knew that what united the team was a desire to win, and a desire to know why their best efforts often ended in defeat. He entered the room, and was introduced by Wriggles who called the team to order.

Loeb began softly, amplifying his voice as he continued to speak, "My wife was making me crazy and was on the verge of losing her job because you guys were losing too many games, so I decided to do something about it."

The men didn't know whether he was joking or serious. Some chuckled, most did not.

"Late one night, I snuck into Wrigley and said some prayers aimed at removing the curse of the Billy Goat, and any other curses on Wrigley Field or on the Cubs. Since then, your record of home games has improved tremendously. Can any of you deny it?"

The men shook their heads back and forth.

"Do any of you have a better explanation than the one I have given? And, if you do, then how can you then explain your record on the road compared to your record at home since my late night visit to the pitcher's mound at the Friendly Confines?

"Now, with the consent of Mr. Post, the GM, and of Manager Wriggles, I have come up with a plan aimed at moving the team toward contention in the divisional playoffs. According to my statistical calculations, that is an unlikely but not an impossible goal. But, I believe, if you follow the plan I've set out, we have a chance of getting there. But, I need your help. Right now, we will take three baby-steps in that direction. First, I will recite with you the twenty-third psalm and the ninety-first psalm, copies of which will now be distributed to each of you. Second, before you leave for the field, Coach Sota will give each of you a magical amulet to wear around your neck. Its purpose is to dispel any curses or spells set against you and to give you some additional power—sort of like steroids, but legal. Third, we will recite together a spell meant to reduce any evil powers around you. The spell we will say is one you all know—*Abra cadabra*. But by reducing the number of syllables each time we say it, we will reduce the powers of evil around us."

Not allowing them any time to react to what he had said, Loeb placed a white skull cap on his head, and began to slowly recite the twenty-third and ninety-first Psalms in English translation. At first, the only voice audible was his own, but as he read on, the teammates began to join him.

Then Loeb said, "Repeat after me: *Abra cadabra, cadabra, dabra, bra, ra, a.*" And they did, until all that was left of the word was an eerie silence.

Before they left the room, Loeb lifted his arms and pronounced a Hebrew blessing upon the team. By the fact that each member of the team bowed his head during the blessing, Loeb knew that he had gotten their attention. As each member left the room to go onto the field, Sota handed him a small metal amulet with Hebrew and Aramaic writing on it, secured by a slim gold chain that each member put around his neck. He also gave each member of the team a single thick thread of red wool for him to place around his wrist—a kabbalistic repellent of evil spirits.

During the game, Loeb remained in the locker room, reciting the Psalms. The Cubs won 9-2. And, they won the next two games against the Pirates as well, after following the pre-game program of prayer that Loeb had set out for them.

When Loeb flew home that Friday morning so as to arrive there well in advance of the start of the Sabbath at sundown, the team was sorry to see him go. They had two more games—on Saturday and Sunday—to play in Pittsburgh. That they lost them pleased Loeb, since it showed the players that they needed his presence and his help. Now, he could implement the rest of the plan he had set out for them. He had won their confidence.

THE NEXT HOME GAME WAS MONDAY night against Los Angeles. At 5:30 that morning, just as the sun was starting to rise, a bus full of Cubs players arrived at the Pratt Boulevard beach on Chicago's far north side. Loeb was already there to greet them. Rather than use the *mikvah*, the ritual bath, Loeb had decided to use Lake Michigan as a *mikvah* to spiritually purify the team members all at once. Reluctant at first, the players and coaches disrobed on the deserted beach, while a block away traffic continued its perpetual flow up and down Sheridan Road. Wearing bathing suits, they each entered the water until it was at least waist high. Carrying sheets to obscure the view from the street, the trainers entered the chilly water. Loeb also entered the water, walked to the far side of the sheets where the players were standing, and asked them to remove their bathing suits, and to place them on their heads, like make-shift skull caps. He recited a blessing, first in Hebrew, and then in English, which the players recited after him. Then he asked them to immerse themselves three times in the water. He then told them to replace their bathing suits and to exit the water, where each was clothed in a white robe with the Cubs insignia on the sleeve. In the pockets of each robe, there were bread crumbs, which Loeb instructed the players to throw in the water while reciting a verse from Scripture, "I will cast my sins onto the waters." Loeb then prayed aloud with the team around him, standing with bowed heads, "We hereby repent of our sins and resolve to try not to repeat them. May God forgive us for our sins against Him, as we forgive those who have sinned against us. May God love all those whom we love, and may God love all those who love us." When their prayers were complete, everyone boarded a bus that took them to Wrigley Field, where a huge breakfast awaited them.

Though tired from being up since before dawn, the Cubs won a double-header later that day against the Dodgers, and then swept the homestand series. Accompanied by Loeb, the Cubs proceeded to go on an extended road trip, winning all of their games, except those that Loeb did not attend because he stayed home to observe the Jewish Sabbath. During the games, Loeb discreetly stayed in the locker room, out of sight. Yet, as the season progressed, Loeb began to worry that his anonymity in the "miracle of the Cubs," as the press was beginning to call it, would soon come to an end. Loeb's participation had been kept a secret at his request. However, he knew that a secret, as someone once said, was something that someone tells everybody to tell nobody.

In the meantime, Loeb attended to the tasks at hand, counseling those players who came to see him privately, encouraging them to do good works, to increase their donations to charity, to spend more time at introspection, and to live spiritually and ethically enhanced lives. By the beginning of August, unlike many previous seasons, the Cubs were not considered to be out of the running for post-season play by the sports writers. Loeb kept repeating to himself the old rabbinic adage, "We do not rely on miracles." Yet, in his heart of hearts, he heard Kalinsky repeating back to him his own words, "God will provide."

Loeb wasn't sure how it happened, but the secret somehow leaked out. The media gave him no peace, no privacy. His secretary screened calls at his office, but the phone ran incessantly at home. Faxes and printouts of e-mails piled up on his desk. He started to wear a variety of disguises when he went out, afraid of being accosted on the street by a reporter hungry for a story. Even the Jewish media, which had generally ignored him in the past, now pleaded for a few minutes of his time. Jewish organizations that in the past had never offered him speaking engagements—and when they did, claimed that they had no funds for an honorarium—now hounded him with lecture requests, and dangled generous honoraria in front of him. Loeb ignored them all.

Loeb went to his office and began to sift through the piles of requests for interviews. Post had advised him, "There's no such thing as bad publicity. All publicity is good publicity because it increases interest. It focuses attention on you in a highly competitive media market, and offers free publicity for the Cubs. It increases ticket sales, TV and radio revenues and the sale of Cubs paraphernalia." But, Loeb refused to be the focus of attention in an ephemeral parenthesis between a TV or a radio commercial.

Loeb thought of a line from the "The Godfather": "A person in my position can't afford to look ridiculous." He expected to be asked embarrassing questions about Tamara's defense of pornography, to be requested to perform magical tricks on demand, to be asked to reveal in a sound byte the results of years of study, to be cajoled into portraying the sacred teachings of the Jewish sages as some form of hocus-pocus.

Loeb sifted through the requests, sorting them into categories: national TV shows, local TV shows, national radio, local radio, Chicago print media, Jewish print media, national and big city newspapers, smaller city newspapers, and magazines. Within a few hours, he was done. He then reviewed the requests from national TV and radio shows. He had heard of some of them, but had watched none of them. During the next few days, Loeb began to watch and to listen to some of these shows to see what transpired there. One show he watched began with a segment of interviews with men who had decided to become women. All of these men had begun to undergo sex change operations, but had decided to stop midway, and to live the rest of their lives as women from the waist up and as men from the waist down, or vice versa. Another show featured teenage boys who had fathered children with their own mothers.

One day, as Loeb began to sift through the piles of papers littering his office, not knowing exactly what he was looking for, an image on one of the e-mails he had received grasped his attention. It was a photo of Kathleen Wyner, the hostess of a show called "The Wyner Report." He had wondered what had happened to her.

During the 1991 war in the Persian Gulf, Kathleen Wyner had been a news anchor on CNN. Loeb would watch her each day to find out how the war was progressing. He had friends who had been called up to serve there. He watched to find out whether any Iraqi Scud missiles were hitting places in Israel where friends of his lived—sequestered in their homes with their children, wearing gas masks. And, when the Gulf War was over, Loeb watched her simply because he liked to watch her. She was not only an incisive reporter and news commentator, but she also was the personification of every Jewish man's wet dream.

Tall and stately, with shapely legs that seemed to go on forever, her adequate breasts often dangled over her news desk as if they were inviting the viewer to fondle them. She had the kind of chiseled aristocratic face that gave her permission to keep her dirty-blond hair cropped short. Her slightly elongated neck reminded him of a marble sculpture produced by a Renaissance artist. Her sparkling white teeth looked like they belonged in a toothpaste advertisement. The shape of her mouth suggested that it had talents for things other than reporting the news. A paragon of Puritan prudence, she nonetheless looked like an explosion in search of the right detonator. In his fantasy life, Loeb yearned to be the trigger.

Loeb knew that Kathleen Wyner had been an Assistant District Attorney in Oklahoma before becoming a judge. Before joining CNN, she had been the youngest appellate judge in her state. He didn't know for sure why she and CNN had had a parting of the ways—although there had been reports that she was let go because of an affair she had been having with a very high U.S. government official. All he wanted to know was what she was doing now, and on what station The Wyner Report was being broadcast. He looked at the e-mail from her producer and saw that it was a small cable station in Dallas of which he had never heard.

Loeb turned on his computer and sent an e-mail to the producer of "The Wyner Report," setting down his terms for an interview. Other stations had offered him various sums of money; yet, he requested none. What he asked for, he knew was unusual.

He wanted a two-hour taped interview, the right to help edit the interview before it was shown, and the option of having segments of the interview sold to other stations for airing. He also demanded that no one other than Kathleen Wyner conduct the interview with him, and that she prepare for it by reading a stack of material that he would send to her. Finally, Loeb indicated that his interview with Kathleen Wyner would be an exclusive. He had no intentions of talking to any other interviewers.

Loeb went into the men's room, affixed one of his disguises and went home, hoping that the study of a kabbalistic text would banish the vision of Kathleen Wyner from his mind—at least, temporarily.

The next morning, Loeb came to the office early, and turned on his computer. A voice boomed out of the machine, telling him that he had mail. In fact, he had a lot of mail—more requests for interviews. Yet, in the midst of the long list of communications that he had received, there was a response from the producer of "The Wyner Report." He had accepted Loeb's terms. The interview would be held in Dallas, at the cable station's studio. An airline ticket was being sent.

Loeb flew to Dallas for his interview. He had been to Dallas before, and was afraid of getting lost in the enormous Dallas airport with its many separate terminals. Loeb was therefore relieved when he saw a man carrying a sign with his name on it when he got to the luggage-claim area. The man was his driver, sent by the studio. He immediately took Loeb's briefcase to save Loeb the trouble of carrying it, but Loeb pulled it back from his grasp. "A lot of our guests are nervous at first," the driver said, "but Kathleen always manages to find a way of relaxing them." A stretch limo took Loeb to the studio, shooting down the LBJ Freeway at almost ninety miles an hour. Loeb had felt safer in a New York taxi. The temperature outside was well above one hundred degrees.

Loeb had been on television before, usually on religion programs that aired at 5:30 A.M. on Sundays. He found this studio comparatively small, but adequate. All the basics were there, but none of the amenities of a network station. He was shown the set, which looked like a library—though the books were not real. He was then taken into a dressing room where a technician put powder on his face and showed him how to sit on the bottom of the tail of his jacket so that the wrinkles in his suit would not show. He was then escorted back to the "library," where another technician "wired him." A glass of water was set out on the table in front of him, and he sipped the water slowly. He looked straight ahead and found himself facing the hem of a bright red dress, out of which extended long inviting legs. He looked up, and saw Kathleen Wyner standing across the table from him, a photogenic smile on her face. Immediately, he found himself like a teenage boy, too embarrassed to stand up because he had an erection.

"Don't get up, Rabbi," she said, extending her hand. "I see that you're already wired up."

Thank God, Loeb said to himself. He shook her hand, and said, "I am enormously pleased to meet you, Ms. Wyner. I've been a fan of yours for many years."

She had matured more than she had aged, making her even more alluring than before. Behind her makeup, he saw a face resplendent in beauty, but fractured by disappointment. He wanted to ask her how she had come to such a pass, but instead he quoted to himself, "The gate to wisdom—silence." Not so long before, her image was being beamed around the world on CNN, and now she hosted a little-watched interview show on a small cable station that most subscribers to cable TV did not even receive.

"You're wondering why I'm not longer at CNN," she said.

"I didn't know you were psychic," he said.

"I'm not. It's just what all of my guests want to know."

"Is it perhaps because of a love affair you had with a high government official?" he asked, forgetting about the Talmudic proverb he had just quoted to himself, and wishing he could pull his words back into his mouth, and her with them.

"Well, Rabbi Loeb, perhaps *you* are the psychic here."

"No. I recall reading something about your alleged relationship somewhere."

"If I can invoke the confidentiality of clergy privilege, I can tell you that it is not simply an allegation, and that I've been paying for it since it was alleged. The network supported me as long as my 'relationship' helped me get information, but once he left office, I was no longer of use, and was let go. I was too potentially embarrassing to have around. They wanted me to report the news, not to make it. So, here I am. Without the man I loved, and who—I believe—loved me, childless, with my biological clock ticking away, and on the verge of being jobless."

"Jobless?" Loeb repeated.

"Almost, until you came along that is. You've saved me—for now— and I wish I could find a way to thank you."

Loeb's fantasies returned. It took all of his self-control to refocus his attention on the interview at hand.

The sound people asked for a voice check, and the interview began. The first few minutes were tense, but as the interview proceeded, Loeb began to relax. Wyner had done her homework. Her questions were on-target, insightful, penetrating. Loeb, who had lived his entire married life with a lawyer, was used to the style of interrogation she used. She was gentle and aggressive at the same time. Loeb couldn't help wondering if she were also that way in bed.

The hours seemed like a few minutes. To Loeb's regret, the interview was now over. Wyner stood up, politely thanked him, removed her microphone and left the room. For the next few hours, Loeb sat with one of the producers in another room, and reviewed the tape, offering an occasional suggestion regarding what to edit and how, and which segments to try to sell to other stations.

Loeb was enormously pleased with the interview, which he ascribed to Wyner's skill as an interviewer, rather than to himself. She had elicited both his learning and often repressed sense of humor. She had encouraged him to clarify issues that at first were not clear enough.

The producer gave Loeb a number of release forms to sign. Loeb read them and noticed that he was being paid one dollar for the interview. He pointed to that statement, and said, "That must be so that the contract can be valid," showing his knowledge of law, gained from having lived so long with a lawyer.

"Yes, Rabbi. To be valid, there must be some financial 'consideration' for your services, but look down at paragraph 16." Loeb looked to the next page on the contract, and found an additional paragraph typed onto the standardized contract. It stated that Loeb would be paid 50 percent of all fees received for selling any segments of the tape to other networks. "We expect this to yield you at least $200,000," the producer said, smiling. "Kathleen insisted on it. She said that it was her way of thanking you for what you've done for her—for us."

Before Loeb could respond, a robotic young woman appeared, and escorted Loeb to a dressing room. He got up to leave, but the producer stopped him. "Forget something?" asked the producer.

"What?" said Loeb

"To sign the contract."

Loeb blushed, reached for a pen, and signed. He then followed the young woman into a small room full of mirrors and lights. She wiped off his makeup, and asked him to wait there for a few minutes. Before she left, she told him that his driver was on his way to the studio to take him to the airport.

Loeb removed his shirt and his undershirt, both of which were drenched with sweat from having sat under the hot TV lights for so long. He removed a new shirt and undershirt from his briefcase. Loeb put on the dry undershirt and let his pants drop beneath his ankles before putting on the new shirt. He then began to pack up his briefcase when he heard the door open. Thinking it was his driver, he didn't bother to pull up and zip up his pants. Standing in his underwear, with his pants down around his feet, he turned around to see Kathleen Wyner standing in front of him. She had a smirk on her face. Her hands were folded beneath her breasts. She looked like she would burst out laughing any second. Not knowing precisely what to do, Loeb sat down, trying desperately to wiggle into his trousers.

Wyner locked the door behind her. She had changed from her red dress into a loose linen blouse and a flimsy cotton skirt. It was too hot outside for her to consider wearing anything heavier. She was braless.

Wyner unbuttoned the top few buttons of her blouse, revealing her breasts. They were even more inviting than he had imagined. She lifted up the hem of her long, wide skirt above her waist, and she sat down on his lap, facing him. Loeb's right arm had been resting in his lap and he felt his own hardness below his wrist, and her dampness above it. She slowly rocked against his imprisoned wrist and said, "There's one more question I have to ask, and I want to ask it off camera. It's something I've been thinking about all during our interview."

Loeb cleared his throat and said, "And, what might that be?"

"Is sleeping with a rabbi a religious experience?" she asked, punctuating each word with a soft sigh as she continued to sway on the top of his wrist.

Loeb struggled for breath as well as for words. He was afraid that he might explode at any moment.

"I don't really know," he finally said with a nervous giggle. "I've never slept with a rabbi."

"Well, neither have I," she said, forcing her tongue through his teeth and kissing him deeply. Loeb was now unsure of his next move, or hers.

Finishing her thought, Wyner continued, "Not yet, not now."

She stood up, straightened her skirt and buttoned her blouse. In rapid-fire cadence, Wyner said, "I know many men who are very handsome and I know many men who are very powerful, and you are neither." Loeb cowered; she softened her voice and continued, "But, what I need now is neither. What I need is a man who is reliable, intriguing, brilliant, and who has integrity, and few men that I know are your match. And, that's precisely why I am leaving now. Things with us might begin well, but where and how will they end? So, let's keep things in the realm of fantasy. That way, there are no disappointments, no recriminations. Let's leave it like this. Goodbye. Thank you."

She kissed Loeb on the cheek, unlocked the door and left. He sat in the chair, speechless. When his driver arrived, Loeb was still sitting in the chair with his pants around his ankles, staring in disbelief at the image of himself in the mirror in front of him.

Loeb flew back to Chicago on the last flight from Dallas. During the flight, he thought about what might have happened with Kathleen Wyner. Arriving in Chicago, he took a taxi home. Loeb entered his darkened house and went into the bedroom. Tamara was asleep.

Though he knew that the holy books forbid a man to think of another woman while making love to his wife, Loeb began to make love to

Tamara. While she was still half asleep, Loeb did everything to Tamara that he had fantasized doing to Kathleen Wyner.

Tamara knew that she had not evoked her husband's lust that night. But, she went back to sleep happy. The passion and the conjugal creativity that he had exhibited during their earlier years together, seemed to have returned. She was less concerned with the cause of his sudden outburst than she was with the result. Tamara had missed the lover whom she had married years before. Early the following morning, Tamara welcomed Loeb back home by doing everything to him that he had fantasized being done to him by Kathleen Wyner.

Loeb was at that age when men begin to worry about why their arteries have hardened while their erections have softened. Prostate problems had begun to annoy him, making urination both increasingly frequent and difficult. He was convinced that he was losing his potency, and his ability for sexual frequency. Now, his fears had been allayed, his fantasies fulfilled. "Don't think you're the only one who can work wonders," Tamara whispered into his ear. "See. You don't need Viagra," she said, "Love is the best potion, the most potent magic. Now, I don't want to hear any more from you about your 'declining years.' You're better than ever."

"And so are you," said Loeb, kissing his wife deeply while fondling her generous breasts.

Tamara giggled and said, "So, should I write a 'thank you' note to Kathleen Wyner?"

Loeb blushed. He knew he had the desire but not whether he had the stamina to make love to his wife again. A sudden loud knock on the bedroom door extinguished his erupting lust. It was Joshua.

"Dad, Dad, come out quick, you're on TV!"

By the time Loeb had caught his breath, put on his bathrobe and sat down in front of the television in the next room, the clip of his interview with Kathleen Wyner that had been shown on the cable sports channel was over.

"How was it, Joshua?"

"Awesome, Dad! Who's the foxy lady doing the interview?"

"Kathleen Wyner."

"She a sports announcer?"

"I guess she is now."

Still in the afterglow of ecstasy, Loeb went back into the bedroom with Tamara, dressed, and packed his luggage for the trip to San Diego. The Cubs would be playing the Padres that evening.

Loeb took Tamara in his arms and hugged and kissed her.

"Do you really love me, Jay?" she asked.

"What's this, 'Fiddler on the Roof'?"

"No, really, Jay. Do you love me?"

"Do you know the joke about Adam and Eve? Eve says to Adam: Do you love me? And, Adam answers: Who else? Tamara, who should I love but you? Who can I love except you?"

"Kathleen Wyner, for instance?" said Tamara, seriously.

"Don't be silly. There's only you." Loeb kissed Tamara again, hugged Joshua, left the house, and walked to Sheridan Road where he hailed a cab. Soon after Loeb had entered the taxi and said, "O'Hare—American," the driver asked, "Didn't I see you on TV this morning?" Loeb replied, "Probably somebody who looks like me."

Traffic was unusually light, and Loeb arrived at the airport within half an hour. After passing through security, he checked the monitor listing departures and went directly to the gate. On a television screen in the waiting area, he saw himself talking to Kathleen Wyner about one of the formulas he had employed in his capacity as the spiritual advisor to the Cubs. It was taken from a prayer in the Jewish High Holyday liturgy: "Repentance, prayer, and charity avert the evil decree." After describing how he had encouraged the players to do repentance, pray, give charity, and perform acts of lovingkindness, Loeb described the spiritual transformation that many of the players had undergone during the baseball season, and the positive effect it had on their performance on the field. Wyner then asked him to expound on the nature of the "evil decree" that had stifled a Cubs victory for so many decades.

Loeb talked about baseball superstitions in general, trying to avoid the specific issue of the Cubs. But Wyner probed, and got him to admit something that he had not even told Cubs management—that he believed that the curse on the Cubs was not the Billy Goat curse, that there had been other, more potent curses, both on Wrigley Field and on the Cubs.

First, at Wyner's insistence, Loeb succinctly reviewed the story of the Billy Goat curse that he had first heard about from Nicklesen. Loeb then went on to explain that in many folkloristic traditions, the curses that are the most effective and that have the greatest longevity are those aimed at redressing a moral wrong, at establishing justice, and at compelling repentance for sins committed—but none of these factors was relevant to the Billy Goat curse.

Cubs management had been within its rights to eject Sianis and the goat from the ballpark. Sianis had no right to have designated "Murphy" as the Cubs' mascot. For good reason, animals were not seated in Wrigley Field, even if someone had bought them a ticket, as Sianis had done for Murphy. Indeed, who would want a goat as a mascot, anyway, Loeb added, since the goat, in European Christian folklore, had been a symbol of the devil and the antichrist?

Rather, Loeb asserted, there were other, more potent curses on the Cubs and on Wrigley Field than the one placed on them by Sianis. One such curse, according to Loeb, was brought upon Wrigley Field by the Cubs fans themselves. Loeb described how his research had convinced him that the Cubs fans' behavior at certain critical junctures, during World Series play at Wrigley Field, ironically had contributed to the jinxing of their own team and their own ball park. Loeb gave two examples: one from the 1932 World Series against the Yankees, and the other from the 1945 World Series against Detroit. Another potent curse, according to Loeb, had already been placed upon the Cubs in 1908 by John McGraw, the manager of the New York Giants, from whom the Cubs had "stolen" the pennant that year.

Speaking about the 1932 World Series against the New York Yankees, Loeb described how the Cubs players and fans had yelled racial epithets at Babe Ruth that eventually got him so angry that he retaliated by hitting his famous "called shot" homerun in Wrigley Field.

Sitting in the stands on that day, in a box seat behind the plate, was the Democratic Party's candidate for president, Franklin Roosevelt. When the Babe smacked the ball into the center field bleachers, Roosevelt laughed and cheered. But, there is no record of Roosevelt's protesting the spurious racial slurs hurled at the Babe during that series, among them "dirty nigger."

Loeb reminded his viewers that the "curse of the Babe" was a force to be reckoned with on a baseball field, and that better known than the curse of the Babe on the Cubs was the curse of the Babe on the Boston Red Sox for "selling" Ruth to the New York Yankees in 1920. Yet, the curse of the Babe on the Sox had been lifted in 2004 for reasons unknown. Some speculated that it was because Ruth's daughter had declared that after 86 years, enough was enough, and forgave the Sox on her father's behalf. But, according to Loeb, the curse of the Babe on the Cubs continued to retain its power.

When Wyner asked Loeb if he believed that the "called shot" was fact or legend, Loeb responded by quoting what Joe Dugan, one of Ruth's teammates, had once said about the Babe: "All of the lies about him are true."

Loeb then focused on the last World Series in which the Cubs had played, in 1945. Here, the issue was something close to Loeb's heart: antisemitism. The place was Wrigley Field. The Cubs' adversary was the Detroit Tigers. And the object of the fans' cruel and unprovoked hatred was the always gentlemanly Tigers first baseman, Hank Greenberg.

Loeb described how, in 1945, the greatest Jewish slugger of all time, Hank Greenberg, had returned to baseball after a four-year-long stint of service as an officer in the U.S. Army Air Corps during the Second World War. Even Tigers fans expected little from the veteran ballplayer when he returned from military service to finish up his baseball career. Yet, Greenberg managed to play in forty-seven games during the 1945 season, and to help the Tigers win the pennant that year. In the World Series against the Cubs, he batted .304 with seven RBIs, two homeruns, and even a decisive sacrifice bunt. In 1946, his last full season of play with Detroit, Greenberg led the American League with forty-four homeruns. Detroit traded him to the Pirates in 1947 where he ended his long and distinguished career as a player. In 1956, Greenberg became the first Jewish player elected into baseball's Hall of Fame.

Though not a particularly religious Jew, Greenberg had refused to play on the Jewish Day of Atonement—Yom Kippur, which his fellow Jewish Hall of Famer, Sandy Koufax, was later to emulate. Greenberg's decision evoked the esteem of many, but the ridicule of many more.

Throughout his career, Greenberg was harassed by antisemites, especially in Detroit. Indeed, many baseball commentators believe that in 1938, when he began to close in on Ruth's record of sixty home runs, Greenberg was intentionally thrown bad pitches because his fellow players and the fans did not want to see Ruth's record broken by a Jew. But, Greenberg never accepted this explanation. Indeed, in 1938, after he had hit his fifty-eighth home run, Greenberg's mother promised to make him sixty-one pieces of gefilte fish, each shaped like a baseball, if he broke Ruth's homerun record. When he failed to do so, Greenberg simply said that he couldn't have eaten that much gefilte fish in any case.

Though antisemitic jibes had plagued Greenberg all during his playing career, the harassment reached a crescendo during the 1945 World Series in Chicago, in "the Friendly Confines" of Wrigley Field. On numerous occasions during the Series, but especially when he came up to bat, the umpires had to halt play because the fans hurled bottles and debris at Greenberg while screaming epithets like "dirty kike" and "Christ-killer Jew bastard." Greenberg's insides must have been churning, but he refused to respond to hate. In 1947, when Jackie Robinson came up to the Major Leagues, it was Greenberg who was the first baseball star to befriend him, and to mentor him in how to deal with prejudice and hatred both on and off the baseball field.

Loeb explained how he had become convinced that it was not the Billy Goat curse, but the sins of hatred and bigotry committed at Wrigley

Field that had caused the Cubs to be cursed. Indeed, it was the effects of those curses that Loeb had exorcised from Wrigley Field on that night in May.

Like a prosecuting attorney with a witness on the stand, Wyner probed further. "What you have told us might account for the curse on Wrigley Field. It might explain why the Cubs have not won a World Series since 1932 or a pennant since 1945. But it does not explain why the Cubs have not won a World Series since 1908. How do you account for that? Was it bad baseball, an unsuccessful 'rebuilding effort,' or something else as well?"

"I believe," Loeb said, "that it was the curse of John McGraw, the manager of the New York Giants in 1908."

Loeb had become so engaged in watching himself on TV that he failed to hear the boarding call for his flight. Indeed, a number of the other passengers had gathered around him, watching him watch himself on TV. Before boarding the plane, a few applauded. Others asked for his autograph. Meanwhile, the impatient airline personnel quickly herded Loeb and his admirers onto the plane.

Loeb was not used to traveling first-class, but Post had insisted upon it. As Loeb settled into his seat, the flight attendant asked him if he wanted anything to drink. Loeb asked for a Diet 7-Up, but just as the stewardess was bringing it to him, the pilot asked the flight crew to be seated for takeoff. Loeb watched the attendant finish his drink as the plane ascended on its way to San Diego.

Loeb was hungry. He had not eaten all day. Yet, despite his first-class ticket, the airline still forgot about his order for a kosher meal. And, so, as he had done so many times before, Jay Loeb had no lunch on a long flight. But because he was travelling first-class, the apologetic attendant brought him three limp salads and four small packages of pretzels, which he washed down with a glass of Diet 7-Up.

Upon arriving at the San Diego airport, Loeb was met by a driver sent by Post to take him to the stadium. Unlike the limo in Dallas, this one had a television. Loeb turned it on and flipped the channels until he found what he was looking for: the image of Kathleen Wyner interrogating her ever-willing subject.

Bored with the sound of his own voice, Loeb lowered the sound and stared at images of Wyner when they came on the screen. Arriving at the ballpark, he went to the locker room where the team was already dressing for the game. Apparently, the players already had seen the entire interview with Wyner, and had caught segments on various news and sports programs throughout the day. Loeb was greeted by a loud round of applause.

"I didn't know that the last Cubs team that won the World Series had two Jewish players. Maybe we need something like that this year—like this Greenberg guy who's on the roster. When is he getting here, anyway, and who the hell is he? No one seems to know. What do you think, Rabbi?" Hornsberry asked.

"Time will tell," Loeb responded, having momentarily forgotten that he had spent an entire segment of the interview with Kathleen Wyner talking about the strange end of the 1908 baseball season, and about the roles played by two Cubs players who were Jews: Jonny Kling and Ed Reulbach.

IN 1906 AND 1907, THE CHICAGO CUBS HAD clinched the pennant by August 1. But 1908—the last year the Cubs won a World Series—would be different. And in the gladiator match of that year's National League pennant race, Jonny Kling and Ed Reulbach would play a crucial role. In his interview with Kathleen Wyner, Loeb explained why he thought that Kling should have preceeded Hank Greenberg as the first Jewish-American inducted into the baseball Hall of Fame.

Kling was an innovator at a time when baseball was still inventing itself. Brought to the Cubs from the New York Giants in 1900, Kling became the Cubs first-string catcher. The great Honus Wagner considered Kling the "all-time catcher" of his era. Kling was the first major league catcher to stay up close to the batter, and one of the first to throw from a crouch. These were some of the many things he had brought to the major leagues from his study of play in the Negro Leagues.

Loeb went on to describe how Kling liked to ingratiate himself with the umpire. He would suggest to the umpire how he should call a pitch.

Kling would then block the pitch from the umpire's view. "It was a strike, right?" he would say, and usually, the umpire would agree.

Kling was considered the Cubs' "brain behind the plate" who led the Cubs to four pennants and two World Series victories during his years with the club. Kling's teammates had a simple nickname for him: "the Jew."

In the 1907 World Series against Detroit, which the Cubs won in five games, Kling consistently shut down the aggressive base running of that icon of the game of baseball, who was also a notorious racist and antisemite—Ty Cobb. However, it was during the frenetic and controversial end of the 1908 season that Kling was at his best. Nonetheless, he left the Cubs after their victory in that year's World Series to invest time and money in his billiard business. Denied entry into the baseball Hall of Fame, Kling went on to become the world's professional pocket billiard champion. Without him, the Cubs failed to win their fourth pennant in a row, and their short two-year-long winning streak in the World Series came to an abrupt halt for the rest of the twentieth century, and into the twenty-first. In 1912, Kling was traded to the Boston Red Sox, which he also managed that year. He ended his playing career in Cincinnati, and then went into real estate, making a small fortune, which allowed him to buy a minor league team in Kansas City that he eventually sold to the Yankees for a handsome profit.

Toward the end of September 1908, the National League pennant race was in a dead heat among the Pirates, the Giants and the Cubs. A double-header was scheduled in Brooklyn on September 26 between the Dodgers and the Cubs that was destined to eliminate the Pirates from pennant contention. The Cubs player-manager, Frank Chance, caught the first game; Kling caught the second, hitting 2 for 3. The Cubs pitcher for both games was Ed Reulbach.

Ed Reulbach was one of the most educated men ever to play professional baseball. Before coming to the majors, he had been a star athlete at Notre Dame. In 1908, he was 24-7. His ERA usually hovered beneath 2.00. For four years he had the highest percentage of wins of any National League pitcher. But, on September 26, 1908, Reulbach did something done never before and never since in major league baseball. He pitched two consecutive games on the same day, and won each with a shutout. The Cubs assistant trainer, Ed Levy, once recalled that when Reulbach came off the mound at the end of the second game on that day, he told Levy that perhaps they shouldn't have played on that day since it was Rosh Hashanah, the Jewish New Year, and that he— Reulbach—was part Jewish. Yet, playing on that day did not seem to faze his Jewish teammates, Kling and Levy.

But, according to Loeb, it was the game the Cubs played against the Giants, a few days before Reulbach's extraordinary performance, that may have determined both the National League pennant race that year, and the fate of the Cubs for the balance of that century, and beyond. And, the key players in that drama came down to three people: a Giants rookie named Fred Merkle, a National League umpire named Henry O'Day, and the Cubs second baseman—Johnny Evers.

On September 23, 1908, the Cubs arrived at the Polo Grounds in Manhattan to play the New York Giants. The Giants were holding on to first place in the National League by six percentage points. Both teams were crippled by late season injuries. Going into the ninth inning, the score was 1-1. The game, the season, and the pennant, were all on the line. Christy Mathewson, the Giants' ace pitcher, stood on the mound like a golden haired god surveying his domain. In the 1905 World Series, Mathewson had pitched three shut-outs—a feat accomplished neither before, nor since, in World Series play.

In the top of the ninth, the Cubs second baseman, Johnny Evers, led off. The first pitch was a fastball that Evers missed completely. The second was one of Mathewson's best curve balls. Evers swung, not even coming close. The third pitch was a fastball that jammed Evers' wrists, going right over the inside corner of the plate. The next batter, Wildfire Schulte, summarily struck out on three pitches, two fastballs and a curve.

Only the third batter, Frank Chance, managed to make contact with the ball—a dribble to the shortstop, who summarily dispatched him with a throw to first base.

Coming to the mound in the bottom of the ninth was the Cubs pitcher, Jack Pfiester. He was in such severe pain from a torn ligament in his shoulder that he had almost fainted soon after coming in from the mound the previous inning. But, in those days, there was no such a thing as a "closer." Pfiester knew that because of his injury, he could not throw his curve ball, and that his fastball lacked its usual pop.

Despite Pfiester's injuries, he got the Giants' first batter to ground out. Devlin, the next batter, swung at Pfiester's aborted curve, punching a clean single to center field. McCormick came to the plate and tried twice to bunt, but failed. Swinging with two strikes, he grounded the ball to second. The Cubs tried for a double-play to end the inning, but got only one runner out. To the fans' surprise, Giants manager John McGraw then let the rookie Fred Merkle bat. Everyone had expected a pinch hitter, but not McGraw. Merkle had succumbed to Pfiester's curve ball his first three times up, but McGraw took the gamble that it wasn't working anymore. Merkle's bat never left his shoulder as Pfiester painfully fired a couple of fastballs across the plate. The following pitch, Merkle poked foul, glazing the Cubs first-baseman's glove. Every fan arose in his or her seat for the next pitch. Merkle swung, and the ball headed again toward the right field foul line. Except, this time it fell in fair territory. There were now two Giants on base: Moose McCormick on third, and rookie Fred Merkle on first. Al Bridwell then came to the plate and smacked the ball into short center for a base hit.

As soon as McCormick's spikes hit home plate, the ecstatic Giants fans began to stream onto the field. They lifted Mathewson onto their shoulders and carried him around the field. Mathewson was carrying a ball that everyone assumed was the winning game ball. The crowd spontaneously began to sing a song that had been written earlier that year by vaudevillian Jack Norworth: "Take Me Out to the Ballgame."

Meanwhile, most of the Cubs ran for safety from the hostile Giants fans. Merkle watched what was happening as he hovered between first and second base, and then he also ran off the field. Thereupon, the Cubs second baseman, Johnny Evers, produced a ball from somewhere, and stepped on second base claiming a force out on Merkle, a third out, and the absence of a Giants' victory. But, for the New York fans, their Giants already had clinched the pennant.

Minutes later, in the safety of the locker room, the Cubs manager, Frank Chance, convinced umpire Hank O'Day that the game was not over, that the Giants had not won, that Merkle was out on a force, and that the run scored by McCormick did not count, that the game had ended in a tie. O'Day called in the Giants manager, John McGraw, and informed him of the decision. McGraw exploded, and began to assault Chance. McGraw appealed the decision to the National League president, Harry Pulliam. The decision was now in Pulliam's hands.

Ironically, a few weeks earlier, on September 4, the Cubs had been playing Pittsburgh. The score was tied in the bottom of the tenth inning. Pittsburgh was up to bat. The bases were loaded with two out. The next batter hit a clean single to center. The third base runner crossed the plate. As was then the custom, the fans invaded the playing field. Most of the players already had vacated the field. The Cubs second baseman, Johnny Evers, called to the center fielder to throw him the ball, which he did. The runner who had been on first base was leaving the field. Evers ran after him to tag him, but when he could not, Evers stepped on second base declaring the player out and the run void. Umpire Hank O'Day, who was walking off the field at the time, ignored Evers' protestations. The Pirates remained the victors. The Cubs appealed to the National League president, Harry Pulliam, but Pulliam upheld O'Day's decision that the run had scored.

Yet, a few weeks later, on September 23, in an almost identical play, O'Day robbed the Giants of the pennant by calling Merkle out and thereby voiding the winning run. In Merkle's case, Pulliam also would uphold O'Day's decision, though it blatantly contradicted his earlier call, only a few weeks before. Pulliam never raised the question of where Evers got the ball that he used to make the put-out against Merkle on second base, as the ball Bridwell hit, never made it back into the infield. The board of the National League, chaired by Pulliam, decided on October 5, after three days of meetings, that the game had ended in a tie, and that for the first time in baseball history, the pennant race had ended in a tie. They had hoped that end of season play in the final days of September might resolve the problem for them by awarding a clear victory to one of the contending teams, but such was not to be the case.

Not knowing what to do in this unprecedented situation of a tie for the pennant, the board of the National League decided that the outcome of the 1908 National League pennant race would be determined by a single playoff game to be held in New York City on October 8, 1908. Rumors began to spread that O'Day had been bribed by the Cubs. The nineteen-year-old Merkle, a Wisconsin farmboy, began to fear for his life on the congested streets of New York. There was blood in the air.

EVEN BEFORE LEAVING CHICAGO FOR New York on the new express train that took eighteen hours rather than the usual twenty-eight, the Cubs had begun to receive death threats from the New York fans. When the Cubs arrived in New York, they were taken under police guard to a hotel in midtown Manhattan. As soon as the New York fans learned where the Cubs were staying, a group of them held an all-night vigil outside of the hotel, blaring horns and making all kinds of noise to try to prevent the players from getting any sleep. The next morning, in order not to attract attention, the players left one at a time through a back door of the hotel, and, dressed in street clothes, some wearing disguises, they took the train up to the Polo Grounds.

More than 250,000 Giants fans surrounded the Polo Grounds that morning, each in hope of getting a ticket to the game. Some perched themselves on pillars of the Eighth Avenue elevated train to get a view of the game. Eventually, the trains had to stop running because of the numbers of fans sitting on the tracks. Speculators sold counterfeit tickets to thousands of fans who surged toward the gates, only to be turned back. Mounted police and patrolmen were everywhere. Even the umpires had trouble getting into the ballpark, and arrived in the locker room an hour behind schedule. National League President Pulliam arrived at the park under heavy police escort.

When the Cubs took the field for pre-game warm-up, they were greeted not only with a cacophony of boos and hisses, but with a deluge of bottles and garbage. When the Cubs' player-manager, Frank Chance, appeared on the field, he was struck by a beer bottle in the neck, and had to retreat back into the dugout to stop the bleeding that gushed onto his uniform. He emerged some moments later with a huge bandage on the back of his neck. Chance would suffer other fan-inflicted injuries by the end of that day.

The Cubs had been promised twenty minutes of practice, but after only a few minutes, the Giants ran onto the field, and to the delight of the crowd, chased the Cubs from the field. Meanwhile, in the right field stands, the crowds pushed down a fence and thousands stampeded onto the field. While policemen and firemen tried to herd people off the field, two men fell to their deaths from the grandstand roof into the bleachers below, and their bodies were carried away in blankets by the police. Meanwhile, Christy Mathewson began throwing warm-up pitches from the mound. He would face the same opponent who had pitched against him in the controversial game of September 23—Jack Pfiester.

It was now 2:00—game time, but it was announced that the game would be delayed until 3:00 P.M. This gave gamblers extra time to place bets on the game, just as a rumor spread through the ballpark that the Giants manager, John McGraw, had bribed the umpires to throw the game the Giants' way.

Finally, the game got underway. In the top of the first inning, Mathewson mowed down the first three Cubs batters who faced him. As the Giants left the field, a sky-splitting roar came from the crowd. The Giants now came up to bat.

Just as the cheers of the crowd were winding down, they escalated as Pfiester's first pitch hit the batter, and his next four pitches to Buck Herzog awarded him a walk. The following batter struck out swinging, but the Cubs catcher, Jonny Kling, intentionally dropped the ball on the third strike, tagged out the batter, and threw to first, nailing Herzog.

Pfiester, who was still nursing his injuries, gave up a double, and walked the next batter. There were two out, and a couple of runners on base. Then, a run scored. Chance came to the mound and called in another pitcher, his ace starter—Mordecai Peter Centennial Brown. Pfiester left the mound crying, either from pain or disappointment, or both. Meanwhile, as Brown fought his way through the hostile fans to get from the bullpen to the mound, a fan perched on a telegraph pole lost his balance and fell off, breaking his neck.

With twenty-nine wins and an ERA well below 1.50 that season, Brown was the perfect choice. Brown had been a coal miner in Indiana. He was known either as "Miner Brown" or as "Three Finger Brown." Brown had lost a finger and the use of one other in an accident when cutting wheat at the age of seven. His remaining good fingers had been broken while wrestling with a hog when he was a boy. But, rather than hampering his pitching, Brown's mangled hand had served him well during his years with the Cubs, beginning in 1903 when he joined the club. Some attributed his almost unhittable "hook" ball and his early version of the split-fingered fastball to his anatomical peculiarities. With Kling behind the plate calling pitches and plays, Chance knew that the game was far from over. Brown came to the mound, threw a few warm-up pitches, and then summarily struck out Art Devlin to end the inning.

The second inning was uneventful. As the third inning began, Mathewson motioned to the Giant center-fielder, Cy Seymour, to back up as Cubs batter Joe Tinker came to the plate. Seymour, however, stayed put. Tinker then hit a line drive to exactly the spot to which Mathewson had pointed. Seymour finally recovered the ball, bobbled it, and threw, but Tinker was already safe at third. Kling then came to bat, and drove in Tinker with a bloop single. Brown bunted, moving Kling to second. The next batter flew out to Seymour, moving Kling to third. Evers came up and was walked. Schulte took his turn at bat and doubled. Then, to a barrage of howls and hisses, the wounded Chance stepped up with two on and two out, and unleashed a line drive into the outfield, beating the throw into second with a masterful slide.

As the anxiety of the Giants fans increased, the game moved ahead uneventfully until the seventh inning. The score was now 4-2. The first two Giant batters singled, and the third walked. McGraw, getting desperate, took Mathewson out of the game and put up Larry Doyle to pinch hit. Doyle hit a high fly foul that looked as if it was heading for the stands behind the plate. Kling jumped up to try to catch it. Suddenly, derby hats rained onto the field trying to distract Kling's attention. Bottles were hurled from the stands at him, as he lunged for the ball. Undeterred and unafraid, Kling somehow managed to avoid the missiles hurtling down at him, and made the catch. A sacrifice fly brought in a run, but when that inning ended, so did the scoring on that fateful afternoon. In the last of the ninth, Brown disposed of three batters with four pitches, giving Chicago both the game and the pennant.

Police charged onto the field as the last out was made. Drawing their revolvers, the police escorted the Cubs to the locker room. Yet, some of the Cubs were injured by the rowdy fans as they left the field. Chance, already wearing a bandage on the back of his neck, was hit in the throat by a fan, causing him to lose his voice for a few days. Pfiester was punched in the jaw and slashed with a knife on his already injured shoulder. Solly Hofman, the Cubs outfielder, was hit across the face with a bottle. Meanwhile, Mordecai Brown changed into street clothes, and with his pitching hand in his pocket, he melted into the crowd and made his way back to the hotel where the Cubs were sequestered under police protection until they left the city the next day for Detroit and the World Series.

The 1908 World Series was only the fifth contest of its kind. The first World Series had been played in 1903, but because of a controversy between the leagues, there was no championship bout in 1904.

The Cubs entered World Series play in 1906 for the first single-city contest in baseball history. For that week, Chicago was the baseball capital of the world. However, during that week there was a miniature civil war in Chicago: the Cubs against the White Sox, the largely German-American population of the north-side against the heavily Irish-American population of the south-side. Even the Cubs roster was heavily populated by players of German origin, including two German Jews—Kling and Reulbach. The Sox roster was punctuated with Irish names like Sullivan, Walsh, Donahue and Dougherty. Not only did both teams have to battle one another, but both teams also had to contend with the frigid Chicago weather and occasional snow.

Brown was in top form for the first game. For the second game, Reulbach threw a one-hitter, leading the Cubs to a 7-1 victory. After Reulbach's victory, the fanatical Cubs fan, Chicago judge Kenesaw Mountain Landis, almost got into a fist fight with a Sox fan. A little over a decade later, Landis would become the Commissioner of Baseball, after the 1919 "Black Sox" scandal, in which the White Sox were accused of intentionally losing the World Series. But, in 1906, the White Sox still managed to win the Series 4-2, despite their low team batting average of .230 during the regular season. The Cubs could not beat the "hitless wonders of the south-side." Rattled by their loss in the World Series after a 116-36 record in the 1906 season, the Cubs resolved with a vengeance to win both the pennant and the championship the following year.

In 1907, the Cubs won the National League championship with a 107-45 record, seventeen games ahead of the second-place Pirates. The Cubs bullpen was having a stellar year. Brown had been 20-6 with a 1.39 ERA, Reulbach had a 17-4 year with a 1.69 ERA, and Pfiester had a league leading 1.15 ERA with 15 victories and 9 defeats. Kling led the league with 499 put-outs. In the World Series that year, the Cubs faced the Detroit Tigers, who won three consecutive American League pennants in 1907, 1908 and 1909. The Cubs knew that they had to shut down the Tigers' Ty Cobb in order to win, and that they did. Cubs pitching held him to four hits during the series. Kling, perhaps motivated by Cobb's outspoken antisemitism, stifled Cobbs' usually effective base running. The Cubs trounced the Detroit Tigers in the 1907 World Series, 4-0.

The 1908 World Series began in a rain-drenched Detroit stadium, with the Cubs winning the first game 10-6. Playing at home the following day, the Cubs won 6-1. The next day, the still-wounded Pfiester collected the only Cubs defeat in the Series which the Cubs went on to win in five games.

Though the Cubs went on to win the pennant in 1910, 1918, 1929, 1932, 1935, 1938, and 1945, and though they won division play in 1984, 1989, 2003, and the "wildcard" spot in 1998, their victory in the 1908 World Series was the last world championship they would win for the rest of the twentieth century, and beyond. Until his death in 1934, Giants manager John McGraw asserted that the Cubs 1908 championship title was tainted because of the Merkle episode, and that the Cubs did not deserve to win the World Series ever again. In McGraw's view, O'Day's decision had been unjust. Pulliam's decision had been unfair. Evers had lied; the ball which he had used to force out Merkle, was not the ball that Merkle had hit.

Loeb was convinced that the Cubs undeserved world championship title of 1908 had tainted their play ever since, that the curse of McGraw had been efficacious, and that its power had been strengthened by the sins against the Babe in 1932 and against Greenberg in 1945. Now, time would tell whether the power of these curses had been removed, whether "repentance, prayer and charity could avert the evil decree," whether the Cubs would now have another chance at the pennant and the world championship title.

Each of the major figures in the Merkle episode ended his life, as if under a curse. The Cubs second baseman, Johnny Evers, was never able to explain where he got the baseball that he used to claim the force out of Merkle on second base. Evers eventually lost most of his money when his investments went sour. He suffered from clinical depression for the rest of his life, and died penniless, miserable and alone. A few months after the "Merkle affair," National League president, Harry Pulliam, went into a private dining room at The New York Athletic Club, put on his dressing gown, lay down on a plush couch, took out a revolver, and blew his brains out. Hank O'Day, the umpire of the Merkle game, became a manager. In 1912, he managed the Boston Red Sox, but was fired at the end of the season. In midseason 1914, he came on to manage the Cubs, who finished fourth in the league that year. His career ended with failure, and was tainted by rumors of impropriety. Ironically, Merkle ended up with the Cubs in 1918—just in time to lose their fifth World Series in five attempts. In 1926, he coached for the New York Yankees, when they lost the World Series. It seems that Merkle was a jinx on any team that he joined.

Loeb completed his historical explanation of how the Cubs had come to be cursed by John McGraw in 1908, a curse that already had held fast for almost a century.

BACK IN TWENTY-FIRST CENTURY SAN DIEGO,
the Chicago Cubs donned their amulets and joined Loeb in prayer before
going onto the field to face the San Diego Padres. As was his custom,
Loeb stayed in the locker room during the game. He had requested that
each player submit a weekly list to him stating how often he prayed,
what charities he donated to, which sins he committed and how he had
sought to repent after realizing that he had committed them, and which
acts of charity and good deeds he performed. Loeb also requested that
Cubs management submit to him the weekly statistics of each player's
performance on the field. As the game proceeded, Loeb studied these
documents.

Loeb knew the contents of each player's file almost by heart. He
was therefore able to compare the lifestyles of the players as the season
had progressed to the lifestyles they each had led when the season had
begun. The more he read, the more pleased he became. Though none of
the players were saints by any means, each had made significant progress
in improving his spiritual standard of living. Loeb further reviewed the

documents and found a clear correlation between the players' moral and spiritual improvement and their performance on the field. In his view, whether or not the Cubs got into the playoffs, each member of the team had become a winner in the task of individual spiritual and moral self-development. Yet, Loeb knew that neither Post nor Wriggles saw things as he did. Their only concern was to see the Cubs in post-season play—no matter what it took.

When the players returned from the field that day, they were smiling. They had repeated in that game what they had done in the first 1984 playoff game against the Padres, a 13-0 victory. In the following days, the Cubs swept the series with the Padres. It seemed that the curse that had prevented them from beating the Padres in the 1984 playoffs had vanished. That contest had probably been lost the moment Cubs first baseman Leon Durham watched a ground ball go right through his legs into the outfield to tie the game that the Padres would eventually win to eliminate the Cubs that season from additional post-season play.

From San Diego, the Cubs went on to Arizona to play the Diamondbacks. By then, the story of Loeb's activities with his now-famous chickens that night in May in Wrigley Field had been embellished upon, exaggerated, and was known by every baseball fan in the United States, and beyond. Despite intense media pressures, Loeb never revealed the fate of his chickens.

Not to be outdone by the Cubs, the Diamondbacks had an Apache medicine man come onto the field just before game time. In full, feathered regalia and with painted streaks on his face, he danced and chanted his way around the infield, invoking the spirits to grant a victory to the Arizona team. By the third inning, it seemed as if his incantations had fallen on deaf ears. The Cubs had already taken a healthy 5-2 lead. But, the medicine man's efforts were not without an effect. During the fourth inning, in the bright blue sky of the Arizona desert, rain clouds suddenly made an unusual, ominous appearance. The skies opened up, showering the ballpark with torrential rains, making unplayable the field that was built without adequate drainage facilities. The umpires called the game. The following day, the Cubs and the Diamondbacks played a double-header in the blistering hot late afternoon Arizona sun. The Pentecostal minister who was supposed to "bless" the field that day was asked not to recite his prayers. The Cubs and the Diamondbacks split the double-header.

From Arizona, the Cubs criss-crossed the west, playing in San Francisco, Colorado, Los Angeles and Houston. They then returned to the Midwest for a game against Milwaukee, and for a long home stand before a bulging audience of old and new adoring fans at Wrigley Field. All across the nation, and even up into Canada, the Chicago Cubs left behind them a trail of victories. It was now mid-September, and to the amazement of Cubs fans—especially, Tamara Loeb, the Cubs were in contention to win the Central Division. The next couple of weeks— when the final games of the regular season would be played—would prove decisive. But Rabbi Jay Loeb had other things on his mind: the Jewish High Holyday season would begin at the end of September, which meant that he had a prior—and higher—engagement than the Cubs.

In early September, during one of the Chicago home stands, Loeb had the rare luxury of visiting his office at the Tribune Towers. His office looked like Santa Claus's workshop just before Christmas. Bags of mail, messages, and printed e-mails were everywhere. His secretary had sorted them for him. On top of one of the many piles of mail around the room was a letter marked "Personal." It was from Kathleen Wyner. The letter read:

> My dearest Rabbi Loeb, or should I say, Jay:
> Some people have good luck. Some people have bad luck. Most people have both. But a very select few individuals are talismans for others. Whatever luck they might have, they bring good luck to the people they care about. And, you, Jay Loeb, are such a person. I don't believe that you make magic for the

Cubs, but that you are *magic for the Cubs because you care about them, and want them to succeed. I believe that those whom you care about—your wife, your son, your friends, your students—succeed precisely because you care. You are their magical charm. Your concern, your passion, is your magical potion. Yet, like all potent forces, passion must be controlled and channeled, lest it erupt as a destructive power. You play with fire, which can both enlighten and provide warmth, but which can also burn and consume everyone and everything in its path. Be careful with your fire, your magic, your passion, lest it engulf you.*

My passion for a man I once adored almost consumed me. My passion for you and yours for me could readily consume us both. That's why I left the room at the studio. And now I see that I was right. Instead of being devoured by the fire, I have been made alive again through the power of the light. You have become my lucky charm. Though you cannot resurrect the dead, you can perform an even greater miracle; you can resurrect the living, which is what you did for me.

As your keen powers of discernment clearly recognized, my life was on the skids, shattering into pieces, falling apart. The worst thing that could happen to a human being was happening to me: I had a past, but no future. My future, my hope, had been taken away from me. But, then, you came into my life out of the blue, and your talismanic powers have worked their magic.

Because of my interview with you, many new job opportunities came my way. Something I have not had in recent years. Something I had learned no longer to expect. I've received offers to anchor the news in a number of cities—nothing big, but more than I have now. Recently, I've received offers from one of the networks to host a new weekly show, "Faith and

Values." And, just when I was about to choose to accept one of the jobs I'd been offered, the "former high government official" about whom you spoke called me.

He told me that he has never stopped loving me. How his position made it impossible for him to continue our relationship. How miserable and how guilty he was. How much he regretted the damage he had done to my life. How much he now realized that he had to make it up to me. How he would try to repay me for some of what I had suffered because of him. I listened, wanting to believe him, but I couldn't. Until yesterday, when the results of his efforts became clear.

The White House called. The President has nominated me for a federal judgeship. It will be rushed through the Senate with bipartisan support. My former lover had seen to it. Soon the hearings in the Senate will begin. Soon I will have a future back in a field I love, and never should have left. I will have my honor, prestige, self-worth, and my security restored. I will be a federal district judge with an appointment for life. And, all of this is because of you, my talisman. What more could I want? Only one thing: a child.

Which brings me to my request. Please, don't be offended. I want you to father my child through artificial insemination. I have been studying the precedents on this in Jewish law, and I understand that your tradition does not necessarily consider artificial insemination by a donor as an act of adultery since no act of intercourse takes place. You see, I have been studying your tradition. In fact, I am secretly and privately studying with a rabbi here in Dallas to convert to Judaism. I don't expect an answer now, but after my judgeship is confirmed, I'll be back to you on this. In the meantime, all my love. Best wishes to you and good luck with the Cubs.

Kathleen

Loeb read the letter over and over again, and he thought of a saying by Oscar Wilde: "In this world, there are only two tragedies. One is not getting what you want, and the other is getting it. The last is the real tragedy." Loeb read the letter one last time and burned it.

On Sunday, September 20, Loeb joined the Cubs in New York for a double-header against the Mets. The Cubs needed four more wins and no more than two losses to clinch the Central Division. A battery of clergy of every conceivable faith had been gathered by the Mets to attend the game to help assure a victory for their team. Before the game, prayers were recited, holy water was sprinkled, communion was given players who wanted it, a confession booth had been set up in the bullpen, faith-healers attended to medical needs of the players in the locker room, some of the ministers spoke in tongues. But, Loeb, as he had done so many times before, prayed with the team and collected reports on their spiritual progress, which he studied during the game. Loeb knew that the players and God, and not him, would bring about either victory or defeat. Loeb also knew that in baseball, as in life, arrogance and pride were deadly poisons.

As Loeb observed the pretentiousness of his fellow clergy at Shea Stadium, the brazenness of the New York fans, and the unearned self-confidence of the Mets players, he quoted to himself the biblical verse, "Pride goes before a fall." By the end of the day, the Mets had dropped the double-header to the Cubs. At the night game the following day, no New York clergy were present, but the Mets lost anyway. The Cubs now needed a single victory to win the Central Division. Ironically, the Cubs were scheduled to return to Chicago for a couple of interleague games with the White Sox. It was like the 1906 World Series all over again, except this time, the Cubs had to win.

The Jewish High Holydays, beginning with the New Year, Rosh Hashanah, would begin that Friday night, and Loeb hoped that the division title would be won before then. He would not attend any games on Rosh Hashanah, even if they were played in Chicago.

Unlike the "hitless wonders" of 1906, the White Sox were now a young, aggressive team, with a powerful offense but a weak defense, playing in a pitcher's ballpark. The Cubs would have to beat them with defense.

Loeb sat out the first game so that he could work on his post-season strategic plan and his sermons for the coming Jewish holydays. Tamara was livid. The Cubs lost their first game at the White Sox's ballpark, and Tamara told Loeb in no uncertain terms that unless he attended the second game, he could forget about his "conjugal rights" during the coming Jewish New Year holiday celebration. Even Joshua gave his father a cold shoulder.

Loeb put aside his work, and attended the second game against the Sox. The game was tied in the ninth inning. With two outs and a man on third, the Sox's pitcher hurled a "passed ball," allowing the Cubs runner to score, and granting the Cubs not only a win and victory in the Central Division, but also vindication for their humiliating loss to the Sox in the 1906 World Series.

After the game, as Loeb was being bathed with champagne in the

Cubs locker room, he was informed that his wife had fainted dead away at her seat. Smelling like a wino, Loeb left the celebration to take Tamara to the hospital emergency room, where she was treated for shock, and kept overnight for observation. Loeb thought of the old adage, "Some people can't take 'yes' for an answer."

Now, for the first time in months, Loeb had some free time on his hands. The divisional playoffs that would determine the National League championship, and who from that league would play in the World Series, were scheduled to begin on Tuesday, October 6, the day after the Day of Atonement, Yom Kippur. Now Loeb could concentrate on the coming holidays and upon his plans for post-season play, including his plans for the arrival of Sandy Greenberg.

The players and Cubs management had been pressuring Loeb to produce the elusive Greenberg. Reporters had come up empty in trying to locate such a player, or even to find evidence that such a person existed. They had looked all over the country, searched in the Mexican and Japanese baseball leagues as well as in the minor leagues and in collegiate teams, but they came up blank. The Sandy Greenbergs that they had located were obviously not the right ones. One was a ninety-five-year-old retired shoe salesman in Ft. Lauderdale. Another was a four-year-old boy in Des Moines. A third, Sandra Greenberg, was a topless waitress in Lake Tahoe. A fourth was an orthodontist in Hartford. Loeb promised Post and Wriggles that he expected that Greenberg would report for play "at the appropriate time." When that would be remained a mystery. Meanwhile, Loeb made a couple of telephone calls that would determine Greenberg's future. One was to London and the other was to Jerusalem.

For years, Loeb had conducted religious services for the Jewish High Holydays—Rosh Hashanah and Yom Kippur—at the small synagogue at his seminary. The few dozen people who usually attended were mostly retired men and women, living on a fixed income, and unable to afford the sumptuous membership fees of the large synagogues that dotted the

Chicago "Gold Coast" and Lake Shore Drive. Each year, they were joined by a handful of students and medical residents from the downtown campus of Northwestern University.

Like all Jewish holydays, the Jewish New Year began at sunset. This particular year, the beginning of the New Year and the celebration of the Sabbath began simultaneously, on Friday evening, September 26, just as it had in 1908, the last year the Cubs had won the World Series. Loeb took this as a hopeful omen, and he was pleased that, unlike 1908, there would be no Jewish players on the Cubs team playing ball on Rosh Hashanah.

Loeb came early to the synagogue to be sure that everything had been prepared for the service. He wanted to review the liturgy one last time with the cantor, and to have adequate time to don his liturgical robes. Though Loeb expected that some additional worshippers might wander in because of his newly acquired fame, he anticipated that everything would proceed routinely, as in past years.

Loeb had not been home very much the past few months, and he relished spending some time with Joshua and Tamara during the holydays. He also looked forward to spending the next two days in tranquility and prayer. But he would soon be disappointed.

As Loeb approached the seminary, he noticed that a mob of reporters and fans had gathered there. Mounted police and police on foot were there in force to restrain them. As Loeb got closer, he was recognized, and the horde surged in his direction. A visibly pregnant woman ran toward him, embraced him, and pointed to her stomach, screaming, "Bless my baby!" A parade of people in wheelchairs and on crutches slowly made their way toward him. Some held makeshift signs, asking Loeb to cure them. A few people, carrying signs that read, "I have AIDS. Help me," tried to force a path through the throng. Homeless people begged for money. Wealthy people called out the names of various stocks, asking for investment advice. Children brought baseballs, gloves and bats that they wanted Loeb to bless. A man with wild eyes grabbed

Loeb's arm and pleaded with him to exorcise the demons that possessed him. A group of men with shaved heads, dressed in orange robes, chanted mantras in some foreign language, while shaking tambourines and beating on tom-toms.

One platoon of reporters and camera crews focused on the crowd, while another tried to break their way through the crowd to get an interview with Loeb. Finally, at Loeb's request, the police escorted him into the seminary through a back door in the alley.

Loeb entered the synagogue, and found it already jammed with worshippers who had been admitted by the frenetic ushers. The entire Cubs team was there, with their coaches, trainers, and even some members of the Wrigley Field ground crew. It was not what Loeb had either anticipated or wanted.

Loeb climbed two flights of stairs, hoping that the door to his small office would be unlocked. It was. He went in and found mounds of unopened mail and messages, practically knee-deep on the floor, and piled up on his desk. The seminary had never bothered to forward Loeb's mail to him.

Loeb dug into the mountain of paper on his desk until he found the telephone. He conjured up a phone number from his memory that he had not dialed in months. He pressed seven buttons on the phone, and was relieved when he heard a familiar voice say, "You're the last person I expected to hear from tonight. You see, I've finally gotten a caller ID on my private line." It was the voice of his friend, Patrick Hood, the Archbishop of Chicago.

"Patrick, I really need your help. I've got a real situation on my hands," Loeb said nervously.

Cardinal Hood interrupted him, laughed, and said with a forced Irish brogue, "And a good evening to you, too, laddie. And, a Happy New Year."

Loeb giggled nervously and heard his friend say, "You know, Jay, I've got a real situation on my hands every minute of every day. Welcome to the club."

The Cardinal's words had put Loeb's situation in perspective, and he began to regain his composure.

"What do you suggest?" Loeb inquired.

"You know, I'm not Jewish," the Archbishop said rhetorically, "but I'm going to answer your question with a question, anyway. One that I learned from you: What do you think?"

"I think," Loeb said haltingly, "that—as you like to say—we've got to find a way of making lemonade out of the lemons that we've have been handed."

"Could you sneak over to my residence after the services tonight?"

"Sure, Pat."

"See you then."

"Thanks much."

Loeb hung up, relieved. He went into a classroom, donned his long white liturgical robes, put on his prayer shawl, and tried to focus his mind on the solemnity of the holyday that was now descending upon the world.

Loeb entered the sanctuary, pleased that seats in the first row had been saved for Joshua and Tamara. But, the seats were empty. Joshua and Tamara had preferred to sit with the team. As Loeb ascended the pulpit, the din of conversation toned down, and the service began. The team members looked incongruous in their skull caps. Joshua wore a Cubs cap.

The noise from outside had died down. The police must have dispersed the crowd, and the media must have left as well. Loeb welcomed everyone to the service and spoke briefly about the meaning of the Jewish New Year celebration. He reminded the non-Jews in the congregation that Judaism was not a religion that actively sought converts. "We have enough problems with the Jews we already have," he said, trying to inject some humor, but no one laughed. He encouraged the non-Jews present to pray at the churches or mosques of their choice, and to recommit themselves to the teachings of their own faiths.

The service began with the chanting of the cantor. The Cubs players looked lost as they tried to follow the service, which was mostly in Hebrew. The plaintive chants of the cantor evoked strange expressions on the faces of the members of the team. Luckily, most of the regular worshippers were not baseball fans, so the service proceeded with a minimum of disruption. However, Loeb was disappointed as he watched Tamara, Joshua and Hornsberry discuss pitching strategies throughout the service.

As the evening liturgy moved toward its conclusion, Loeb arose to deliver the sermon. Looking at his audience, especially at the members of the team, he discarded the sermon he had prepared, and began to speak extemporaneously.

Loeb began by telling a story about Yogi Berra. Yogi was once asked, "What time is it?" He looked at his watch and replied, "It's now." Loeb explained that Yogi had it right. *Now* is all we really have. He told of a Hasidic master who was once asked by his disciple, "What is the most important thing a person can do?" The disciple expected the master to say something like giving charity, observing the Sabbath, studying the Torah. But instead, the master said, "The most important thing a person can do, is whatever he happens to be doing at the moment—because *now* is all we have for sure. Each moment is an opportunity that we might never have again."

Loeb went on to relate this idea to an analogy between baseball and life. "As in baseball, so in life," Loeb continued, "time passes and often nothing really happens. You train for years and you practice before each game. Then, during each game you wait and wait for something to occur, sometimes almost for the entire game. Meanwhile, others around you do important things, make decisive plays, and receive the cheers of the crowd, while you stand alone and forgotten, fighting boredom somewhere out in right field. But then, usually when you expect it least, a decisive moment arrives. The outcome of the game hangs in the balance. And in that moment, everything depends upon what you will do in that situation, in that 'now,' at that place. To meet the challenge of the moment, the player must always be ready. To make the decisive and often difficult play presumes long hours of grueling training and practice, many minutes of unrewarded waiting. But, when the crucial play arrives, the moment, the situation and the place converge. And what one does then and there during that decisive moment proves critical because you may never get a second chance. In that instant, there is only 'now.'"

Loeb adjusted his prayer shawl, and looked directly at the members of the team. He said, "In our lives, we sometimes reach a juncture, a moment, a 'now,' that—depending upon what we do—will effect every future moment for the rest of our lives. Each of us finds ourselves at this point sometime during our lives. Baseball players find themselves in such a situation many times during the course of their careers. And, even baseball teams can find themselves in such a situation during their team's lifetime. Such a moment in the history of the Chicago Cubs was in 1908. So was 1945. And so is now." Loeb looked directly at Post and Wriggles, and he said, "*Now* is all you have. Use it well. The most important thing you can do, is what you are doing *now*."

The service ended with a concluding hymn. While the congregation sang, Loeb and the cantor marched to the back of the synagogue to greet the worshippers as they left, and to wish each of them that they "be written in the Book of Life for the coming year." As each member of the team left, looking out of place in a business suit, he bowed his head to receive Loeb's blessing. Loeb blessed each of the players, and wished them success in the upcoming playoff series. Soon, the synagogue was empty except for Loeb and his family. Seeing how tired Jay was, Tamara encouraged him to go directly home to eat and to rest up for the lengthy liturgies that would be recited in the synagogue during the next two days. But Loeb told Joshua and Tamara that he had a previous engagement.

Surprised, Tamara asked, "With whom?"

"With Patrick Hood. Where else would you expect a rabbi to be going on Rosh Hashanah than to see the Archbishop?" asked Loeb, smiling.

"I will not ask why you're going there," Tamara said.

"Don't," said Loeb. "I'll walk home as soon as Pat and I have made some lemonade."

"What?" Tamara asked.

"Don't ask. I'll see you two at home, later."

Loeb kissed his wife on the lips and his son on the forehead, and went out the seminary's back door into the alley. He walked up La Salle Street to North Avenue, and then a few blocks eastward to the Cardinal's residence.

Loeb climbed the steps that led to the huge gothic mansion that had served for decades as the home of the Archbishop of Chicago. He knocked on the door, which was soon opened by a cheerful nun in a black habit.

"Good evening, Rabbi," she said. "His Eminence is waiting for you in the living room." Loeb followed the nun through the foyer, and was led into a large living room decorated with portraits of the former archbishops of Chicago. There, sitting in a lounge chair, dressed in jeans, a polo shirt and slippers, was the Archbishop of Chicago. When he saw Loeb, he put down the writing pad on which he had been making notes, stood up, and walked briskly toward his guest. The men embraced. Pointing to the portraits in the room, the Cardinal said, "I have them looking over my shoulders at everything I do. Let's go into the dining room. It's less crowded in there."

The men walked together through a sitting room, and entered a large dining room with a long, mahogany dining room table. Within seconds, a second nun emerged with coffee, tea, and platters of cake. "Don't worry, Jay, it's all kosher," Hood said, as he and Loeb sat down facing one another across the immense table. Above them, a large chandelier seemed to hang down precariously from the high vaulted ceiling above.

"I've been following the reports of your exploits the past few months, Jay. So, I'm glad we can have this time together. We haven't seen one another for too long. I miss our talks. They're a kind of mini-vacation for me. All day, I'm in meetings, at official functions. Not very much time to think, write, or read. When I took this job, one of my academic colleagues said to me: The first year, you'll stop writing. The second year, you'll stop reading, and the third year, you'll stop thinking. Well, as you know, I'm now beginning my third year, and I'm beginning to see what he meant.

"But once I started to hear about what you've been up to, mostly from TV, it got me reading, writing and thinking again. It encouraged me to apply my academic knowledge and training to many of the diverse situations that I have to deal with every day. Until recently, I had separated what I used to do as an academician from the administrative and pastoral tasks of my present job. But lately, I have come to see how my past studies can be helpful in my current duties. In fact, just before you arrived, I was making notes for a scholarly book inspired by your recent experiences—even though I know I'll have no time to write it."

Loeb sipped his coffee and listened to his friend speak. At first, it sounded to him like the ramblings of an overburdened and lonely man running a huge corporate enterprise, but soon the Cardinal's discourse began to focus in a very precise way on Loeb's situation. As Loeb listened, he was proud to have this man among his closest friends.

"I've been re-reading the Gospels and the Hebrew Scriptures, trying to find a framework for understanding your situation, and for understanding what your situation can tell us about how to strengthen religious faith. And, though I certainly don't see you as another Jesus Christ, or even as one of the Hebrew prophets, there are certain lessons I think we can learn from them that apply to you, to us. Here's what

I've come up with. See what you think. I'm giving you the short version. I'm sure you can fill in the rest. Didn't you once quote to me a Talmudic saying that it's enough to give a wise man a hint because from that hint he can figure out the rest?"

Loeb put down the coffee cup. He cradled his head in his hands and listened.

"The Hebrew prophets came with a profound moral and spiritual message, as did Jesus after them," the Cardinal said.

Loeb nodded, and said, "Yes, they wanted the people to repent of their sins, to do good works, to lead moral lives, and to worship God."

"And you and I are in the same business, so to speak. Are we not?" Hood asked rhetorically. "Only we do not claim that we receive revelations directly from God as they did, but the goal is essentially the same—to improve the quality of people's moral and spiritual lives. Yes?"

Loeb nodded.

"Prophets like Jeremiah had a great message, but the people didn't accept it, right?"

"Yes," said Loeb. "They not only ignored the message but they persecuted him, abused him, and even threw him into prison. Almost killed him. His message was too powerful, too threatening."

"But some of the prophets got their message across, like Elijah and Elisha. And Jesus managed to convince at least some people to follow his teachings. Why?"

Loeb was silent as he reviewed chapter after chapter of Jewish and Christian Scriptures in his mind. Suddenly, he looked up, knocked over the coffee cup by accident, and with a smile of discovery on his face, he said, "The people heeded their moral and spiritual teachings because they believed in their ability to work wonders."

"Precisely," said Hood. "Few people will disregard the moral and spiritual teachings of someone they believe has the power to work wonders—to heal, to make things happen that others can't seem to make happen. A person like this is a person to heed. A guy like this is not someone to mess with."

"But when the people do not believe that the religious leader has those powers, they have no compelling reason to listen to them. It's just nice talk, clergy chatter, homiletics," Loeb added.

"And, I think, that's why our people—yours and mine—no longer take our teachings seriously anymore," Hood went on. "We clergy are no longer wonder-workers. We have become 'facilitators,' administrators, managers, counselors, social workers, politicians. So, the people have no reason to take our teachings, and those of our religious traditions, very seriously. We've lost our leverage. And that leverage is the people's belief that we can work wonders, whether in fact we can or not. It's like psychotherapy—half of the cure is in the patient's belief that the therapist can cure him.

"As reluctant as I am to admit it, I think that if Jesus did not do all the miracles that the Gospels ascribe to him, and only preached his message, few would have followed him."

"Now that I think about it, you may be right," Loeb said. "The Pharaoh didn't listen to Moses to let the Israelites go until he performed big-time miracles. And I'm sure that the Israelites wouldn't have listened to Moses if he had not performed wonders in the Land of Egypt and in the wilderness. No one listened to Elijah when he inveighed against worshipping idols until he performed wonders and miracles. And closer to our own times, the Hasidic masters were able to convey their message to the people because the people believed in their abilities to heal the sick, cure the infertile, predict the future, and to do other wonders as well. I never thought about it before, but maybe you're right—the medium gets across the message. The message is a moral one, and the medium is the miracle."

"Our parishioners look to science and technology for miracles, but not to us anymore," Hood said. "They go to employment agencies rather than to us when they need help finding a job. They go to psychologists when they have spiritual and emotional problems. They turn to pills and drugs in situations in which prayer might help. But your recent experience demonstrates the validity of my thesis: when the people believe that clergy have magical powers—whether the clergy actually possess them or not, the people will more readily follow the clergy's moral and spiritual teachings, especially when the clergyperson is a paradigm of learning and virtue—like you, Jay. Is this not what has happened with the Cubs? Besides, even if we really possess such powers, we know that those powers are not really our own; they are God's, and we are only God's channel for expressing them."

Loeb blushed and said, "You hit the nail on the head. When I was a scholar, researching and writing books to convey the teachings of my tradition, no one took me seriously. I was ignored, considered an irrelevant anachronism by my rabbinic colleagues and by my religious community. Now, suddenly, leaders and organizations in the Jewish community that wouldn't have given me the time of day all want my attention, my endorsement, my advice. But where do we go from here? What do we do with the lemons?"

"We make lemonade, of course. What else, Jay? I have to think about this some more in terms of how it can be applied to my own ministry and to the recruitment, training and retraining of priests. But, as for right now, here's what I propose to do.

"I'm going to call the Mayor tomorrow and ask him to declare Monday, October 5, which happens to be Yom Kippur, a citywide day of prayer and repentance on behalf of the Chicago Cubs. Since he's a White Sox fan, this might take some doing. But the Archbishop of Chicago is not without clout in this town. A lot of people owe me a lot of favors. Sure, we'll get flak from the Sox fans, from the ACLU, and probably from some of your Jewish 'advocacy' organizations. But I'm sure the Mayor will consult with his lawyers to make things constitutionally kosher. Maybe, he'll just ask employers in the city to give workers off part of the day to go to their respective houses of worship to attend special services that will be held around the city."

"Will there be special services held around the city?" Loeb asked sheepishly.

"I think so," said the Cardinal. "Because, before I call the Mayor, I will convene an emergency meeting of the Chicago Council of Religious Leaders, and ask for their help. They're always looking for some common cause, and here we have one. They're also always looking for a way to get people into their houses of worship, and here's one. And, they're always looking for good publicity, and this will do it. And, after I tell them that I will be celebrating a special noon mass that day at the cathedral, and that special masses will be celebrated in every Catholic Church in the archdiocese, I think they'll go along. Once they agree, when I tell the Mayor that mid-day religious services will be held throughout the city in every church, synagogue, mosque, Buddhist Temple, etc., I think he'll jump on the bandwagon. Also, I'll have my communications people get the media on board as well."

"I guess there are some advantages to being the Catholic prelate of Chicago," Loeb said. "It's a great idea, Patrick. I couldn't have thought of a better one myself."

"Leave it to me," said Hood. "I'll call you on Monday or Tuesday, when everything is in place. So, you see, your magic has brought about an opportunity to encourage people to pray and to improve the moral quality of their lives. After all, that's what we're in business to do, are we not?"

"Patrick, no wonder you're a Cardinal!"

The Cardinal walked his friend to the door, opened it, and said, "Now, you know Jay, that if the Cubs don't win the World Series, we're both going to look awfully silly. So, I hope you've got some more tricks up your kabbalistic sleeves."

"I hope so, too, Pat. Thanks again. Thanks so much. I knew I could count on you."

"Happy New Year, Jay. Regards to Joshua and Tamara."

The Archbishop of Chicago closed the door, and Loeb began the long trek home. The route he chose took him past the Children's Zoo, where he recited a prayer that his chickens be "inscribed in the Book of Life" for the coming year. Loeb reviewed the long liturgy for the next day in his mind as he walked, and by the time he had come to the end of his review, he was almost home. He opened the door and went into the bedroom to find Tamara fast asleep. Joshua was in living room, practicing pitching mechanics that Hornsberry had described to him during the religious service earlier that evening. Loeb went into the kitchen and ate the cold dinner that Tamara left out for him. He recited the Grace after Meals, washed up, and went to sleep thinking about Sandy Greenberg.

LOEB ENJOYED THE REST OF THE holydays that weekend, especially since Tamara had restored his conjugal rights. The following Monday evening, just as he had promised, Patrick Hood called. Loeb was at his desk at home, sifting through the satchels of mail that had been delivered from his office at the seminary. Many of the letters were from synagogues and Jewish organizations inviting him to lecture at handsome fees. There were also a few invitations for visiting professorships, and requests from publishers that had always turned him down in the past, pleading with him to write books for them on any subject of his choosing.

The Cardinal reported that everything had gone according to plan. There had been some opposition at first, but things had fallen into place. That year, not only Jews would be praying and repenting on Yom Kippur. The entire city and parts of the suburbs would also be focusing that day on spiritual concerns. Loeb was delighted.

He hung up the phone and went back to reading and sorting his mail. It was already after 9 P.M., and soon he would have to leave for the airport to meet the British Airways flight that would be carrying his two colleagues: Rabbi Sinai from London, and Rabbi Katz from Jerusalem.

Loeb arrived at the International Terminal at O'Hare Airport well ahead of the flight. He was overjoyed when he saw his colleagues, Rabbi Sinai and Rabbi Katz. He drove them to his home. Rabbi Sinai would sleep on the pull-out couch in his study and Rabbi Katz would sleep in Joshua's room. Tamara and Joshua were already fast asleep, Joshua on the living room couch. Loeb invited his colleagues into the kitchen, where they ate herring and drank vodka, and talked about the challenges they would jointly face in the days ahead.

Loeb had met Rabbi Yitzhak Katz in a bookstore in the Old City of Jerusalem years before. They had each come there at precisely the same time to purchase the same kabbalistic book. The conversation they began in that store had continued over many years—sometimes in person, but more often by telephone or mail. Much of their discussion centered around the sixteenth-century mystical rabbi Judah Loew of Prague, who, according to a popular Jewish legend, had created a Golem—a powerful creature in human form—to defend Prague Jewry from pogroms and other threats of physical harm. The legends describe how learned and pious rabbis of past generations had not only failed in the attempt to create a Golem, but also how, in the process, some had lost their mind, their faith, or even their lives.

Rabbi Yitzhak Katz and Rabbi Moshe Sinai were each in their seventies. Each presided over a small yeshivah in which both Talmudic and kabbalistic studies were taught. Katz's school was in the Old City of Jerusalem. Sinai's was in the Golders Green section of London.

Sinai was born in Lublin, Poland. During the Second World War, he had been hidden by Polish farmers in a barn on the outskirts of Lublin, not far from the Nazi death camp at Majdanek. He had seen his parents shot by the Nazis, and was later told that all of the Jews of Lublin had been gassed to death at Majdanek.

Sinai's fair skin and blue eyes allowed him to "pass" for a young

Pole. During the days he worked on the farm, taking care of the livestock. But, because he spoke Polish with a strong Yiddish accent, he was told to pretend that he was a mute. For the years of the war, Moshe Sinai lived mostly in silence and alone in his hideout in the barn with the cows, chickens and hogs, to whose needs he attended. Like each of them, he was in constant danger of being slaughtered by the German invaders.

After the Jews of Lublin had been turned from flesh and blood into smoke and ashes, Sinai sneaked back into the city to retrieve as many Hebrew books as he could carry. Despite the risk, he made many such trips, and soon he had accumulated his own library, which he hid in various secret places in the barn. Some of these books were kabbalistic, and during the long nights, he studied by candlelight, memorizing as much as he could. When the war ended, he left the farm in search of surviving Jews. He found a group of Jewish partisans and joined them as they made their way westward toward Germany. There he ended up in a British "Displaced Persons Camp," and eventually he was taken to England.

Soon after his arrival, Sinai went to the headquarters of the Chief Rabbi of the British Empire in London. There, a panel of rabbis examined his knowledge of Talmud and Jewish law. On the basis of that examination, they granted him a rabbinical ordination, and assigned him to a small synagogue in the Golders Green section of London, where most of the members of the congregation were, like him, Jews who had survived the Holocaust. Sinai soon established a yeshivah in the synagogue, where through the years, a trickle of students came to study Talmud and Kabbalah with him.

Loeb and Sinai had first met through the mail. Soon after Loeb had published a book on the thought of Rabbi Judah Loew of Prague, Sinai wrote to him, disputing Loeb's interpretation of one of Loew's writings. Loeb wrote back, demonstrating why his interpretation was correct, and that Sinai had not been aware of an unpublished work by Loew that was preserved only in manuscript in the British Library in London. Sinai went there, checked the manuscript, and wrote Loeb a letter of apology. Frequent correspondence then ensued. But Loeb and Sinai were to meet for the first time that night at O'Hare airport.

The following morning, the rabbis prayed together, ate together, and spent most of the day studying and discussing kabbalistic texts. By the time Joshua and Tamara had arrived home for dinner, they were out walking along the shores of Lake Michigan. As the sun began to set, they entered the house while still engaged in an animated discussion of the meaning of some recondite medieval text. Tamara knew that few things stimulated her husband as much as being engaged in the study of old sacred texts with scholars who shared his insights and erudition. There were few who did. She was happy to see him happy. Yet, her husband had not revealed to her the reason for their visit.

For three days, the three rabbis studied together during the day, and they went to the lake to walk each afternoon. On Friday morning, Rabbi Sinai and Rabbi Katz left to spend the Sabbath and the Day of Atonement with other colleagues whom they knew in Chicago.

That Monday, October 5, the Day of Atonement, the people of Chicago, of all faiths and creeds, gathered in their respective houses of worship, just as the Cardinal had hoped they would. Religious services of many faiths and denominations were broadcast on television and radio for those who could not attend in person. For at least a few hours that day, there was city-wide prayer, peace and harmony.

Few people other than Loeb remembered that on October 5, 1908, the board of the National League led by Harry Pulliam had made its decree to uphold O'Day's decision in the Merkle incident, a decision that had contributed to the decades-long misfortune of the Cubs. Loeb hoped that the city-wide day of prayer and contrition on behalf of the Cubs would remove any remnant of the curse on the Cubs by John McGraw. After all, on the evening of Tuesday, October 6, the Cubs would begin their post-season play in Wrigley Field against the winner of the National League's "wild card" spot that year: the Giants.

The following day, at 4 A.M., Jay Loeb was jolted out of a deep sleep by the sound of his alarm clock. Since the sun had not yet risen, it was too early for him to recite the morning prayers. He was still hungry and thirsty from the long Yom Kippur fast the day before. Yet, Loeb refrained from eating breakfast because he knew that he was required to fast that day—at least until the kabbalistic ritual he was about to perform had been completed. After a brief sojourn in the bathroom, Loeb dressed quietly in the darkness. He took his prayer shawl and his phylacteries, as well as some kabbalistic books he had set out the night before. Loeb put everything in his briefcase, and tiptoed out of the house so as not to awaken Joshua and Tamara. The brisk early morning air invigorated him. After the long Yom Kippur day of fasting, repentance and prayer, he felt unusually clean and pure. Perhaps, as the liturgy for that day stated: "Repentance, charity and prayer can remove the evil decree."

Loeb hated to drive. Perhaps it was his technophobia. Perhaps it was because he had learned to drive when a teenager in congested New York City. He went to the garage and started his car, a big, brown 1985 Buick. Like an elderly person suddenly awakened, the car struggled to get moving. Its well-worn motor groaned and sputtered at first, but soon settled down to a soft hum. Loeb put the car in drive, stepped gently on the accelerator, and headed north along the lake to a secluded beach in suburban Wilmette. Awaiting him were his colleagues, Rabbi Yitzhak Katz and Rabbi Moshe Sinai.

There, they would attempt to enact the ritual they had been studying together the week before. There, they would attempt to perform a kabbalistic ritual that had not been performed for a very long time. It was a ritual that few had even dared to try, and that even fewer were believed to have successfully accomplished. Indeed, many scholars believed it had never been done at all, but was only a legend. That morning, these rabbis would attempt to create a Golem—a humanlike creature with superhuman physical powers.

When Loeb had invited his colleagues to join him in this perilous enterprise, each reluctantly agreed. Creation of a Golem was a serious undertaking, both physically and spiritually dangerous. But, at their advanced stage in life, both Rabbi Katz and Rabbi Sinai felt that this might be their one and only chance to try to do what each had dreamt of doing for so many years. Though sanctioned by Jewish tradition, creation of a Golem was strongly discouraged. However, if successful, it promised to be an experience like no other.

"Was not God described in Scripture as the Creator? And, are human beings not described in the Bible as having been created in the image and likeness of God? What better way to articulate the human being's ability to emulate his Creator, than by becoming a creator oneself? Only in creating a Golem could a kabbalist share in the divine rapture of the ultimate kind of creativity—the creation of life from inert matter." It was with these words that Loeb had convinced his colleagues to travel so far in order to join him that early morning on a deserted beach in Wilmette, Illinois, in order to work wonders.

The three rabbis embraced as a beam of sunlight shot across the dark waters of Lake Michigan. The sun was about to rise. They had been brought together that early morning, not only by a common challenge, but also by a shared legacy. Not only was each of them the most recent links in the long chain of kabbalah-masters; each of them was also a direct descendant of the legendary creator of the Golem—Rabbi Judah Loew ben Bezalel of sixteenth-century Prague.

They each undressed and entered the chilly water, reciting the appropriate prayers, as they purified their bodies for the task ahead. They dried themselves off and dressed in white linen garments. Now that the sun had arisen, they were permitted to recite the morning prayers. They each donned their prayer shawls and phylacteries and said the morning prayers, adding special kabbalistic meditations. To settle their minds, they each intoned a variety of kabbalistic mantras that echoed softly across the otherwise silent beach in suburban Chicago. Each looked pensively at the others as they began the ritual of creating a Golem.

Rabbi Moshe Sinai had brought a walking stick with him that he had taken from the ruins of the Jewish ghetto of Lublin years before. It had belonged to the nineteenth-century wonder-working Hasidic master known as "The Seer of Lublin." With this staff, he drew the figure of a human being in the smooth sand of the Wilmette beach. He drew with the skill of an accomplished artist until the facsimile of a human form appeared in the sand. Then, the rabbis began to intone the secret names of God found in the kabbalistic treatises they had studied together earlier that week.

Each had studied these texts for many years. Now, they would utilize the power of the divine names and the sacred words that comprised those texts to try to create life out of inert matter. Now, they would share in the rapture of the Creator in creating life by becoming themselves creators of new life.

According to the Bible, God created the world with words. "God spoke . . . and there was." Similarly, the three rabbis recited the letters of one of the most sacred words known—the mysterious forty-two-letter name of God, preserved for generations by the kabbalistic masters, and passed down in secret from master to disciple in centuries past. They intoned each consonant together, precisely pronouncing it with the appropriate vowel, exactly 310 times: for in Hebrew the letters are also numbers, and the letters corresponding to the number 310 spells the Hebrew word "*yesh*"—"that which is."

As they pronounced each of the letters, they emanated the sound from their mouths as they simultaneously envisioned the shapes of each of the consonants and vowels in the deepest recesses of their minds. And, as they spoke the sounds and contemplated the shapes of each of the Hebrew letters they intoned, they walked in a series of circles—first counterclockwise seven times and then clockwise seven times—around the form that lay dormant in the sand. As the three rabbis circled the figure, each of the sacred letters they pronounced seemed to animate one of the limbs of the figure embedded in the sand.

Rabbi Sinai took a cup of water and poured it on the chest and nose of the figure and blew upon the spots where he had poured the water. He then recited a verse from the biblical account of the creation of Adam: "A flow would well up from the ground and water the whole surface of the earth—the Lord God formed man from the dust of the earth. He blew into his nostrils the breath of life, and man became a living being."

As Rabbi Sinai spoke, the figure became progressively detached from the sand in which it had been drawn. Hair grew on its head. Nails sprouted on its fingers and toes. Rabbi Katz cautiously approached the figure, and under its tongue he placed a small parchment slip on which the words "*Adonai Emet*—the Lord is Truth," were written. Like his colleagues, Katz knew that only the power of God, and not their own power, could bestow life.

Breath now entered the Golem's nose and chest. Its eyes opened and sparkled in the young sunlight of the day being born. A jolt of energy surged throughout its massive bulk. Firmly, Loeb commanded, "Golem, stand." And the Golem arose from the sand, looking like anyone arising from a deep sleep.

The body of the Golem looked like Michelangelo's sculpture of David—tall and strong, with muscles and sinews of fashioned marble, ready and able to confront any physical challenge that might lie ahead.

Loeb dressed the Golem in a Cubs baseball uniform that Wriggles had given him. At Loeb's insistence, it had the number 18, which in Hebrew numerology spells *Hai*, meaning "life," on the back.

"Now that you have come into the world," said Loeb to the Golem, "your name will be Sandy Greenberg. You have been created to play baseball, and I have named you after the two greatest Jewish baseball players: the slugger, Hank Greenberg, and the ace pitcher, Sandy Koufax. If you fulfill the reason for which you have been created, we who have created you will be given the funds to create a school for the training of Jewish scholars. This new generation of scholars will help ensure that the teachings of our tradition will be passed down to generations yet to come."

Like Golems before him, Greenberg was human in every way—except that he lacked the power of speech and the ability to procreate. He also lacked a human soul, having instead a soul like that which most animals might have.

"You will obey Rabbi Loeb's every word," Rabbi Sinai said to the Golem. "If you disobey him, you will be returned to the earth from which you came."

Though fear flashed across the Golem's eyes, he nodded humbly to Rabbi Sinai, showing that he understood what had been said. The Golem then repeated this gesture to Rabbi Katz, and finally he bowed to Rabbi Loeb.

Each of the rabbis then collapsed onto the sand on the still deserted beach, out of exhaustion and ecstasy. Meanwhile, the Golem stood immobile on the beach, as if he were guarding them from any danger that might befall them. When the rabbis had recovered, Loeb spoke to the Golem, "Now, come with us," and the Golem followed the rabbis into the car. Half an hour later, they arrived at Loeb's home. Luckily, Joshua and Tamara had already left for the day. Loeb prepared breakfast for his guests. He and his colleagues ate sparingly. But, the Golem, for whom food was a new and delightful experience, ate everything laid out before him. The rabbis watched the Golem eat. They looked like the doting parents of a newborn child who find their baby's every bodily function, no matter how mundane, to be an act of wonderment and delight. The rabbis recited the Grace after Meals, and then Rabbi Sinai and Rabbi Katz arose to leave. The elderly rabbis embraced Loeb, kissed the Golem on the forehead, and left. Loeb walked them to the door, and said in Yiddish, "If everything goes according to plan, we will meet again in about five weeks in New York at the synagogue of the 'Old Rebbe.' Thank you, my friends, for all you have done."

"And you, be careful," said Rabbi Sinai in Hebrew. "You know the power of the Golem. You know that his power can turn against you. Be careful. I hope we have done the right thing in bringing this creature into the world."

"I hope so, too," said Loeb, who stood by the door waving until he saw his colleagues get into a taxi and drive away.

LOEB WAS EXHAUSTED. HE WENT INTO his study and retrieved a videocassette that he had prepared for the Golem to watch. It was a six-hour-long tape that contained instructional videos on all aspects of baseball, as well as clips of the best plays of baseball's best players, including Hank Greenberg and Sandy Koufax. Loeb ordered the Golem to sit in the large lounge chair facing the television, and the Golem complied. Loeb turned on the television, inserted the cassette, and turned on the VCR. He sat down in another chair and watched the Golem learn about the game that was his destiny. Loeb said to the Golem, "This is baseball. I want you to watch this and to learn as much as you can. I am going to sleep for a few hours. You stay here and watch and learn. Do you understand?" The Golem nodded, and Loeb went into the bedroom where he fell into a deep sleep. It was about 10 A.M.

About four hours later, Loeb was awakened by the sound of a woman screaming. He jumped out of bed and rushed into the living room. The Golem was still sitting in the chair watching the tape, but nearby stood Loeb's hysterical housekeeper cowering for safety in the corner of the room. She had entered the house, and started to straighten up the living room when she saw the immense hulk of a strange man sitting there staring into the television. She spoke to him but received no reply. When she spoke to him again, diverting his attention from the screen, he must have given her a forbidding look. Loeb explained that he was the Cubs' new player, Sandy Greenberg, that he could not speak, and that he would be staying with the Loebs for an indeterminate period of time. The housekeeper ran into the kitchen, muttering to herself.

Loeb looked at his watch and he realized that the first game of the playoffs against the Giants would begin that evening at 7 P.M. He dressed in jeans, a sweatshirt and gym shoes, went into the living room, turned off the television, and ordered the Golem to follow him to the car.

Loeb drove with the Golem to a baseball field in the far northern end of the city that he hoped would be vacant that day. Luckily, it was. He gave the Golem a bat, had him stand at the plate, and pitched him the ball. The Golem remained immobile. Loeb then said, "I will throw this ball towards you, and I want you to hit it with the bat." Loeb pointed to the wall at the end of center field, about 300 feet away. Then, Loeb pitched the ball, and the Golem hit it to the exact place to which Loeb had pointed. Loeb repeated this exercise a number of times, and each time had the identical result. Loeb then said, "I will throw the ball, and I want you to hit it as far as you can." Loeb threw as hard as he was able. The Golem swung effortlessly, and the ball rose in a high arc and soon disappeared from sight. Somewhere in the distance, Loeb heard the bleeping of a car alarm.

Loeb took a catcher's mitt in his hand, crouched behind home plate, and ordered the Golem to throw a variety of pitches from the mound: a fastball, curve ball, slider, knuckle ball, screw ball, split-fingered fastball— each at a different speed. And, the Golem complied just as he had been instructed to do, and as he had learned to do by watching the instructional videotapes on pitching. Loeb then ordered the Golem to throw a number of pitches that Loeb had invented himself, and the Golem complied.

Earlier that week, Loeb had consulted with his friend, Dr. Marshall Rosenberg, a leading sports physician, about a question that had concerned him: How fast would a fastball have to be thrown so that even the most skilled batter could not have quick enough reflexes to hit it? Rosenberg—who had written a study explaining why even such a great athlete as Michael Jordan could not learn how to become a major league slugger—had been researching this question for quite some time. Rosenberg told Loeb that no hitter, no matter how good, and no matter how fast his reflexes, could hit a fastball that exceeded a speed of 116 miles per hour. "But, of course," added Rosenberg, "I know of no pitcher who can throw a ball that fast. So the issue is really theoretical." But, with regard to the Golem, it was not theoretical.

Loeb recited a prayer, crouched behind home plate, and ordered the Golem to throw what Loeb called "the off-speed fast fastball." The Golem went though his windup. Loeb held his breath, and the Golem released the ball.

The ball moved out of his hand, as if in slow motion. It looked easier to hit than pitches thrown at Little League batting practice. But, just as the ball had made about half of its trek between the mound and the plate, it suddenly accelerated enormously, arriving in Loeb's glove with a pop. Loeb recited a blessing of thanksgiving to God, and placed an ice pack around his now-swollen left hand. He and the Golem went to the car, and Loeb drove to Wrigley Field. Every muscle hurt. Loeb knew that he needed a sauna and a visit to his chiropractor at the first available opportunity.

It was still a couple of hours before game time, and the mob scene around the ballpark reminded Loeb of the prophetic vision of the ingathering of the exiles. Loeb was met at the door to the Cubs locker room by a frenetic Wriggles and an agitated Post.

"Rabbi, where the hell have you been?" yelled Wriggles. "I've been trying to reach you all day. The team's all warmed up. They need you to lead them in some prayers. Without you around, they feel they can't win. Maybe, you're some kind of amulet yourself."

Post extended his hand to the Golem and said, "You must be Sandy Greenberg," The Golem turned around, showing Post the name "Greenberg" and the number 18 on the back of his uniform.

"Sandy's been a mute from the time he came into this world," Loeb explained, directing his remarks to Wriggles. "But, he's ready to play today. I warmed him up myself this afternoon. But, start him off slowly, maybe as a pinch hitter. He's not yet up to speed."

Wriggles turned to Post and said, "I'm not going to let this kid play today. I don't know what he can do."

Post looked at Loeb, then at the Golem, and then at Wriggles, and said, "Sorry, Wriggles, Sandy's in today. Jay knows what he's doing. He's got us this far, wouldn't you agree? We'd both already be out of job if not for him. Besides, every sports reporter in the country is here to see who Sandy Greenberg is, and what he can do. Sandy's in—if only as a pinch hitter."

Loeb smiled.

Wriggles was angry. He turned to Loeb and said sarcastically, "With all due respect to you, Rabbi, I don't think you know how to warm up a player—especially for post-season play."

"You're right, of course," said Loeb. "But, just give the kid a chance to bat, even if it's only once in the game."

Wriggles nodded, reluctantly.

Post, Loeb, Wriggles and Greenberg entered the locker room. When the team members saw them, they spontaneously applauded.

Wriggles quieted them down, after which Post said, "We've gone farther this season than anyone expected us to go. We've surprised all the sports reporters. Delighted all our fans. So, even if we lose, it's OK." Post hesitated and quickly added, "But it's even better if we win." The players clapped their hands and cheered. Post continued, "We've all played a part in getting us here. But I think we'll all agree that we wouldn't have gotten here without the help of our spiritual advisor and friend,

Rabbi Jay Loeb."

The players cheered, threw their towels and baseball caps into the air and started to chant, "Let's go, Jay! Let's go, Jay!"

Loeb stood on one of the benches in the locker room, and put his index finger over his mouth, asking for quiet. At once, there was dead silence. Loeb spoke,

"Have you all said your prayers today?"

Everyone nodded.

"Did each of you attend one of the prayer services held all around the city yesterday?"

Everyone nodded.

"Have you all given to charity this week?"

Once more, everyone nodded.

"Have each of you done good deeds this week?"

And, again everyone nodded.

Loeb raised his voice, and yelled, "And, are we going to beat the Giants?"

Everyone yelled, "Yes!"

Loeb elevated his voice, and said, "And, are we going to go on to win the pennant?"

And everyone yelled, "Yes!"

And, then Loeb screamed, his voice cracking in mid-sentence like a teenage boy, "And are we then going on to win our first World Series since 1908?"

And everyone yelled, "YES!" Everyone, except, of course, Greenberg, whose placid face was an inscrutable mask.

Loeb continued, "And now, I want to introduce you to your new teammate, Sandy Greeenberg. You all know that we've been carrying him on the roster for most of the season. You've all been wondering who he is, and what he can do. Well, friends, believe me when I tell you that he was brought into this world for only one reason: to play baseball. He's still a little green, but by the time we get to the World Series, I think you'll understand why I wanted him on our team. So, please welcome him to the Chicago Cubs."

The players applauded, and each went over to the Golem to shake his hand, but he just stood there.

"Sandy's a bit shy, guys. And, unfortunately, he's a mute from birth and cannot speak," Loeb said.

Loeb then looked at the Golem and said, "Sandy, shake hands with your teammates." The Golem smiled shyly and went around the room shaking everyone's hand. His height and physique were imposing, even when compared to the other athletes. Like Hank Greenberg, he stood at a full six feet four inches. Though he was slim and lanky, each of his taut muscles bulged through his skin.

"We've all got our amulets on, Rabbi," Sota said, displaying his own.

"Then, it's time to pray," said Loeb.

The team members lowered their heads, and Loeb recited a short invocation, a few psalms, and then he raised his hands, and blessed the players. It was time for the Cubs to take the field.

The Giants had already come onto the field to the jeers of the Cubs fans. Now, it was the Cubs' turn to enter the field. As they ran in, the crowd roared like an agitated ocean at night during a storm. Dignitaries and members of the press jammed the sky boxes and the first few rows of seats. The sports reporters were all anxiously awaiting to see one person: the elusive Sandy Greenberg. Meanwhile, seated in her usual seat, along the third base line, was Tamara Loeb, dressed in all her Cubs paraphernalia, screaming her lungs out.

Until Loeb directed him to follow his teammates onto the field, Greenberg remained standing in the locker room. He was visibly afraid of going outside without Loeb being with him. So, for the first time since his midnight visit to the pitcher's mound months before, Jay Loeb walked onto the field. Following him walked Sandy Greenberg.

When the crowd saw them, they erupted with applause. Loeb and Greenberg stood with the team as "The Star-Spangled Banner" was sung, after which Loeb led Greenberg to the dugout, where they sat together as the game began.

By the bottom of the ninth, only one run had been scored. Both pitchers were in top form. But, in the fifth inning, Hornsberry had made a potentially fatal mistake. He threw a high fastball right across the plate that had been knocked into the basket in left field by the Giants' clean-up hitter.

In the bottom of the ninth, the Cubs led off with a walk. The Giants pitcher was beginning to show signs of fatigue. Hornsberry was due up next, but Wriggles called him back to the dugout, and motioned for Greenberg to go to the plate.

"Greenberg's 'now' is *now*," Wriggles yelled in Loeb's direction, reminding him of the sermon he had preached on Rosh Hashanah. Loeb and Greenberg walked across the dugout toward Wriggles. Wriggles said to Greenberg, "I want you to bunt the runner over to second." The Golem looked questioningly at Loeb.

Loeb gasped, "I forgot to practice bunting with you earlier today. Do you know how to bunt? Did you see it on the videos?"

The Golem nodded, picked up a bat and squared off to bunt to show Loeb that he understood. Loeb said, "Then go out there and bunt as well as you can."

The Golem smiled and marched out toward the plate. Wriggles turned to Loeb and said, "Well, thanks a lot, Rabbi, you just had him show the other team what we plan to do."

Loeb went back to his seat in the dugout, and sat down. The infielders moved in, prepared for the bunt. The catcher was ready to spring for the ball. As the Giants pitcher went into his windup, Greenberg stood at the plate and squared off to bunt. The crowd began to jeer.

It wasn't clear as to whether their displeasure was directed at Wriggles for ordering Greenberg to bunt his first time up; or, whether it was at

Greenberg for not having appeared until now. Needless to say, there was considerable skepticism about Greenberg, both among the fans and the sports reporters. No one had ever seen him play. No one had been able to find any information about him. No one understood why he had been kept hidden until then. They expected a slugger, another Hank Greenberg. They didn't come to see Sandy Greenberg bunt. Was he the superstar, the "Cubs' secret weapon," they had been promised; or, was he simply another rookie with potential rather than proven ability? They had forgotten about Hank Greenberg's decisive bunt in the 1945 World Series in which the Tigers had defeated the Cubs.

The pitch came in, and Greenberg pushed the ball downward onto the ground. But, because he had never bunted before, he did not know how much force to use, so he used too much. Rather than pushing the ball a few feet up the line and having it slowly roll forward, the ball struck the grass and abruptly stopped. The power of Greenberg's thrust had pushed the ball through the grass, deep into the sod below. The ball lay buried in the turf, out of sight.

The third-baseman ran in, and fell to his knees, desperately trying to find the ball, while the pitcher ran over to cover first base. The catcher used his mitt to dig for the ball. By the time he found it and dislodged it from the turf, the runner on first already had scored.

At Loeb's command, Greenberg was chugging for home plate, like a locomotive out of control, moving much faster than the Giants catcher ever expected that a man that size could move. Greenberg was not going to slide—first, because he had not yet learned how; second, because Loeb had not told him to do so. Meanwhile, Wriggles was frantically yelling, "Slide, slide!" And from the stands, Loeb heard Tamara screaming, "Slide, you moron. Slide!"

The Giants catcher knew that to save the game, he had to defend the plate with his own body. He had to tag Greenberg out as he made his way toward the plate. The catcher clenched the ball in his glove and put his right hand over it to prevent it from being dislodged from the force of the inevitable impact. He dug his spikes deeply into the base path in front of home plate, and braced himself, ready to make his play, which would send the game into extra innings. But Greenberg kept coming. He ran right into the catcher, hitting him with such force that the catcher was catapulted more than a yard backwards, slamming into the home plate umpire. The catcher's hand jerked back against the umpire's mask and he dropped the ball. Greenberg crossed the plate with the winning run. The crowd went wild.

That night on the television news, the sports reporters all spoke about "the shortest homerun by the biggest man," and about "the Cubs' new secret weapon—The Incredible Hulk." Greenberg watched himself on television, and was highly confused. How could he be here and there at the same time?

After the ten o'clock news, Loeb took a hot shower and Tamara gave him a Ben-Gay rub to ease the pain in his muscles from his "workout" with Greenberg earlier that day. Loeb then led the Golem into his study, and had him lie down on the opened couch that would serve as his bed, and he introduced the Golem to another one of life's great pleasures—sleep. Earlier that evening, the Golem had devoured, with delight, a dinner that could have easily fed a dozen hungry sailors.

Loeb sat with the Golem until he had fallen asleep. Not having slept before, the Golem seemed frightened, not knowing what would happen to him. But, soon he drifted off into a serene rest. Watching him, Loeb remembered how he would sit with Joshua when he was a baby, while Joshua struggled to stay awake until he reluctantly, but eventually, dropped off into a deep sleep. Loeb sat for a while with the Golem, contemplating the events of the extraordinary day that was now coming to an end. He wondered whether a Golem can dream. And, after a while, Loeb went into another room and called Minnie Sota at home.

"Minnie, I have a favor to ask of you," Loeb said.

"Ask away, Rabbi," Sota said.

"But, you have to promise me not to talk to Wriggles about this."

"If that's what you want, sure. What is it?"

"I want to bring the boy to the park early tomorow morning, and I want you to work with him. He's still a little raw. I'd like you to review some fundamentals with him. Check out his mechanics. Give him some tips. He's got great natural abilities, but he needs some grounding in the fundamentals of the game. I don't know if I'm making sense; am I?"

"Sounds like Sammy Sosa when he came up to the majors. I worked with him then, you know," Sota said. "Sure, Rabbi, I'll work with him. How's 7 A.M.?"

"Fine, Minnie. See you then. And thanks. Thanks a lot."

THE FOLLOWING MORNING, LOEB AND
Greenberg met Sota at Wrigley Field. The lesson for the day was batting.
Sota explained that in the craft of baseball, there are two major tools:
the bat and the ball. The goal of the hitter is to effectively hit the ball
with the bat. The goal of the pitcher is to prevent it. A major weapon in
the arsenal of the pitcher is fear.

A hard sphere is being hurled at you, sometimes at speeds in excess
of ninety miles an hour. If it hits you in the head, it can kill you. If it hits
you in the hand, it can break a bone. If it hits you anywhere, it will hurt.
If it hits you in the funny bone of the elbow, the pain will be excruciating.
Greenberg listened attentively, but showed no fear. Sota seemed pleased
and moved on to his next point.

"In baseball, you need to cultivate certain virtues. One virtue is
courage, the courage to stand up and have the ball thrown at you. For
the hitter, however, the main virtue is patience. The hitter must wait for
the right pitch to hit or for the pitcher to make a mistake. If he decides
to swing, the hitter has very little time to translate his decision into action,

often less than two one-hundredths of a second.

"And when the hitter swings, everything must be in synch—from the balls of the feet, to the shifting of weight from one leg to another, to the movement of the hips, to the glide of the arms, to the flex of the wrists—as the bat moves across the plate to meet the ball."

As Sota spoke, he demonstrated how to swing the bat. Greenberg took a bat, and copied his swing. Sota had Greenberg repeat the exercise many times, until he was convinced that the rookie had it down pat.

Sota then showed him various ways to hold the bat, like how to choke up. He showed him how to shift his feet to get different results, like hitting to the opposite field. After Sota was convinced that Greenberg understood, he turned to the next fundamental feature of hitting. "In hitting, timing is everything. The goal of the pitcher is to throw off the timing of the hitter. One way the pitcher does this is by throwing the ball at different speeds. Another is by throwing it at different locations. A third is by making the ball do unexpected things. A fourth is by putting different kinds of spins on the ball. The pitcher has a whole arsenal of magical tricks to throw the batter off. The better the pitcher, the more stuff he has. The better the pitcher, the better he is at using what he's got.

"A pitch begins to come in looking one way. The batter gets ready to hit it. Then, suddenly, the pitch that's coming at you magically turns into another pitch. You swing at the first pitch you saw, but it seems like it's another pitch that crosses the plate, and you miss it.

"That's why the hardest thing to do in professional sports today is to hit a baseball. Hitting is a game of failure. Even the best of hitters, like Ted Williams, failed more than sixty percent of the time. Most batters fail a lot more. To become a successful hitter, you must be prepared to fail about seventy percent of the time.

"And, there's one other thing to keep in mind when batting: Don't think. You don't have the time. By the time you're finished thinking about whether to swing, the ball's already in the catcher's mitt."

Sota was going to ask Greenberg if he had any questions, but remembered that he was a mute, so instead he asked, "Do you understand most of what what I've been telling you?" The Golem nodded that he did, and he began to swing the bat in different ways to show that he was ready to try to apply what he had learned.

Greenberg stepped to the plate, and Sota stood behind a pitching screen on the pitcher's mound. Sota lobbed the ball directly over the plate, but Greenberg stood there and watched it go by.

"Why the hell didn't you hit that? It was right over the plate!" Sota angrily yelled.

Loeb walked out of the dugout to the pitcher's mound, and said to Sota, "You have to tell him what you want him to do, and try to be as clear and as precise as possible."

Loeb left the mound. Sota said, "I want you to try to hit this pitch in fair territory along the third base line." Sota wound up and delivered. Greenberg hit a flash into left field that skipped along the third base line onto the grass, fair by about a foot. Sota yelled some instructions to Greenberg about how to hold his hands on the bat and how to position his shoulders. "Now, do it again," Sota said. He let the ball go, and Greenberg hit a blistering grounder that went down the line, fair by no more than six inches. Sota watched in amazement and scratched his head. "Now, wait for a good pitch before you hit it, and when you get the right pitch, bloop it into short right field." The right-handed Greenberg shifted his feet as Sota had shown him in order to go to the opposite field. Sota wound up, and with all his strength, he aimed right at Greenberg's head and let the ball fly. Rather than hit the dirt as most hitters would do, Greenberg made a sudden movement that looked like a boxer artfully dodging a jab, and the ball sailed harmlessly by. He smiled like a defiant little boy, playing a game of "chicken." There was no fear in his eyes. Greenberg reset his stance and waited for the next pitch—a curve ball that he looped over the head of an imaginary second-baseman into short right field. So far, Sota seemed pleased, but that would soon change.

Sota had arranged for the pitching machine to be placed on the field earlier that morning. The machine had been calibrated to throw a variety of pitches at different speeds. Unlike the balls Sota had been throwing, the machine simulated major league pitching. Sota said, "Now, Sandy, this machine is now going to pitch to you. It'll throw a lot faster than I can. It'll throw different types of pitches at different speeds. It'll throw bad pitches, too. Try to hit only the good ones. Pretend this is a real game and that there's a team on the field. Try to get as many base hits as you can. If you see a pitch that you think you can knock into the stands, then go for it."

Greenberg stood at the plate as Sota turned on the pitching machine. The first pitch came in low; the machine had been set for a shorter man. Greenberg let it go by. "Good eye, good eye," Sota said, trying to encourage Greenberg. The second pitch jammed him, though it sailed over the inside corner of the plate. "Watch out for those," Sota said. The third nicked the outside corner, but Greenberg let it go by. "You've got to try for them," said Sota. After more than twenty pitches, Greenberg still had not hit the ball. Loeb saw that Sota was getting frustrated and he walked out to the mound.

"What the hell is going on here?," Sota said. "You told me the kid knows how to play. He's standing there like he never saw major league pitching before."

"Minnie, I want to let you in on a little secret. Don't tell anyone; he hasn't. Yesterday was his first baseball game."

"Then, what the hell is he doing here? You said he was a little green, not that he'd never played before. You promised Post that Greenberg would help us win the World Series, but the kid doesn't know his ass from a hole in the wall about playing baseball. I thought you wanted me to tune him up, to bolster his confidence, to test his fundamentals, to teach him some fine points of the game. Bullshit. This is like Little League. This kid's a fake. He doesn't know baseball.

Yesterday must have been a lucky break. What the hell's going on here? What are you trying to pull?"

"He's learning," said Loeb. "Didn't you just tell him that patience is a central virtue of baseball? Take your own advice. Give him one more try."

"OK. One and only one, and if he screws up, the deal's off. I go right to Wriggles and Post and tell them the truth about your wonderboy," Sota said with a mix of anger and sarcasm.

"OK, Minnie," Loeb said. "One more chance, and that's it. Let's fill up the batting machine and try again. If you still have doubts, I wouldn't stop you—I can't stop you—from talking to Post. One more chance, a few more minutes. What harm could it do?"

"All right, Rabbi, but as you always say: We don't rely on miracles."

Sota and Loeb filled up the hitting machine, which soon started to fire pitches at Greenberg. Like a machine responding to a machine, Greenberg hit the first pitch into left field for what would have been a clean single. He lined the second pitch right over second base for what would have been another hit. Then, he pulled the next ball deep into right. The ball bounced into the stands for what would have been a ground-rule double. The next pitch was a high fastball, which Greenberg slammed into the next to last row in the left-centerfield bleachers. Sota watched in amazement as Greenberg seemed to be recalibrating his stance and swing with each individual pitch. His timing was impeccable, his swing singularly appropriate for each pitch. He seemed able to hit the ball with pinpoint accuracy to any place in the park that he wished. He had learned well.

Loeb turned off the pitching machine and said to Sota, "The only reason the last pitch did not go out of the stadium was because you told him that he should knock the ball into the stands if he could. You did not give him permission to knock it out of the ballpark."

Loeb stood with Sota behind the pitching screen and said to the Golem, "Now, Sandy, when you get a pitch you like, hit it out of the ballpark."

The first pitch came in low, and Greenberg let it go by. The second was inside, and he pushed it down the third base line, just like he had done to the earlier pitches that Sota had thrown to him. The next three pitches, he hit what would have been base hits, into each of the three sections of the outfield—left, center and right—as if he were following the routine of a computerized program. The next pitch must have been the one he was waiting for. He swung off the balls of his feet, his hips in front of his hands, his weight shifting from leg to leg, his wrists breaking with exquisite timing and unleashed power.

The ball sailed upward and outward like a rocket leaving the launching pad. It headed for the clock that sat perched over the scoreboard that stood high above the bleachers in center field. But, it sailed still higher, over the clock, as if it were being carried on the wings of some mythical bird towards parts unknown. Sota watched the flight of the ball, and whispered a phrase from "Star Trek": "Where no one has gone before."

"You mean that no one has ever hit a ball out there before?" Loeb asked.

"No one else has, and I doubt if anyone else will," said Sota, who just stared at center field, his eyes ablaze, and his jaw hanging open in sheer amazement. As Sota stood trying to absorb what had just happened, Greenberg kept hitting the balls that were unleashed in his direction by the hitting machine. Finally, Sota turned to Loeb and said, "I guess he's learned all he can from me. See you tonight."

Sota walked slowly off the field. Loeb turned off the hitting machine and walked to the plate.

"You did well, Sandy. Congratulations. I think you're ready for the game tonight."

Loeb took the Golem home and fed him an enormous brunch. The Golem must have especially liked the lox and cream cheese sandwiches on a bagel. He devoured sixteen of them, and washed them down with three two-liter bottles of Coca-Cola. After brunch, Loeb had the Golem sit in front of the television again and he put a tape into the VCR that dealt with base running and pitching. The Golem watched intently while Loeb went into his study to attend to his seemingly endless backlog of correspondence. Within a few hours, it would be time to leave for Wrigley Field for the second game against the Giants. Loeb knew that he would have to protect Greenberg from the growing media attention.

Loeb had arranged with Matalón to let him and Greenberg sneak into Wrigley Field through a door on the loading dock. In that way, they would avoid the media and the fans. Matalón led them through hallways and doors until they arrived at the players' locker room. A few team members were already there, as was Wriggles. Greenberg started to get dressed in his uniform. Sota greeted Loeb and Greenberg with a knowing smile on his face. When Greenberg had finished dressing, Sota and Loeb led him outside for batting practice. As he had done earlier that day, Greenberg repeated his exercise. The first good pitch cruised along the third base line, barely in fair territory. The second was a clean hit to right, the third a blooping hit over second base into center field, and the fourth a long shot that bounced into the stands in right field. Not wanting Greenberg to hit anything out of the park quite then, Loeb told Greenberg that he had enough practice. They returned to the locker room to await the start of the game. But Greenberg was hungry. He hadn't eaten for a few hours.

Six kosher hot dogs were brought to Greenberg from a stand near the ballpark that served only kosher products. Greenberg sat in the locker room, happily eating his hot dogs, and washing them down with glass after glass of Gatorade.

"Who d'ya t'ink you are, Babe Ruth?" one of Greenberg's teammates asked as he watched him devour hot dog after hot dog. But Greenberg only smiled.

It was still more than an hour to game time, but Greenberg did not look well. He went over to Loeb, put his hand on his stomach and grimaced, as if in pain. It took Loeb a few minutes to understand what was wrong. Greenberg was having another new experience: a stomach-ache. Loeb further realized that though Greenberg had eaten his first meal the day before, he had not yet gone to the bathroom. Loeb had neither instructed him to do so, nor had he shown him what to do in the bathroom.

Loeb got a bottle of antacids from the trainer and gave some to Greenberg to swallow. He then took him to the bathroom, and explained what a person does there and how. Greenberg nodded that he understood, though he was visibly apprehensive. Loeb thought back to when he had toilet-trained Joshua—only Joshua was then a tiny boy, and not a muscular giant. Greenberg looked both surprised and relieved as he underwent still another new experience—in the bathroom. By game time, the antacids had kicked in, and he was fine.

WRIGLEY FIELD WAS PACKED. SOME OF the fans held signs: "We love Sandy." "Let's go, Hulk." When Loeb and Greenberg came onto the field, a roar went up. Tamara waved proudly at her husband. "The Star-Spangled Banner" was sung by a local blues singer, who did not know the words. The crowd applauded, and the game was underway.

The Giants exploded in the second inning with five runs, but the Cubs came back with one in the third, two in the sixth, and two in the seventh, as Cubs relief pitching kept the Giants scoreless. In the ninth inning, the game was tied 5-5. The Giants scored a single run in the top of the ninth on a walk, an error and a single.

Already in the sixth inning, when the Cubs had come to bat, the fans had begun to chant, "We want Hulk. We want Hulk." By the bottom of the ninth inning, the chant had reached deafening proportions. Wriggles ignored the fans, and put in a couple of pinch hitters in the bottom of the ninth who did part of their jobs. They tied up the game, but could not win it. The game went into extra innings.

In the top of the tenth, the Giants threatened early with two base runners. A bunt and a sacrifice fly led to a run scoring. A double scored a second run, but a strikeout ended the top of the inning. It was now 7-5. The chant, "We want Hulk," began again as the top of the Cubs lineup came up to bat in the bottom of the tenth.

The first Cubs batter hit a slice along the third base line, barely fair, for a base hit. The next batter got a clean single in left field, but the following hitter hit into a double play. The runner at third scored. The clean-up hitter hit a check swing blooper into short center field that fell in for a single. The next hitter slammed the ball into right field, and the ball bounced into the stands for a ground-rule double. There were runners at second and third. Greenberg looked at Sota and smiled. The pattern looked familiar.

The din of the chant "We want Hulk" seemed to shake the stadium. Sota went over to Wriggles and asked him to let Greenberg bat. Loeb looked at Wriggles' expression as Sota and Wriggles argued, and for the first time Loeb saw things in Wriggles' face that he had not seen before: jealousy and pride. Loeb had read in the press that Wriggles was jealous that Loeb was getting much of the credit for what Wriggles believed to have been the product of his managerial skill. Loeb had disregarded the reports as media gossip. But now he saw that the reports were true.

The conference between Wriggles and Sota was over. Wriggles sat down in the dugout and folded his hands defiantly. Sota walked over to Loeb, and said, "The skipper says that the kid can hit. But it's no favor. Wriggles knows the odds in a situation like this, and the odds are strongly against the kid. He wants the kid to humiliate himself by making the last out. He wants the fans out of his face, and into yours."

"You mean Wriggles resents Sandy and me so much that he would risk losing the game?" Loeb asked, astonished.

"He doesn't dislike you or the kid, only the publicity you've been getting that he thinks should rightfully be his," Sota said. "The skipper's got a huge ego. And he's pissed off that you're getting all the credit for the team's success while he's still being blamed for their failures of last season and at the beginning of this one. So, now, he wants to show everybody that you and your wonderboy are only a fluke, a publicity stunt, a fleeting bit of good luck, and that he's gotten the team to where they are now. Not you. And certainly, not the kid. He's been around for a long time. Seen flashes in the pan before."

Loeb went over to Greenberg and handed him a bat.

"Do you feel OK now?" Loeb asked, like the doting father that he was. The Golem nodded.

"And you know what you have to try to do now?" Loeb asked. Greenberg nodded, smiled at Sota, and went to the plate. The crowd erupted at the volume of a volcano.

Greenberg let the first two pitches go by. One was a ball, low and outside, a teaser meant to tempt him to swing. The other was a strike that just caught the inside corner, jamming him. The third pitch was meant to hit him in the arm, probably the elbow, but Greenberg artfully dogged it. When Greenberg's teammates saw that the pitcher was trying to hit him, they started out of the dugout onto the field. But Loeb restrained them. The last thing they needed was a rumble. The Golem could go berserk and cause a lot of damage.

Greenberg stepped back into the batter's box, his gaze intent. Thinking that he had intimidated the rookie batter, the pitcher let loose his best "heat," a bit high, but right over the plate. Like an uncurling spring, Greenberg hauled off and smacked the ball with all his strength. The fans stood up, as an eerie silence swept across the ballpark.

The wind had been blowing in that day at Wrigley Field, which was why few long balls had been hit, and why Wriggles had agreed to let Greenberg go up to bat. Yet, despite the wind resistance, which would have knocked another ball down onto the field to be caught, Greenberg's missile continued to climb. Somewhere over deep center field, the ball ejected its white cowhide casing into the green ivy growing up the outfield wall, and like a rocket shedding its fuel tanks, it continued to climb higher. The taut string between the cover and the inner cork unraveled and dropped somewhere over the center field bleachers, while the ball's inner core fell harmlessly onto Sheffield Avenue outside the park. It bounced upward, shattering a window on the third floor of a residential building, startling the people inside, who were simultaneously watching it all on television.

In a silent stadium, full of awestruck fans, Greenberg slowly rounded the bases, thereby allowing the other base runners to score ahead of him. As Greenberg stepped on home plate, the faithful fans exploded with appreciation. Sota ran out of the dugout to hug Greenberg, while Wriggles cowered in the dugout next to the water cooler. Greenberg entered the dugout, seeking Loeb, who told him to get back out onto the field and to tip his hat to the crowd. Loeb looked across the dugout at Wriggles, and a biblical citation from the Book of Proverbs came to mind, "Pride goes before a fall." Despite Wriggles' attempts at sabotage, the Cubs had won.

That night at home, Greenberg and the Loeb family saw the sports highlights on various television channels. As they watched, the Loebs ate hot dogs and beans that their housekeeper had prepared. Following the New York custom, Loeb ate his hot dog with a mountain of sauerkraut. Greenberg, who had fearlessly stood up to a ninety-five-mile-an-hour fastball aimed right at him earlier that day, painfully flinched at the sight of a five-inch-long hot dog. Loeb explained to Tamara what had happened in the clubhouse, so she prepared another dinner for Greenberg: ten soft-boiled eggs, six slices of white toast, and a pitcher of strong hot tea.

The following day, Friday, was a travel day for the Cubs. The next two games would be played in San Francisco. However, neither Loeb nor Greenberg would accompany the team for the Friday night and Saturday games. On that Friday night, not only would the Sabbath begin, but also the Jewish festival of the Feast of Booths, *Sukkot* in Hebrew, the holyday that celebrated God's providential care over the Israelites as they wandered in the wilderness from Egypt to the Promised Land. Though the holiday lasted more than a week, only its two first and two last days were observed as being especially sacred, and the first two days ran from that Friday night to sundown on Sunday.

That Friday morning, Greenberg and Loeb went to Wrigley Field. Sota had stayed behind to coach Greenberg in base running. Sota would take a later plane out to San Francisco for the Friday night game. He showed the indefatigable Greenberg how to run the bases, how to slide, how to steal a base, how to read the coach's "signs" while on base. By early afternoon, when Sota had to leave for the airport, Loeb was tired just from watching Greenberg run the bases. He took the Golem home to prepare for the Sabbath and the holyday that was soon to begin.

That evening, after a traditional Sabbath dinner, where special prayers for the Feast of Booths were recited, Loeb lay down on his bed to catch up on his reading. As he began to read a scholarly journal, he felt like a fish that had been caught, but that had now been returned to its natural home.

Loeb had not told either Joshua or Tamara that Greenberg was a Golem. He had only told them that Greenberg was an orphan and a mute whom he had secretly helped since birth, and that Greenberg had grown up in a number of foster homes which Loeb had arranged. Tamara welcomed Greenberg into their home, but was disappointed that she could not discuss baseball with him because of his inability to speak. Tamara was also wary, if not sometimes afraid, at how the young athlete sometimes leered at her, so she was always carefully dressed in his presence. Joshua's feelings, however, were clearly ambivalent.

Jay and Tamara Loeb always had been guilty that they had not been able to have more children. They felt that Joshua had gotten a bad deal, being an only child. When he was very young, Joshua seemed to mind being alone while most of his friends had brothers and sisters to play with. But, as he got older, Joshua was content with not having rivals for his parents' affection. Though he was pleased to have a baseball player living with him and his family, Joshua wondered why his father was treating this stranger like an adopted child, but tried hard not to surrender to full-blown sibling jealousy.

Loeb refrained from watching television on the Sabbath and on Jewish religious holydays, but Tamara, Sandy and Joshua went into Tamara's study to watch the game in San Francisco. As Loeb read in his study, the game began. A TV camera zoomed in on Wriggles, standing regally on the steps of the dugout, like an absolute monarch in firm control of the inhabitants of his domain. Had Loeb been watching, he would have realized how happy Wriggles was that he and Greenberg were absent.

Before each commercial break, the film clip of Greenberg's home run the day before flashed on the screen, with an accompanying explanation of why Loeb and Greenberg were not with the team for the third and fourth playoff games. The sportscasters tried, with difficulty, to explain to the viewers the meaning of the biblically ordained festival known as "The Feast of Booths."

Tamara's shrieks and screams, and the sounds of things being slammed down on the desk and floor emanated from her study. Meanwhile, Loeb lay in bed and continued to read, only disturbed that he could not fall asleep reading because of the tumult. Two hours later, Tamara came into the bedroom, and demanded, "Jay, you've got to do something about this."

"About what?" Loeb replied.

"It's the old Cubs all over again."

"Like what?" Loeb calmly asked.

Tamara responded in a loud, agitated voice, "Like what? Like nineteen Cubs runners stranded on base without scoring. Like our relief pitcher tripping on his way in from the bullpen, falling down, and dislocating his shoulder—without even throwing one pitch. Like his successor, who didn't have adequate time to warm up, giving up three home runs in a row. Like one of our outfielders colliding with one of our infielders when they went after the same fly ball in short center—with the ball falling right between them. Like a grounder coming right at our first baseman, and just as the ball comes in reach, it hits something on the turf and bounces over his head into short right field. It was like watching the Little League, except there, when the players screw up, it's cute. It was just pathetic, tragic, sickening. Like watching three sets of the 'Three Stooges' pretending they're playing baseball. Maybe the curse has returned. Maybe you never got rid of it to begin with."

Loeb put down the journal he was reading, stood up, and embraced his wife, trying to comfort her. But, her body was stiff, and failed to respond to his embrace. She pushed him away, and said, "Well, don't just stand there. Do something."

Loeb started to lose his temper, but reined it back in.

"I will do something," Loeb said. "As soon as the sun goes down Sunday night when the holiday ends. In the meantime, we have a holiday to celebrate, a festival that our liturgy calls 'the season of our joy.' So lighten up, and don't ruin the holiday for the rest of us with your childish tantrums. Don't you understand that all that happened is because of Wriggles' arrogance and pride, all because he's jealous of the adulation by the fans and the press that Sandy and I are receiving? I'll talk to him and to Post after the holiday, and not before, and that's the way it's going to be."

Tamara turned around, went into her study and slammed the door. Seconds later, Joshua and the Golem made a hasty retreat from the precincts of her room.

"I think Mom's going to sleep in her study tonight, Dad," Joshua said. "You know how she gets sometimes. We learned about it in Sex Ed."

Loeb was rattled, and he responded to the situation the same way that any Jewish man would. He led Joshua and Sandy into the kitchen, and said, "Let's eat." Ten minutes later, a couple of large vats of sherbet had been emptied. Joshua went to his room to go to sleep. Loeb took the Golem into his study, and began to teach him how to read. But, after about an hour, both the teacher and the student were tired. Loeb waited until the Golem had fallen asleep, and then he lay down in his bed with his partner for the night, a new scholarly work in Hebrew about the Seer of Lublin, written by his friend, colleague, and collaborator in the creation of the Golem, Rabbi Moshe Sinai.

FOR MANY YEARS, LOEB FOLLOWED A
similar pattern on the Sabbath and on most of the Jewish festivals. He
would rise early in the morning after a long night's sleep. If Tamara
were awake, there might be a few quick moments of lust, with neither
foreplay, nor afterplay, but with a cosmic mutual release of pent-up
tensions. If she were not awake, he would go to his study to peruse
some recondite commentary to the scriptural reading assigned to that
day. Most of the time, he would go to the synagogue, returning a few
hours later for a big lunch with Joshua and Tamara. He would then
take a nap—his soundest sleep of the week. Afterward, he'd go out for
a long walk, and return just as the sun was setting and the holy day was
coming to an end. Upon arriving home, he would say the afternoon
and evening prayers. After which, he would gather Joshua and Tamara
to recite in plaintive tones the *havdalah* that declares the passage from
the holy day to the regular days of the week. And, then, he would
adjourn to his desk to start his work week.

But this week was different. The end of the Sabbath did not lead to
the work week, but to the second day of *Sukkot*, which Loeb stringently

observed. Though it did not have as many restrictions as the Sabbath, it was still a holy day on which Loeb neither worked, nor wrote, nor traveled, especially by car.

Though that Saturday morning he had awoken refreshed from his long sleep, Loeb found himself alone in bed, and knew that he would be celibate that morning. The Golem was still asleep in his study, so he could not venture in there to retrieve a book, for fear of waking him. Now that he had become somewhat of a local celebrity, Loeb hesitated before venturing outside—either to the synagogue or even for a walk.

Loeb opened his front door and looked outside. It was raining hard. He took the newspaper that sat perched on his front porch, and took it out of the blue plastic bag in which it was wrapped. On the front page, there was a photo of Wriggles, the blood drained out of his face, looking suicidal.

Loeb took the newspaper inside, read it, and hid it from Tamara. He donned his prayer shawl and recited the lengthy liturgy for that day. After breakfast, he retrieved Rabbi Sinai's book from the bedroom, sat down in the living room, and read. Within the hour, both Joshua and Greenberg got up and sauntered into the living room. Loeb made them both breakfast, after which he asked Joshua to join him in teaching Sandy how to read. Joshua was glad that his father had included him in this task, and that reading was something that he could do better than his newly-adopted sibling.

Eventually, Tamara appeared, still angry from the night before. She went to the closet, put on her coat, and said, "I'm going out for a walk."

"But it's pouring outside," Loeb observed.

"Frankly, darling, I don't really give a damn," said Tamara, who disappeared outside into the windblown downpour, slamming the door behind her. By the time she returned, Greenberg had learned the fundamentals of reading, and she had clearly caught a cold.

Greenberg was delighted with his newly acquired skill, elemental though it was, but he was clearly frustrated that he could not speak the words that he was reading. Tamara was miserable, chilled and constantly sneezing. Loeb made her some tea with honey, and tucked her into bed under a hill of blankets. He then found some echinacea tablets in the medicine chest, giving two each to Joshua and to Greenberg, and then chewed two himself. None of them could afford to catch a cold that week. Loeb and Greenberg still had post-season play to worry about, and Joshua had the upcoming SATs.

The rest of the day was quiet. Tamara stayed in bed nursing her blossoming cold. The Golem stayed in the living room, reading through a pile of Joshua's old children's books that Joshua had found in a box in his closet. Loeb was in his study reading. Joshua reviewed vocabulary lists for the SATs.

As the afternoon progressed, each took a nap. When Loeb awoke, it was already dark outside. He recited the afternoon and evening prayers, waited for the rest of his family to wake up, fed them a late lunch, and conducted the special *havdalah* ceremony that makes the transition from the Sabbath/festival to the rest of the festival. Meanwhile, on the west coast, where it was two hours earlier than in Chicago, Wriggles was in the locker room addressing the team.

"Post isn't here, so get it through your heads that I run this team. I'm the manager, the boss. You listen to me. There'll be no more voodoo by some nerdy rabbi. No more praying in this smelly locker room. No more stunts by the rookie superjew. Only good, basic baseball. We don't need any outside help. No more bullshit. Just get your heads together. Get out there and win this series." The players quietly finished dressing, and when the time came, they went out to the field.

As Tamara went into her study to watch the game, Loeb went out for a walk with Sandy and Joshua. The streets were quiet, almost deserted. The rain had stopped, and the dying leaves on the ground gave the air a sweet and pungent aroma. When they returned home, they heard Tamara's yells, punctuated with coughs, sneezes and wheezes. It appeared that the game was not going well for the Cubs. Actually, it was going even worse than it had the previous evening. Joshua and Sandy sat down at the kitchen table, where Loeb joined them in dinner. After they had eaten, Loeb brought something to eat and drink into Tamara. Her only response was: "They suck. They really suck. Suck big time. Even worse than last night, they suck." Loeb put down the food tray, and went back inside.

The following morning, after reciting his prayers, Loeb contemplated what he might do that day. It was the second day of the holiday, and he had no plans. He retrieved both the Sunday *New York Times* and the *Chicago Tribune* from the front door, and looked at the front page of each. The *Times*'s front page mostly reported on foreign affairs and the ongoing health care crisis in the United States. The *Tribune*, however, focused only on one theme: the Cubs. The headline read: "Wriggles' Ego Bubble Bursts, Drowning Cubs."

The phone in Loeb's house had rung sporadically the previous day, but because of Sabbath observance, he didn't answer it. That morning it rang constantly, but he still would not pick it up in observance of the holiday. Eventually, Loeb turned off all of his phones, lest they wake up his sleeping family.

By mid-morning everyone was awake and fed. Tamara returned to bed, and the two boys returned to their reading, as did Loeb. The front doorbell rang. Loeb told Joshua to answer it, and to tell any reporter who might be there, that it was a Jewish holyday, on which he would not give an interview. A few seconds later, Joshua entered Loeb's study, and said, "There's a man outside. He says he's not a reporter, but a Jew in trouble who needs your help, and that the police had suggested that he see you. What should I do?" Loeb put down his book, rose from his chair and said, "It may be a trick. I'll take care of it."

Loeb went to the front door. Standing there was a lean, handsome man, with a dark, healthy complexion. His hair was only slightly thinned out and was almost all gray. He was probably about seventy, but his athletic physique gave him the appearance of a much younger man. He was casually, but well dressed. He wore a polo shirt covered by a windbreaker, expensive, crisply-pressed slacks and running shoes. He took off his sunglasses, put out his hand, and said, "Rabbi Loeb, Rabbi Jay Loeb? Hi, I'm . . . Sam Klein."

Loeb shook his hand, and said, "Look, sir. If you're a reporter, you should know that I wouldn't grant an interview today. Today is a Jewish holyday—"

"*Sukkos*," the man said, reciting the name of the holiday with a Yiddish inflection.

"So, you are a Jew?" Loeb asked in Yiddish.

"Yes," the man said.

"Religious?" Loeb asked.

"Not really," the man said.

"My son said something about the police."

"Yes," Klein said. "A policeman told me that you live here, that you are a rabbi, that you might help me. I really have nowhere else to turn right now."

"Why is that?" Loeb asked.

"I was mugged earlier today. They didn't hurt me, but they had guns. They wanted my car and my wallet. They got both. And my luggage was in the trunk of the car. They got that too."

"Are you a tourist?" Loeb asked.

"Here for the sporting goods show at McCormick Place. Own a sporting goods shop near L.A. Flew in this morning. Rented a car at the airport. Drove downtown. Too early to check into my hotel, so I stopped at a restaurant to have breakfast. Came back to the car. They were waiting for me. They got everything. In broad daylight. Few minutes later, a cop car came by. Flagged it down. Cops wrote up a report. Took me to the hotel, but they wouldn't check me in without a credit card. Called American Express for a new one, but it'll take awhile. One of the cops remembered you from the TV or the newspapers. Irish cop. Dropped me off here. Said you were sure to help me out, that Jews take care of their own. So, here I am."

"A little piece of plastic gives you the keys to the kingdom, but without it you're an instant beggar. Strange world," said Loeb.

"Yeah, with a credit card, it's all 'Yes, sir. At your service, sir,' but without it, it's 'Get lost, buddy.'"

The man was extremely serene for a person who had just been mugged. His voice was as soft as velvet and as smooth as honey dripping from a jar. Loeb looked outside, but no police car was in sight. Loeb thought of the old Jewish legend about the prophet Elijah who roams the world, testing people's generosity, compassion and hospitality by pretending to be an indigent, a blind man, or a person just down on his luck. *Perhaps*, thought Loeb, *the prophet Elijah is here to test whether I am true to my convictions.*

"Please, come in, Mr.—er—Klein. Come in. We can continue this conversation inside," said Loeb, embarrassed that he had not made the offer before. *After all*, Loeb thought, *I have my Golem in the house. No one can harm me with him around.*

Klein entered the house, and Loeb asked, "Coffee, tea, soda pop, orange juice, lox and bagels? What can I get you?"

"Well, I've already had two breakfasts today," Klein said. "One on the plane and one downtown. A little vodka with ice would be nice. It's been a rough morning. Do you mind? Wouldn't you join me? After all, it's *yontif*, a holiday."

"I'll get it right away. Please, take off your jacket and sit down." Klein complied and looked around the room as Loeb fetched his drink.

"You don't talk like you're from L.A.," Loeb said.

"Lived in L.A. many years. Moved out the same year as the Dodgers and Giants, '58. Originally from New York, Brooklyn."

"Bronx, myself," said Loeb.

"So, we're fellow New Yorkers as well as fellow Jews—*landsleit* as well as *yiddin*," Klein said.

"Must have been a Yankee fan?"

"*Vous noch*, what else? You, a Dodger fan?"

"Of course."

"But, I rooted for the Dodgers when Koufax pitched," said Loeb. "No one like him. I read somewhere that Ernie Banks said that he always knew which pitch Koufax would throw and where he would throw it, but that he couldn't hit it anyway, for love or money."

"Could be true," Klein said.

"And how about when he refused to pitch on Yom Kippur in the '65 World Series? That took guts. It was a defining moment in American Jewish history. Like when Gore picked Lieberman to run for Vice-President. We Jews finally felt we belong here, that we're real Americans, like everyone else. I read that Koufax did it, not because he was religious, but because he felt he had to serve as a role model to others. Koufax is a great Jewish hero in America."

"Eh, it was no big deal," Klein said. "Hank Greenberg refused to play on Yom Kippur already in the thirties when antisemitism was much more prevalent than in Koufax's time. Unlike Koufax, Greenberg even refused to play on the first day of Rosh Hashanah, and he only played on the second day of Rosh Hashanah because he got rabbinic permission to do so. But today, Greenberg's a forgotten hero while Koufax is an elusive, living legend. The more reclusive he is, the more of a legend he becomes. Look, even that big *haya*, the wrestler, Goldberg, didn't wrestle on Rosh Hashanah and Yom Kippur. So, Koufax's not so special."

"And what about his perfect game?" Loeb said. "Wasn't that something?"

"Nah, it really shouldn't even count," said Klein.

"Why is that?" Loeb asked.

"Look at who he won it against. The Cubs," Klein said.

"But what a pitcher he was. Never seen anything like it," Loeb said.

"'Cause Mathewson was before your time. Before mine, too. I think Mathewson was the best, ever. Also, what about Gibson, Marichal, Ryan, and many others? Koufax was great, but so were others."

"But he was the youngest player ever inducted into the Hall of Fame," Loeb said, showing signs of exasperation.

"Only because he blew out his arm so young. No big deal," Klein said. Klein sipped his vodka, as Joshua and the Golem entered the room.

"You've already met my son, Joshua, Mr. Klein. And this is our friend, Sandy Greenberg. He plays for the Cubs. You may have heard of him. He's been in the news a lot lately."

Klein shook hands with Sandy and Joshua.

"Can't say that I've heard of him. Don't keep up much with baseball lately, but it's an interesting name. You named after Sandy Koufax and Hank Greenberg?"

The Golem nodded, and Joshua explained to Klein that Sandy could not speak.

Klein stood up and patted the Golem on the shoulder as if to apologize. He looked him over and said, "You pitch?"

Greenberg nodded his head.

Klein said, "Could be a good pitcher. Has the height, the back muscles for strength. Long arms for leverage, and long fingers for extra spin on the ball."

"You know much about sports, Mr. Klein?" Loeb asked.

"Played basketball and baseball in college. Played a little since. Own a sporting goods store, like I told you. Pick up tips here and there," said Klein. "Sandy related to you, Rabbi?"

"No, but we've sort of adopted him. He has no parents," said Loeb.

"Was adopted myself," said Klein. "My father ran out on my mother. She re-married and I was adopted by her husband. He's the only dad I ever knew. Was a good father to me in every way. Both dead now."

"You have a family, Mr. Klein? Someone we could call about your plight when the holiday is over tonight?"

"No, sis passed away a few years ago. I'm divorced, no kids. Already called the appropriate person: American Express. Hope they come through. Don't think I'll get my stuff back, though. Need to cancel my other credit cards, and to buy some things."

Tamara emerged from the bedroom, carrying a fist full of tissues. When she saw Klein sitting there, she retreated back into the bedroom.

"My wife," Loeb explained to Klein. "She's under the weather. Excuse me."

Loeb went into the bedroom and explained the circumstances that had brought Klein to their home. Tamara was too sick to care. She took some medicine to make her sleep and to relieve her congestion, and returned to bed. Loeb closed her door and returned to the living room.

"Is playing basketball permitted on this holiday?" Klein asked. "Maybe we could go to the park and shoot some hoops. I've got nothing better to do."

"It would have been forbidden yesterday on the Sabbath. But not today. I'll tell my wife we're leaving."

Joshua got a basketball from his room, and Loeb went to the bedroom to talk to Tamara, but she was already asleep. Loeb affixed a disguise on himself and on Greenberg and they left the house.

"Trick or treat?" asked Klein. "You're a little early for that, aren't you?"

"Prudence," said Loeb.

"With a big *bouvon* like Sandy around, what are you afraid of?" Klein inquired.

"Being recognized. Like I told you, Sandy plays for the Cubs."

"Know what you mean," Klein said. They left the house and walked toward the lake and the basketball courts.

"PLAY MUCH BASKETBALL?" KLEIN asked Joshua as they walked along to the basketball courts.

"A little in school. Prefer baseball," Joshua answered.

"And what about Sandy?"

"He's never played," Loeb interjected.

There were a few young men shooting hoops on the basketball court. Klein led Greenberg to the other side of the court. Klein began to dribble and to shoot, while explaining the fundamentals of the game to Greenberg, who just watched and listened.

"Let's challenge those guys to a game," Klein said.

"You crazy?" Loeb said. "We wouldn't stand a snowball's chance in hell. I'm in no shape to play. Sandy's never played before. Joshua, frankly, is not so good, and you're forty years older than those guys. I doubt whether they'd waste their time playing us, anyway."

"Have any cash?" Klein asked.

"We don't carry or use money today. It's a holiday, remember?" said Loeb, a bit perturbed.

Klein reached into his pocket and pulled out a key case. He opened it, reached into some secret compartment and extracted a number of neatly folded bills.

"Emergency funds," he said, looking apologetically at Loeb.

Klein took out a twenty, went over to the three guys shooting hoops, and said, "Twenty bucks. Three of us against you three. Whoever gets to seven first, wins."

"You sure you want to do this, grandpa?" one of the young men asked.

"Only way I'll get a game today," Klein responded.

"Easiest money we'll make today," one of the men said. He pulled a ten from his pocket and put out his hand to his friends, each of whom put a five in his palm. "Well, here's our money. Let's go. We'll let you have the ball first, and you can use your ball. OK?"

Joshua stood behind the line, near the basket, and threw the ball to Greenberg, who was standing at half court. Greenberg held the ball, unsure of what to do. "Throw it into the hoop," Loeb yelled, pointing to the basket, as one of their opponents started to move toward Greenberg with the clear intention of stealing the ball. Greenberg put his massive hand under the ball, and heaved it underhanded toward the basket. The ball went right through the hoop.

"Lucky shot, big guy," one of the men said. Now it was their ball.

One of the young men passed the ball to his teammate who dribbled it around the confused and immobile Greenberg. Joshua lunged to steal it, but the man was too fast and too skilled. He went in for a lay-up, and when he approached the basket he jumped over the top of the rim, stuffed the ball into the basket, and hung on the rim triumphantly with one hand. Loeb just shook his head, confirming the expected imminent defeat of his team. But Klein seemed unruffled. One of the men threw Greenberg the ball.

Greenberg stood behind the line, and, at Loeb's command, passed it to Joshua, who then passed it to Klein. As two of his opponents ran towards him, Klein dribbled into a corner. But just when he looked trapped, Klein elegantly arched his left arm, shooting and sinking a seemingly impossible hook shot.

"Where'd you learn to do that, old man?" one of the young men asked, as his teammate easily scored a second basket.

"Brooklyn," Klein responded.

"No wonder, that's where Michael Jordan was born," one of the young men said.

On the next play, Klein faked the same hook shot, and then turned and made a jump shot. "You're not bad, for an old dude," one of the young men said. "But these guys," he said, pointing at Joshua and Sandy, "they ain't very good." Greenberg was getting frustrated, and he pulled off his shirt, showing that now he meant "business." One of the young men looked at his muscles and yelled, "Damn, you didn't tell us that he was that Goldberg pro-wrestlin' motherfucker."

Greenberg stole the ball from one of his opponents, and, copying Klein's hook shot, made one of his own. Within a few minutes, the score was 7-5. Klein had led his neophyte team to victory. "Keep your money," he said. "I just wanted to get a little exercise."

"Thanks, man. Good game. See you around."

Klein shook hands with each of his opponents, and Sandy and Joshua did likewise.

"Why didn't you join us?," Klein asked Loeb.

"Well, frankly," Loeb said, "I was trying to teach Sandy how to pitch the other day, and I've been paying for it ever since." Loeb put his hand over the small of his back indicating that he had pain there.

"Know anything about pitching?" Klein asked.

"Not very much," Loeb said. "You?"

"Haven't pitched for over thirty years," Klein said. "But, it's like riding a bicycle. You don't forget how. Only the body doesn't cooperate as well as it once did."

"Joshua, I'd like you to run home and bring back two mitts and a ball. We'll wait for you here," Loeb said. "It'll only take you about twenty minutes."

"Do I have to, Dad? I don't really feel like it. I've got to study for the SATs."

"Yes, Joshua, you have to. Maybe Mr. Klein can give Sandy some pointers. Maybe you could learn something yourself. And, when you're home, see how mom's doing. Because of the holiday, I couldn't write her a note about where we went."

Joshua left, reluctantly, and returned a half-hour later with the items Loeb had requested.

"Now, I'm going back home to study," Joshua said, and with a tone of hostile jealousy, he added, "Stay here with your precious Sandy. I'll take care of mom."

Klein found a piece of ground with a slight elevation. He told Greenberg to stand on the elevated part, and then he paced off the distance from where Greenberg stood to where home plate would be. Klein removed Loeb's cap, and put it down on the ground, simulating home plate. Loeb handed Greenberg one of the gloves that Joshua had brought, and gave the other mitt and the ball to Klein.

Klein, who was crouched behind Loeb's hat, threw the ball to Greenberg and told Greenberg to throw a few. He said he wanted to watch Greenberg's mechanics. Greenberg looked at Loeb for approval, and Loeb said, "OK, Sandy, throw a few—but not too hard." The Golem nodded, and began to throw.

After a few throws, Klein stood up and went over to Sandy. "Show me how you're holding the ball," he said. Greenberg did.

"Just as I thought," said Klein. "You're holding it too tightly. Ease up. Used to do the same thing myself. Now, try again." Klein crouched again behind the cap, and Greenberg started to throw again. The ball sailed smoothly through the air, like a dewdrop blown by the wind.

"Now, let me see your fastball. Go for accuracy, not for speed," Klein said with authority.

Greenberg fired a fastball that must have been traveling over ninety miles an hour into the target that Klein had made with his glove. Klein got up, walked toward Greenberg, and said, "Not bad, kid, but you could be a lot better. With your strength, and with fingers as long and as strong as yours, you could do a lot of things."

Klein worked with Greenberg for the next few hours, showing him a variety of things. He showed him how to hold his fingers on the ball for different kinds of pitches. He demonstrated how to manage the spin on a curve ball, by using his long fingers in certain ways. He explained how to aim with precision for a spot on the outside corner of the plate. He made Greenberg throttle back a little when releasing a fastball to provide better control. He taught Greenberg how to make the ball run away from the hitter by changing the landing spot of his foot by about an inch, and by letting his fingers come off slightly toward the inside half of the ball. Klein dug a groove into the ground where Greenberg stood, simulating the pitcher's rubber, and illustrated how to push off with the ball of his foot in the dirt and the heel of his foot on the rubber.

Klein was a gentle but firm teacher, and Loeb saw that Greenberg had taken a liking to him. Greenberg listened intently to everything Klein both said to him and showed him, frustrated that he could not express his appreciation in words.

"The kid's a quick study," Klein said to Loeb. "And, not a smart-ass know-it-all, like most kids today."

Klein went to sit on a bench to rest while Greenberg practiced the various motions that Klein had taught him. After a while, Klein got up, took his glove and crouched again behind the hat. "Now, let's see what you've got," Klein said. The Golem looked to Loeb for approval. Loeb nodded and the Golem began to throw. He had learned his lessons well. Klein was pleased, and so was Greenberg.

"I'm getting kind of hungry," Klein said. "Haven't had a workout like this in months."

"Haven't had one in years," Loeb said.

"You look it," said Klein laughing.

"Maybe, you'd be kind enough to look at a pitch I taught Sandy, before we go?" asked Loeb. "I'd like to know what you think of it. OK?"

"Sure," Klein said. "What kind of pitch is it?"

"A change of speed pitch," Loeb said. "Thought it up myself."

Klein knelt again, put up the glove as a target, and said, "Give it your best shot, kid."

Greenberg went into his windup, careful to show that he was using some of the techniques he had just learned. He let the ball go, and it sailed slowly toward Klein. "You call this a major league pitch?" Klein started to say. However, as the ball arrived at about midway the distance between Greenberg and Klein, it abruptly accelerated to what must have been over 120 miles an hour, hitting what would have been the outside corner of the plate, and landing in Klein's glove with a loud *pop*.

"Never quite saw anything like that before," Klein said, astonished, shaking the sudden soreness out of his gloved hand. "Don't think I have to worry about you anymore, kid. Just keep practicing what I've told you, and take a few hints from the old baseball alchemist over here," he said, pointing to Loeb.

The men walked back home. Loeb went into the bedroom to check on Tamara. She was feeling somewhat better, but still preferred to stay in bed. She was not up for company.

"I'll bring you something to eat," Loeb said, and he left the bedroom. Loeb went into the kitchen to prepare something to eat, but Klein was already there, looking around.

"I see you have a kosher kitchen, but not a gourmet one," Klein observed.

"My wife's not big on cooking," said Loeb. "And, I'm a bit out of practice myself. The housekeeper does most of the cooking, but she's off today."

"Then, maybe I can rustle something up?" Klein asked.

"If you like," said Loeb. Just remember not to mix up the meat and dairy stuff. This is, as you said, a kosher kitchen."

"Don't keep that kosher stuff myself," Klein said. "But, my grandma did. So I know about it. Don't worry."

Loeb left Klein in the kitchen, and went into Joshua's room, where he found him studying. Greenberg was in the living room, practicing various stances, motions and grips on the ball that Klein had taught him earlier that day. Loeb lay down on the living room couch, and fell asleep. The fresh air had tired him out.

When Loeb awoke, the table was set, and a dinner of rolled cabbage, salad and steamed vegetables was set out on the table.

"Got up just in time," said Klein. Loeb went into the bathroom, washed his hands and face, called Joshua and Sandy to the table, and brought a tray of food into Tamara.

"Where did this come from?" she asked.

"Our guest made it," Loeb said, and he went inside to eat.

"On this holiday, it is customary to eat in the *Sukkah*," Loeb said. "But, since you prepared everything in here, we'll eat in here. But before we sit down, let me show you our *Sukkah*."

Loeb took his guest out the back door, and showed him the fragile hut, covered with branches and decorated with fruits and vegetables that stood in the small back yard. There was a fold-up metal table and some metal chairs, and a few unlit lanterns. "This booth, this hut, this *Sukkah*," Loeb explained, "is to symbolize God's providence over our people as our ancestors traversed the wilderness from slavery in Egypt to freedom in the Promised Land."

"Haven't seen one of these in years, since I was a kid in Brooklyn," Klein said.

"And, there is a kabbalistic tradition," said Loeb, "to invite mystical guests, including the Patriarchs of Israel, to the Sukkah." Loeb recited the blessing that speaks about the obligation to occupy such huts during the festival.

When he was done, Klein said, "Well, Rabbi, I guess this year, you have a real live mystical guest—me." Loeb smiled, and invited Klein back into the house for dinner.

The food was delicious. Loeb was grateful. Joshua was surprised, and the Golem had to restrain himself from eating everything on the table.

Klein tasted the rolled cabbage, smiled, and said, "Just like grandma used to make."

As they ate, the sun had set. When the meal was over, Loeb led the others in the Grace after Meals, which seemed new to Klein. Loeb said the *havdalah* prayer, marking the end of the holyday. Joshua returned to his room. Greenberg went into the living room to watch his tapes. Loeb helped Klein clean up from dinner, and then turned on the phones. Almost immediately, the phone rang. It was Sota. Loeb excused himself, and retreated into his study to take the call.

"Waited 'til after sundown to call you, Jay. Just got back from San Francisco. Guess you heard what happened there?"

"Yes," Loeb said, mournfully.

"Skipper's off the wall. Post told him to take tomorrow off, though it's a make-or-break game. Put me in charge. Skipper's mad as hell."

"I can imagine," Loeb said.

"Blames it all on you and the kid," Sota continued.

"I know," said Loeb. "Maybe I should talk to him. What do you think?"

"Don't think so. How's the kid?" said Sota, changing the subject.

"Great. Fine. Ready to play."

"Good," said Sota. "Have him at the park early tomorrow morning. I'll have some of the coaches work with him on base running and fielding. Want him to play right field tomorrow night. Also want him to learn to play first base. Think he can handle it?"

"What do you think, Minnie?"

"Think so. Be at the field at 7 A.M. Tomorrow's going to be a very long day."

"I know, Minnie. Good luck. I know you've got a lot on your shoulders."

"See you, Jay. Good night."

"Night, Minnie. Thanks for calling."

Loeb hung up the phone, and he began to replay the conversation with Sota in his mind, but Joshua came in and interrupted him.

"Is Mr. Klein in here with you, Dad?," Joshua asked.

"No," said Loeb. "I left him in the kitchen."

"Then where did he go?" asked Joshua.

Loeb went into the kitchen and the living room, looking for Klein. He checked the bathrooms, but they were all vacant. In one of them, however, he found a handwritten note:

"Best of luck—S.K."

Loeb checked the house again, including his bedroom. Klein was gone, apparently having left while Loeb was on the phone with Sota. Loeb ran out the door and looked down the street in both directions. Klein was nowhere to be seen. He had disappeared as suddenly as he had come. Loeb phoned the police, identified himself, and asked whether they had had a report of a mugging earlier that day of a certain Sam Klein of Los Angeles who had come to Chicago to attend the sporting goods show. After checking his Caller-ID and verifying that it was indeed Rabbi Jay Loeb who was calling, the desk officer informed Loeb that he would check the computer. A few seconds later, he told Loeb that no such report had been made that day.

Loeb went into the bedroom, and told Tamara what had happened. She blew her nose, coughed, and said, "From what you've told me, there are three possibilities: either you've had your long-awaited visit from the prophet Elijah, or, there's some kook running around named Sam Klein." Tamara sneezed.

"And what's the third possibility?" Loeb asked.

"Tell me everything that happened today, since he arrived," said Tamara. Loeb took over an hour to review every detail since Klein's arrival: from Klein's appearance, to his dress, his manner of speech, his hook shot, his pitching instruction, and finally, his abilities in the kitchen. He then showed her Klein's farewell note.

Tamara thought for a while, and finally she said, "From what you've told me, the third possibility—since all of the pieces seem to fit together, is that your guest was 'Mr. Pitcher Perfect,' 'the left hand of God,' 'the nomadic ghost of Dodgers past.'"

"You're not making sense," Loeb said. "What in the world are you talking about?"

"I think your visitor today was none other than Sandy Koufax in the flesh—and I missed the whole fucking thing!"

Loeb was beyond astonished. "You really think it could have been him?"

"Who else?" Tamara said, as she erupted in a concerto of coughs and sneezes.

THE FOLLOWING MORNING, LOEB WAS awake by 5:30. Tamara wanted to stay home and rest, in order to preserve her strength so that she could attend the game that evening. Loeb washed and dressed, recited the morning prayers, woke up Joshua and Sandy, and prepared breakfast for them. It was all he could do not to say anything about his suspicions about the identity of their mysterious visitor of the day before.

Greenberg had been practicing his reading, and he showed Loeb a book he had found in the house on sign language. He pointed to the book, then to Loeb, and then to himself, indicating that he wanted Loeb to study the book. Greenberg pointed to his throat and to his mouth. He seemed to be saying that he wanted a way of "speaking" and of Loeb understanding him, and that sign language might provide him with a means of self-expression. Loeb told him that after post-season play, he would study the book, so that Greenberg could learn how to commun-icate with him. Greenberg then went to Loeb's study and returned with a pen and paper, and he started to scribble, indicating that he also wanted to learn to write. "And I'll teach you how to write, too, Sandy," Loeb said. "But, now we have to concentrate on baseball." Greenberg seemed satisfied, and he dug with gusto into the six-egg omelet that Loeb had prepared for him.

Joshua was lethargic. Loeb knew that in the next few days he would have to have a heart-to-heart discussion both with Joshua and with Wriggles. They were suffering from the same maladies: jealousy and ego.

After dropping Joshua off at school, Loeb drove to Wrigley Field where Greenberg spent the entire morning being drilled in base running and fielding. They returned home about 1 P.M. Tamara was up and around. The housekeeper came and made them all a late lunch, which they ate in the *Sukkah*. Luckily, that day, Chicago was enjoying a taste of Indian Summer.

Loeb made Greenberg rest up for the remainder of the afternoon. Greenberg lay in his bed, trying to teach himself sign language, and how to shape the letters of the alphabet with his pen. At 5 P.M., Loeb and Greenberg were ready to leave for the ballpark. Loeb urged Tamara to stay home, not to go to the game, and to take care of her cold. Tamara refused, saying, "If they win tonight, I'll feel a lot better. If they lose, I'll feel a lot worse anyway." By 5:30, Loeb and Greenberg were in the locker room. The players greeted them coldly. Wriggles' jealousy had even begun to infect the team.

Sota invited Loeb into the manager's office near the locker room and closed the door. "As you can see, we have a bit of a problem here," Sota said.

"Do you have a recommendation as to what we should do?" Loeb asked.

"It's a spiritual matter," said Sota, "and you're our spiritual advisor. It's your call, Jay."

"I'm going to call Post and have him force Wriggles to see me. I'll handle him. Some one-on-one pastoral counseling. You let Sandy play, but I'll tell him not to do anything 'heroic' unless the game is on the line."

Loeb called Post from the office and explained the situation. Post put him on hold for a few minutes, and then came back on the line. Loeb could visit Wriggles at home, right away, if he wanted to. Loeb agreed. He would be there in an hour. Loeb went into the locker room and gave the Golem his instructions for the evening, and explained that he had to visit Wriggles, who was sick, and that he would return during the game. The Golem looked apprehensive, but nodded that he understood. Sota gathered the team in the locker room, and Loeb spoke to them, softly but firmly, just like Klein had spoken to Greenberg.

Loeb talked about the sin of jealousy, how it harmed the person who was jealous more than it affected the person he was jealous of. How it was like a tumor that grew inside of a person, making him sick, and unable to function, until it became irreversibly destructive. He spoke to them about the sin of pride, about how it was more important for a person to manage his ego even than to manage his business affairs. He spoke about how the ego can create barriers between one person and another, between a person and his own self, between a person and his most important goals. He talked about how an ego can destroy an athlete's performance, how it can unravel a team's solidarity. Finally, Loeb related his observations to the situation at hand, and to the two disastrous losses the Cubs had suffered in San Francisco. As he spoke, the players nodded their heads, indicating that they not only understood, but that they would amend their attitudes and behavior accordingly. Loeb then announced that he was off to talk to Wriggles. He led the players in prayer, wished them luck, and left for Wriggles' apartment.

Three hours later, Loeb returned with Wriggles. Loeb had convinced Post, after speaking with Wriggles, that Wriggles was now fit to manage the rest of the game. By the time they arrived, it was already the bottom of the eighth inning. The Cubs held onto a 2-1 lead. Loeb explained the situation to Sota, who, in his usual gracious manner, handed the reins of leadership back to Wriggles. But, when the fans saw Wriggles in the dugout, they began to jeer and boo. Only Tamara Loeb, sitting in her usual seat, was quiet. She had laryngitis.

Loeb asked Sota how Greenberg was playing. Sota told him that he had caught two routine fly balls in right field, and that the Giants were playing it safe when he came to the plate. They had given him an intentional walk each time. They could afford neither another bunt that turned into an inside-the-park home run; nor did they want another outside-the-park home run blast. Loeb was pleased that the Golem had followed his instructions. As Sota and Loeb spoke, the eighth inning came to an end. Though they had runners on the corners, the Cubs had failed to score. The Giants came to bat in the top of the ninth. The Cubs began to savor the taste of victory that had eluded them for so long. But, in baseball, as in life, fortunes can change in an instant.

The Giants quickly loaded the bases. A seasoned pinch hitter was put in. Everything rode on his shoulders. Wriggles pulled the outfield in. The batter fouled off the first four pitches and then looked at two balls. The next pitch was launched into deep right center field.

Greenberg turned around and ran as fast as he could toward the ivy-covered wall. The Giants runners looked to the third base coach, who looked to the manager. The manager signaled to the coach, who signaled to the players to start running. As the third base runner crossed home plate, Greenberg continued running toward the wall. His hat fell off.

As the ball flew over Greenberg's shoulder, he extended his arms, which seemed to grow longer as he ran. Greenberg lunged for the ball, barely trapping it in the webbing of his glove. While still off balance, he turned and fired an assassin's bullet right into the waiting glove of the Cubs catcher, who caught the next Giants base runner in a rundown and tagged him out. The catcher then threw the ball to the third baseman, who touched third base—a triple play. The run did not count. The Cubs had won.

History had repeated itself because the Giants' scored run didn't count, just as in Merkle's game. But the difference here was that the last out was legitimately made, unlike in the Evers deception of 1908.

There was sudden pandemonium in Wrigley Field. A woman, wearing a tee shirt that read, "I love Sandy," tore it off, exposing her breasts. Strangers bathed one another with beer, kissed and hugged. A man in an elegant business suit dropped his pants and "mooned" the Giants. Meanwhile, the sports announcers were showing split-screen replays. On one side of the screen was Willie Mays's famous over-the-shoulder catch and perfect throw home during the first game of the 1954 World Series. On the other side of the screen was Greenberg's more recent series-winning play. As generations of bottled-up glee erupted at Wrigley Field, the commentators argued with one another, comparing the two great plays.

Frightened by all the noise, Greenberg ran into the dugout as fast as he could. But Loeb made him go out to tip his hat to the crowd, which immediately broke into their mantra-like chant: "We love Hulk! We love Hulk!" Loeb took Wriggles by the hand and led him to where Greenberg was standing. He put Wriggles' hand in Greenberg's and told them to raise their arms, which they did. Wriggles made the "victory" sign with his free hand, jutting his fingers into the air. The crowd cheered him for the first time that season. Wriggles turned toward Loeb, and a broad smile shone on his face.

With the Cubs' well-earned and honest defeat of the Giants, the metaphysical slate had now finally been wiped clean. The shenanigans of Johnny Evers, the duplicity of Hank O'Day, and the curse of John McGraw had been consigned to the archives of history. A new era for the Cubs was about to begin. They had been "written in the Book of Life."

The next chapter in that book was to be the National League pennant playoffs against the Atlanta Braves. The birthday of the new Chicago Cubs would take place on October 13, the day of their first playoff game against Atlanta. But the new birth would have a painful delivery.

THE CUBS WERE EXHAUSTED, PHYSICALLY AND emotionally, from their struggles with the Giants of the past and the present. They were weary from travel to Atlanta the day after having dispatched the Giants in a trying contest. When the Cubs lost their opening game to Atlanta, fickle sportswriters predicted that Atlanta would win the pennant playoffs in four straight games. They foretold how the "miracle of the Cubs" would dissipate into thin air, how Greenberg would burn out like a comet and be consigned to the realm of baseball oblivion, and how a Cubs defeat was simply in the natural order of things—like the annual autumnal transition to the harshness of winter. Jay Loeb knew otherwise. But Tamara Loeb did not share her husband's optimism. The next playoff game would take place on October 14—an annual reminder of the Cubs' abject humiliation in times past.

In 2003, the Cubs had delighted their fans by winning the Central Division. They were favored to win the National League playoffs against the Marlins. In Game Six on October 14, in the eighth inning, the Cubs were five outs away from their first pennant and World Series appearance since 1945. Precisely then, hope abruptly dissolved into abject despair.

The Cubs led 3-0, moving toward the pennant with a shutout. A Marlin batter launched a ball into left field that began to curve into foul territory. Cubs left fielder Moises Alou drifted over, poised to jump up to catch the ball. Suddenly, a fan's hand grabbed for the ball from the stands, preventing Alou from moving the Cubs one out closer to World Series play. Cubs pitching precipitously collapsed; the Marlins scored eight runs in the eighth inning, and soon after won the game. The following day, the traumatized Cubs lost again. The Marlins won the pennant, and later the World Series against the New York Yankees. Few now doubted that the Cubs had been cursed in perpetuity.

Alou was forgiving, but others were not. The fan received death threats. Governor Jeb Bush of the Marlins' home state offered the fan asylum in Florida. Another fan ended up with the ball, and auctioned it off for over $100,000. Fans demanded that the ball be destroyed, to once and for all remove the curse on the Cubs. Some fans petitioned NASA to launch the ball into outer space. Others wanted it dropped off the top of the Sears Tower. In February 2004, the ball was publicly "executed" by explosion, which was broadcast on TV. Cubs fans hoped, but did not believe, that with the destruction of the ball the curse had been neutralized. But, as another playoff game, on another October 14, was about to begin, Cubs fans like Tamara expected that it would be "Dèja vu, all over again."

Loeb had instructed Greenberg to fail at the plate at least once during the first playoff game against Atlanta. To have a rookie batting 1.000 was not only unseemly, but downright suspicious. Loeb wanted the team players to rely on their own abilities, rather than on Greenberg's heroics— except when calling upon Greenberg's singular capabilities became an absolute necessity.

Loeb wanted Greenberg to be the object of his teammates' admiration, not of their jealousy or disdain. To accomplish this, Greenberg had to become one of the team, and not a team unto himself. Loeb understood that baseball embodied the American proclivity for the individual's striving for excellence within the context of a community effort for the common good.

At the end of the October 14 game, anxious Cubs fans all over the country breathed a collective sigh of relief when history was made, rather than repeating itself. The Cubs caught their second wind, and sailed to a one-run win in Atlanta. The following day was a travel day, which meant that the next three games would be played at Wrigley Field. But it also meant that Greenberg would be absent from at least two of those games. The first home game was on Friday evening, the Sabbath, and the second was on a Saturday evening that marked the beginning of the Jewish holiday called *Simhat Torah*—Rejoicing over the Torah.

Rested from a day off from play, feeding on the psychic energy of their fastidious fans, and feeling liberated from the curses that had fettered their play in the past, the Cubs surprised their critics, and crushed the Braves twice in the "Friendly Confines," which were finally friendly to the home team. The Cubs now led 3-1 in the series. One more victory, and the pennant was theirs.

The next game was scheduled to begin on Sunday evening at 7 P.M., just about the time that the Jewish festival would be coming to a conclusion. Greenberg dressed for the game, awaiting Loeb's instructions. From Loeb's house, they could get to Wrigley Field within fifteen minutes.

Despite Tamara's protests, Loeb did not leave for the ballpark as soon as the holiday had ended. Instead, he turned on the television to check the score. It was only the second inning, but the Cubs already had a sizable lead. Hornsberry was in top form. Loeb would wait until he was convinced that Greenberg was absolutely needed. But the occasion never arose.

The Cubs won the game, and, for the first time since 1945, the pennant. Loeb was happy that Post and Wriggles could bask in the limelight and that the members of the team could claim their share of the glory. Yet Greenberg seemed forlorn. He wanted to share in the victory as well, but Loeb explained to him that the most important victory was yet to come. The pennant was but the penultimate battle. It was the World Series that would determine the final outcome of the war. Not merely winning the pennant, but being victorious in the World Series would be the complete fulfillment of the dreams of generations of unfulfilled Cubs fans. And Loeb further assured Greenberg that this ultimate victory could not take place without the employment of the "secret weapon" of the Chicago Cubs; namely, Sandy Greenberg. The Golem listened and seemed content. Tamara's only comment was, "From your mouth to God's ears." Meanwhile, people cheered in the streets, cars honked their horns, and fans throughout the city stormed into bars and got drunk. Too intoxicated with joy, few Chicagoans seemed to care that Greenberg had not participated in the pennant-winning game.

The next day, Cardinal Hood offered a thanksgiving mass in Holy Name Cathedral. People streamed into houses of worship to gratefully acknowledge that miracles can still occur in the twenty-first century. Tamara Loeb stayed home that day. The doctor diagnosed her condition as "acute shock."

The following Saturday night, October 24, the World Series would begin. As winners of the National League pennant, the Chicago Cubs would be on the playing field, something that had not happened since 1945, the year Loeb was born. But this time, the Cubs' opponents would not be the Detroit Tigers. The players they would now face would not be the bottom of the baseball barrel, a bunch of players deemed ineligible for military service because of age or disability, as had been the case in 1945. Rather, their adversaries, as in 1932, would be the "Bronx Bombers," The New York Yankees.

NO TEAM IN THE HISTORY OF BASEBALL had been in as many World Series, and had won as many, as the Yankees. The Cubs had been in ten, losing all but two. By the time the Yankees had arrived in World Series play for the first time in 1921, the Cubs already had won their first and last World Series championships, in 1907 and 1908. Every decade since the 1920s had been replete with Yankees World Series victories. Meanwhile, the Cubs had languished, winning an occasional pennant between 1910 and 1945, but denied final victory by a combination of cruel fate and the strength of their adversaries.

The Cubs would play the Philadelphia Athletics in two World Series contests, in 1910 and in 1929, and be routed each time. In 1910, despite coming into the Series as the strong favorites of the odds makers, and in spite of the legion efforts of players like Kling, Pfiester, Brown, Reulbach and Tinker, the Cubs would drop the Series in five games. In 1929, the Athletics took the Series in five, behind the powerful arm of Lefty Grove.

In 1918, the Cubs faced the Boston Red Sox. Many of the players had applied for exemptions from military service, as World War I wound down to an end. But, as baseball was declared "a non-essential war industry," the players were given a "work or fight" order by the War Department.

To demonstrate their patriotism at a time of war, during the seventh inning stretch, the fans and players sang "The Star-Spangled Banner" — the first time that song was sung at a World Series game. The custom caught on, and in subsequent baseball games, it was sung before the start of every game. In fact, singing "The Star-Spangled Banner" at various public occasions became increasingly popular around the country. As a result, in 1931, the U.S. Congress declared "The Star-Spangled Banner" to be the official national anthem of The United States of America. Nonetheless, the 1918 Series did not go well for the Cubs.

In the first game, the Cubs were shut out 1-0 by a young Red Sox southpaw named Babe Ruth. The Cubs didn't get to Ruth until the eighth inning of the fourth game, when they rallied, and ended Ruth's streak of 29-2/3 consecutive scoreless innings in World Series play—a record that would stand until the Yankees' Whitey Ford surpassed it in 1960. Eventually, the Red Sox took the 1918 Series in six games. It would be the last World Series they would win until 2004, after languishing for eighty-six years under the "curse of the Bambino."

In 1932, Ruth led the Yankees to crush the Cubs in a four-game World Series—this time, not as a pitcher, but as a hitter. In the third game at Wrigley, the legend of Ruth's "called shot" home run was born. Ruth, Gehrig and Toni Lazzeri put on a home run derby that day, which occasioned not only the defeat of the Cubs, but their humiliation as well.

In an interview with a Chicago reporter during the 1932 Series, Lou Gehrig reminisced about how he had played in Wrigley Field, years earlier, in a national high school championship game. In doing background research for his story, the reporter discovered that the self-effacing Gehrig had failed to tell him that at that game, the seventeen-year-old Gehrig had smacked a home run way out of Wrigley Field onto the street.

In the 1938 World Series, the Yankees again beat down the Cubs in four games, outscoring them in the Series 22-9. Despite the efforts of the Cubs hurler, the great Dizzy Dean, the Cubs fell to a Yankee offense led by a veteran Lou Gehrig and a young Joe DiMaggio, and to Yankee pitchers the likes of Red Ruffing and Lefty Gomez.

In 1935 and 1945, the Cubs tried to repeat their 1907 and 1908 World Series victories over the Detroit Tigers. But the Tigers got their long-awaited revenge, winning both contests. The Cubs would have to wait until 2000 to beat the Tigers again—this time in regular season interleague play.

The Cubs had been able to clinch the National League pennant against Atlanta by winning the last three games of the playoffs without either Greenberg or Loeb. This pleased Wriggles. It had proven that the Cubs could win on their own, without "extra help." For precisely these reasons, Loeb decided, that he and Greenberg would not join the team for the first game of the World Series in Yankee Stadium.

The opening game of the Series would be played on Saturday night, October 24. Loeb knew that there was no way he and Greenberg could fly to New York from Chicago after the Sabbath had ended, and arrive there in time for the game. Even if they got there on Friday before the Sabbath and stayed at a New York hotel for the Sabbath day, he and Greenberg would not be able to be at Yankee Stadium until the game was well underway.

Loeb also had to take into account the Jewish law of *marit ayin*, "the appearance of impropriety," which prohibited doing something that might be perceived as a violation of the requirements of the law, even though in fact it was not. Playing that Saturday night might appear as if they had violated the Sabbath in order to get to the game.

Post was not happy with Loeb's decision, though Wriggles was. The players and the press were beginning to give Wriggles some of the credit that he believed he deserved. But Tamara was livid.

"Can't you make an exception, just this once?" she asked Loeb over and over again.

But Loeb was adamant. "As you very well know, we can only violate the law if someone's life or health is at risk. The first game is not decisive, anyway," Loeb said.

"What about *my* mental health?" Tamara countered.

"I think you'll survive the first game," Loeb shot back.

"But," protested Tamara, "the sixth game next week may well be decisive. Friday is a travel day. But the sixth game will be played at Yankee Stadium on Saturday night. What will you do then?"

"Time will tell," said Loeb.

Saturday night, after the Sabbath had ended, Greenberg and the Loeb family watched the game. By the time they turned on the television, the game was already in the third inning. It was an hour later in New York. The Cubs were losing 3-1.

As the game progressed, it became apparent to Loeb that the Cubs were simply out-gunned by a stronger adversary. Every time the Cubs scored a run, they were beaten back by multiple-run scoring by the formidable Yankee lineup. The precision and efficiency of the fine-tuned Yankee machine left the Cubs no margin for error. The overpowering presence of the Yankee bullpen stretched the competitive abilities of Cubs pitching to the outer limits of their talent and experience. In the top of the ninth, the Cubs scored two runs, but it was not enough. The Yankees, playing at home, won the first game of the World Series 11-6. Tamara went into her study and slammed the door, but not before turning to Loeb and screaming, "It's all your fault!"

Unlike Tamara, Greenberg took the defeat in stride. He went to Loeb's study to practice reading and signing his name. Loeb began to pack. He and Greenberg would be flying out the next day to join the team.

THE FOLLOWING MORNING, A LIMO
came to take Loeb and Greenberg to the airport. Joshua and Tamara
would follow later on that day. Luckily, none of the airline personnel
asked Greenberg for a photo ID, as he didn't have one. This time,
the airline served Loeb his kosher lunch. Greenberg got one, too.
But the huge Golem was hungry, so Loeb gave him his lunch. Loeb
had to be content, as usual, with a few small salads and some tiny
bags of pretzels.

The stewardesses had tried to keep the fans in the plane away from
Greenberg in order to ensure his and Loeb's privacy. They especially
tried to keep the coach passengers from invading the first-class
compartment, and clogging up the aisle while they served refreshments.
But some of the passengers managed to get through anyway.

One was a small boy, about eight years old. He approached
Greenberg wearing a miniature baseball jersey with the Cubs emblem
on the front, and the number 18 and the name "Greenberg" on the
back. The boy pointed to Greenberg, to himself, and then to his shirt.

Greenberg understood that the boy, like him, could not speak.

Greenberg took the boy on his lap, took a baseball out of one of his pockets, signed it for the boy, and gave it to him. The boy's face lit up with joyous thanksgiving.

The boy's mother was standing in the aisle nearby, and she said, "You don't know what this means to my son. It gives him hope. You give him hope. Thank you, Mr. Greenberg. Thank you so very much."

Greenberg got up, and put the boy down in the aisle. He bent his tall frame down, and kissed the boy on the forehead. Loeb moved from his seat into the aisle, squeezed past Greenberg to where the boy was standing, and put his two hands on the boy's head, and blessed him. There was a tear in the eye of the boy's mother as she led him back to his seat in coach. As he walked down the aisle, gazing backwards at his hero, the smiling boy proudly showed everyone who cared to look his newly-acquired prized posesssion.

Once the plane came to the gate at LaGuardia, Greenberg and Loeb were whisked off by a detail of New York City police, who cordoned them off from the many fans and representatives of the press who had congregated once they saw who was coming off the plane. Used to dealing with celebrities, the police deftly guided Greenberg and Loeb into a waiting limo, and, with sirens blazing, a police escort led the limo into Manhattan, to the hotel that was serving as the Cubs' home while they were in New York.

At the hotel, Greenberg and Loeb received a warm reception from Wriggles and Sota. In private, they expressed their doubts to Loeb about whether the Cubs could win the Series. Wriggles bit his lip, looked downward at the floor, and asked Loeb for help. Loeb told him not to worry.

Soon, the team was aboard the bus to take them up to the Bronx for the second game of the World Series.

As soon as he entered Yankee Stadium, Loeb was struck by pangs of nostalgia and guilt. He had not been there since he used to go there as a child with his father and grandfather. He wondered whether his father and grandfather would have been angry with him for working to help the Chicago Cubs beat their beloved New York Yankees.

Loeb sat in the locker room, and watched Greenberg dress for the game. Some of the players asked to speak to Loeb privately, either about a personal problem, or simply to help them calm down, or to have Loeb give them a blessing, a new amulet, or a short prayer to recite either before or during the game. Finally, it was time for the Cubs to take the field. As each player was introduced, he ran onto the field only to be met by a cacophonous choir of hisses and boos from the Yankees fans. Greenberg nervously stood with Loeb, waiting his turn.

As Loeb looked at Yankee Stadium, he realized how much it had changed since he used to go there as a boy. The monuments in center field were no longer visible on the playing field, but were now hidden behind a wall. The hitting dimensions of the ballpark had been altered. Though much larger and much more august than Wrigley Field, Yankee Stadium somehow looked smaller than it used to look when he was young. Perhaps it was because he had gotten bigger, or, just older.

Loeb took his binoculars from his briefcase and looked at the grandstand in left field. That was the only place where he could get a ticket for Tamara and Joshua. There were so many dignitaries and season ticket holders to accommodate that he was unable to get them anything closer. He perused the stands and was relieved to see them sitting there, munching on kosher hot dogs with sauerkraut. Tamara looked unusually calm. Joshua sat next to her, poised at the edge of his seat.

Loeb swept the massive stands with his binoculars. In the box seats near the field, he saw the Mayor of New York, senators and congressmen whom he recognized from television, famous actors from the movies and television, well-known composers, writers and artists. But what truly astounded him was the huge Jewish presence that pervaded the stadium. It looked to him like a Jewish love fest, and the object of their affection was one person: Sandy Greenberg. The great cathedral of baseball, the

"House That Ruth Built," looked like an enormous synagogue.

Jewish Yankee fans had adopted Greenberg as their hero. Though they would not root for the Cubs, they would root for one of their own, as they had when Sandy Koufax pitched for the Dodgers against the Yankees in the 1963 World Series.

As Greenberg's name was called, he ran onto the field to take his place along the foul line with his fellow Cubs. The organist began to play the Israeli tune, *Hava Nagila*, and thousands of people in the stands began to sing the Hebrew words in unison. It was like an enormous Bar Mitzvah celebration. People in the stands held up signs welcoming Greenberg to New York and to Yankee Stadium. A well-dressed woman in a box seat held up a placard that read, "Sandy, have I got a girl for you!" Elsewhere in the stands, there was a group of Hasidic Jews with side-curls, dressed in large black hats and long black coats, holding up a sign that read: "The Bobover Rebbe Bestows His Blessings on Sandy Greenberg." Other signs said: "The Hadassah Chapter of Great Neck Loves Our Sandy," "Gay and Lesbian Jews for Greenberg," "Greenberg for Mayor."

Besides the usual peanuts, popcorn, beer and drinks, the roving concessionaires sold "Kosher Polish Sausage," "Amulets from Jerusalem," "Hummus, Techina, Falafel," "Thai Glatt Kosher Chop Suey." Even the Mayor and the other politicians rose from their seats to cheer for Greenberg, knowing that to do otherwise might cost them votes in the next election. There was even a sign that read, "The New York Board of Rabbis Welcomes our Colleague, Rabbi Jay Loeb."

Wriggles had decided to bat Greenberg in the seventh spot, so he did not come up to bat for the first time until the third inning. Meanwhile, Greenberg played his first base position efficiently, as the Cubs were mowed down inning after inning, and while the Yankees easily scored a couple of runs.

When Greenberg came up to bat, the crowd became unhinged. But their excitement soon waned when Greenberg was given an intentional walk. After stealing second, to the delight of his fans, Greenberg was able to score on a single by the Cubs third baseman. It was now 2-1, Yankees. In the fourth, the Yankees picked up another run, but the Cubs came back with one of their own. Greenberg was given another intentional pass his next time at bat, and the Yankees fans began to boo their own manager. By the end of the eighth inning, the Yankees were leading 5-4.

The Cubs managed to get their first batter on base in the top of the ninth, but the next two struck out. It was now Greenberg's turn to bat again. Loeb climbed out of the dugout with him. Loeb looked through his binoculars, and once again, he located his son, sitting in the upper left field grandstand. Loeb handed the binoculars to Greenberg, told him where to look, and asked him to locate Joshua in the stands.

"Do you see Joshua?" Loeb asked. Greenberg nodded.

"I want you to hit the ball to him. Do you understand?" Again, Greenberg nodded, turned, and walked toward the plate. As the pitcher began his wind-up, the catcher extended his hand, indicating that still another intentional walk would be given Greenberg. The Yankee manager was playing it safe. The crowd was not pleased.

After the second pitch, the Golem stepped out of the batter's box, looking disoriented and confused. Wriggles called "time," and he and Loeb went over to talk to Greenberg. Loeb repeated his instructions. But the Golem, knowing that he should only swing at pitches in the strike zone, became even more confused. When Wriggles told him, "Look, kid, a walk's just as good as a hit," his confusion only intensified.

Loeb put his hand on the Golem's shoulder, looked deeply into his eyes, and said, "Just hit the ball to Joshua. He has a glove and he will catch it. Do you understand?"

This time, to demonstrate that he understood, instead of nodding, the Golem extended his left hand, and pointed with his index finger toward where Joshua was sitting in the stands. This time, it was Loeb who nodded. But, thinking that Greenberg was repeating Babe Ruth's legendary "called shot" in the 1932 World Series between the Yankees and the Cubs, the fans rose like a single person and began chanting, "Sandee, Sandee!"

Greenberg returned to the batter's box. Fifty-five thousand fans held their breath, along with millions watching on TV and listening on radio. But when the Yankee catcher put out his arm again, indicating that they would proceed with the intentional walk, everyone relaxed—except Loeb.

The pitch came in slowly, aimed at a target about a yard beyond home plate. As it came in, Greenberg's long and lanky frame bent over the plate, forming an "L" shape. He held the bat in his extended right hand, and cocked his wrist. Somehow, Greenberg kept his balance long enough to swing.

The ball left his bat like a high line drive that seemed destined to drop somewhere in left field for a hit. But, as if it had been scooped up on the wings of an invisible eagle, the ball began to soar aloft, upwards and outwards, until it floated into the glove of a teenage boy in the upper grandstand in left field. Joshua held his glove up in triumph as Greenberg rounded the bases.

The Yankees pitcher threw his glove to the ground. The catcher just stood immobile behind home plate with his mouth open, gazing into the left field stands. Wriggles scratched his head. All across the ballpark, Loeb could hear people reciting the Hebrew blessing: "Blessed are You, our God, Master of Worlds, who has kept us in life, who has sustained us, and who has allowed us to reach this moment."

Now, the legend of the called shot was no longer a legend. Sandy Greenberg had actually done what Babe Ruth was alleged to have done. The curse of the Babe on the Cubs had now been removed. Awed by what they had witnessed, the fans silently contemplated whether what they had just seen, had actually occurred.

The umpire yelled, "Play ball!" The Yankee pitcher called over his manager and asked to be relieved. A new pitcher and catcher were brought in. The rest of the inning proceeded without incident. The Cubs won.

After the last Yankee out, Loeb told Greenberg to go out of the dugout and tip his hat to the crowd, which he did. The fans gave him an extended standing ovation. Some tried to jump on the field, simply to see if Greenberg were real. Meanwhile, in the left field grandstand, Tamara Loeb had fainted dead away in her seat.

The next day was a travel day. The Loeb family and Greenberg flew back to Chicago on the team's chartered plane. The headlines in the *New York Times* that day looked like the headlines at the end of World War II. Giant letters read: *V-G DAY.* Underneath, somewhat smaller letters said: GREENBERG CHOPS DOWN YANKEES, WINS NEW YORKERS' HEARTS. The *Chicago Tribune's* headlines were more direct, but not smaller in size: HULK SLAYS YANKEES.

WORLD SERIES PLAY RESUMED ON TUESDAY
evening at Wrigley Field. Since the Yankees saw that they could not
pitch around Greenberg, they had no choice but to pitch to him. For the
next three games in Chicago, Greenberg dutifully and efficiently played
his position at first base. At the plate, he would knock out a variety of
hits, occasionally steal a base, and when asked by Wriggles, he would
drag a sacrifice bunt or lift a sacrifice fly.

Loeb had explained to Greenberg that self-sacrifice was one of the
virtues taught by the game of baseball, that sometimes a person had to
put his interests aside for the sake of others, that sometimes the needs of
the many were greater than the needs of the one.

Between games, Greenberg privately practiced his pitching with Sota,
who was astounded at everything the rookie had learned from the owner
of a sporting goods store in L.A. When the time came to travel back to
New York for the last games of the Series, the Cubs were leading in the
Series 3-2. In Chicago, the Cubs won two, the Yankees won one. Friday
was a travel day, and Loeb had a problem. Should he allow Greenberg
to play that Saturday night in New York?

Loeb asked to meet with the Yankees manager and with Post. He had an unusual request. He explained to the Yankees manager the problem posed by Sabbath observance, and he asked if Greenberg and the Loeb family could stay at Yankee Stadium for the Sabbath, so as to be able be there in time for Greenberg to play on Saturday night. The manager called the head office in New York, and permission was granted. Thinking of the adverse publicity should he refuse, the Yankees General Manager had little choice but to accede to Loeb's request.

Loeb thanked the Yankees manager, and then he turned to Post, reminding him about the problem of "the appearance of impropriety."

Post asked, "What do you want me to do, Jay?"

Loeb said, "I want you to put full-page ads in tomorrow's and Saturday's New York and Chicago newspapers, and to get a story on the national news informing the public that Sandy and I will not be violating the laws of the Sabbath in order for Sandy to play in Saturday night's game, but that we shall be staying at Yankee Stadium during the Sabbath as the grateful guests of our gracious and generous hosts, The New York Yankees."

"The newspapers are no problem. TV, I can't promise, but we'll give it our best shot."

Loeb thanked Post and once again, he thanked the Yankees manager. On Friday morning, Greenberg and the Loebs flew to New York, and were escorted upon arrival, by a police motorcade, to a deserted Yankee Stadium. A number of sky boxes had been set up like hotel rooms. The refrigerators were stocked full of kosher food. Security staff was on hand to protect them from any intruders. A staff of uniformed valets and waiters was assigned to attend to their every need.

The following morning, Loeb recited the Sabbath morning prayers and then he went down onto the playing field for a walk. As he paced, he thought about his father and grandfather, and kept looking into the stands, somehow hoping to find them sitting there. A few hours later, he returned to the sky box for lunch, read a little, and took a nap. When he awoke, it was almost 6 P.M., and the sun had begun to go down. Fans already had begun to arrive. He said the afternoon and evening prayers, and, with Greenberg and his family with him, Loeb recited the *havdalah* that declared the Sabbath to be at an end. They shared a light dinner. After the Grace after Meals, Loeb and Greenberg went to the Cubs locker room. Joshua and Tamara would watch the game from one of the sky boxes in which they had stayed. Loeb looked at the stands, and he noticed a sign with Greenberg's picture on it. It read: "The Second Coming."

Loeb had asked Post to order Wriggles not to place Greenberg in the starting line-up, but to hold him in reserve as a relief pitcher. Loeb knew that Wriggles would receive this request with skepticism, but that he would have no choice but to comply. Loeb also knew that the fans would not be pleased. When they saw Greenberg sitting in the bullpen, the fans were unhappy and confused. Greenberg just smiled, and began to throw some routine pitches.

Unlike other sports that are played to the authority of the clock, baseball is a game with the potential of extending a single game into eternity. Being the last Saturday night of October, that evening was unusual because it was on the cusp of the year's only twenty-five-hour-long day, the evening when the clocks are set back, and an hour is re-lived. It was also the night of Halloween, and Loeb noticed that some of the fans had come dressed to look like him and Greenberg. In some cases, the resemblances were quite remarkable.

The pitchers on both sides were tired and the game turned into a bi-partisan slugfest. In the bottom of the ninth, the game was tied 13-13, and went into extra innings. Scoreless play extended until the fifteenth inning, when the Cubs put two more runs on the boards, but the Yankees came back with two to end the inning. In the sixteenth, the exhausted teams produced one run each, and the deadlock persisted. The score was now 16-16.

The seventeenth inning was scoreless, but in the top of the eighteenth, the Cubs rallied and scored a run, and, helped by a rare Yankees error, the Cubs scored a second run before the inning came to a close.

The two bullpens, which had been full at the beginning of the game, were now depleted. The Yankees had only one pitcher left. Sitting alone in the Cubs bullpen was a solitary Sandy Greenberg.

Despite the lateness of the hour—it was almost 1 A.M. —few of the fans had left the ballpark, but some had dozed off in their seats. Yet, when Greenberg started out to the pitcher's mound in the last of the eighteenth, the sudden eruption of the crowd jolted them out of their slumber, as if a giant alarm clock had just gone off in the crowded stadium.

Greenberg came to the mound, and he began to throw left-handed. As he took his warm-up pitches, the sports commentators reminded the fans that he batted right-handed like Hank Greenberg, but would pitch southpaw, like Sandy Koufax. As he threw, "We love Sandy" signs were lifted above the heads of fans throughout Yankee Stadium. Meanwhile, somewhere in Los Angeles, a dark, slim, gray-haired man who had been following the game on television, stood up and paced the room, like an expectant father awaiting the birth of his first-born child.

The first Yankees batter came up to the plate, rubbed dirt on his hands, knocked his spikes with the bat, dug in with his right foot, and faced the unknown.

The Cubs catcher gave Greenberg a sign, but Greenberg shook it off. He gave a second sign, but Greenberg shook it off as well. After Greenberg had shaken off the fifth sign, the Golem looked toward the dugout where Loeb stood. Loeb nodded to the Golem, who nodded back to Rabbi Loeb.

Greenberg went into his motion and released the ball with his left hand. The ball moved toward the plate almost in slow motion. The crowd gasped. *Was Wriggles crazy, or did he have no choice but to use Greenberg here?* was the question that entered the minds of Cubs fans who were watching from both near and far, including Tamara Loeb. In Chicago, the archbishop made the sign of the cross and held his breath.

Suddenly, as the ball began to approach the batter, it started to spin in tight, winding spirals. As the ball approached the plate, the batter lunged at it helplessly. Strike one. The crowd gasped. No one had ever seen a pitch like that before. It surpassed even Hoyt Wilhelm's best knuckleball.

The home-plate umpire called "time" and went out to the mound to look Greenberg over. The other umpires came to the mound as well. They checked the Golem's hands, his cap and his uniform. They practically undressed him, looking for Vaseline, nail files, for anything that could make a baseball move like that. Finding nothing, the umpires let play continue.

Greenberg went into his wind-up, and, while still facing first base, he let the ball go. At first, it looked like the ball would go into the dugout along the first base line. When Tamara saw it, she said to herself, "What are you up to now, Jay?" The batter relaxed, figuring that it would be a wild pitch and regretting that no one was on base. Yet, suddenly, the ball curved abruptly, and moved toward the plate, hitting the inside corner and jamming the batter. Strike two.

The batter dug in, determined to hit the next pitch, no matter what it might be. The catcher gave the fastball sign, and Greenberg nodded. As he went into his windup, you could hear a pin drop in Yankee Stadium. The Golem let loose a fastball that crossed the dead center of the plate. The seasoned batter swung, his reflexes fine-tuned with precision. But the ball was already in the catcher's glove. The pitch was clocked at 119 miles an hour. It was a pitch that was heard but not seen. One away.

The next Yankee batter came to the plate. Wriggles sent Sota out to the mound to confer with his catcher and pitcher. Sota said to Greenberg, "I've been in baseball a long time, but I've never heard of the pitches the rabbi wants you to throw to this guy—but here it is. Throw him a regular fastball, a lob ball and then a dirt ball. Do you know what I'm talking about? Because I as sure as hell don't."

Greenberg nodded to Sota, and then he looked toward the dugout at Loeb. Loeb nodded to the Golem who nodded back.

"What if we need more than three pitches to get this guy out?" the catcher asked Sota. "He's this year's American League batting champion, fer Christ's sake."

"The Rabbi says not to worry," said Sota as he walked off the mound toward the dugout.

While the Cubs coach and catcher were conferring, Greenberg reviewed in his mind the lessons he had learned from Sam Klein.

The catcher took his position. Greenberg pushed off with the ball of his foot on the dirt and the heel of his foot on the rubber, throttled back a bit and released the ball, just as Klein had taught him.

The first pitch crossed the plate at 120 miles an hour, not even giving the startled batter time to swing. The batter dug in, waiting for another fastball. Greenberg went into his windup, and lobbed the ball toward home plate. The ball arose in an arch, looking like the kind of pitch a father would throw his nine-year-old son in Little League hitting practice. The batter cocked his bat, awaiting the ball, ready to jettison it like a missile out of the ballpark. But, as he swung, the ball suddenly dropped like a rock in front of him, bouncing off home plate. Strike two.

The Cubs catcher quickly returned the ball to Greenberg, who went into his windup and fired an eighty-mile-an-hour fastball that looked like it was destined for the bleachers, but then it curved sharply away from the batter and rolled into the dirt along the first base line. But it was too late. The batter had already "gone around." Strike three.

The Yankee manager appealed the call, claiming it was a checked swing. The plate umpire looked to his colleagues, but they all agreed that the batter had "broken his wrists," and had "gone around." It remained a strike. Two outs. The sports commentators argued about the call, but the instant replay showed that the umpires had made the right decision.

The Yankees' top slugger now came to the plate. He had led the American League that season in home runs and extra base hits, though not in batting average. He was a veteran clutch hitter, and the disposition both of the game and the Series had fallen into his lap.

Greenberg looked toward Loeb, who made a gesture three times with his hand that he often made when arguing an issue of Jewish religious law. Greenberg smiled and nodded at Loeb.

The batter came to the plate. The fans stood up in expectation—they knew not of what, and they held their breath. Greenberg delivered three identical pitches. Each one left his hand looking like a regular fastball traveling between eighty-five and ninety miles an hour, which the batter squared off to pummel into the stands. But, as each pitch approached the plate, it suddenly accelerated and crossed the plate at 125 miles an hour—or more. The dumbfounded batter threw his bat and hat down in disgust. Three up. Three down.

In the Chicago announcers' booth there was pandemonium. No commentary, only a few grown men jumping up and down and screaming at the top of their lungs, "CUBS WIN, CUBS WIN!" In the Yankees press booth, there was only startled despair. And, in a sky box in Yankee Stadium, an ecstatic Tamara Loeb jumped up and down screaming, until she collapsed in a dead faint on the floor, with her son desperately trying to revive her.

Many dejected Yankees fans began to filter out of Yankee Stadium, while others stayed and chanted, "We want Sandy! We want Sandy!" Meanwhile, all over Chicago, people opened their windows in the middle of the night, and yelled, "CUBS WIN, CUBS WIN!"

Cars throughout Chicago honked their horns despite the late hour. People ran out of their houses onto the already crowded streets to celebrate. Chicago police and the Illinois National Guard were everywhere to prevent rioting.

Meanwhile, in Yankee Stadium, the Cubs locker room was the scene of unrestrained rejoicing. Wriggles was drenched with champagne. The players were singing, shouting, squirting champagne on one another, and dancing around in various states of undress, snapping towels at one another like teenage campers. An army of reporters invaded the locker room, interviewing whomever they could, while looking for Greenberg and Loeb. But they were not to be found.

AS SOON AS LOEB HAD RETRIEVED HIS briefcase from the dugout, he and Greenberg blended themselves into the crowd that was making its way out of Yankee Stadium. As they left, Loeb and Greenberg received many compliments for their great Halloween costumes, for being great look-alikes of Loeb and Greenberg. Eventually, Loeb and Greenberg managed to get onto a crowded "D" subway train, and they headed southward towards Manhattan. Arriving at West 50th street, they got off the train, walked up the stairs to the street, and caught a taxi to the upper west side. Loeb entered a small hotel on 85th Street. And there, sitting in the lobby waiting for them, were Rabbi Katz and Rabbi Sinai. When Greenberg saw them, his eyes lit up, and a huge smile covered his face. He seemed as happy to see them as he had been to win the World Series.

Rabbi Katz and Rabbi Sinai shared a suite of rooms in the hotel. They had reserved a second suite for Loeb and Greenberg under fictitious names. They led Loeb and Greenberg to their rooms. The small kitchen in the suite already had been stocked with food. While the rabbis talked,

Greenberg ate with one hand, and practiced signing his name with the other.

Early the next morning, though he was still exhausted from the events of the previous evening, Loeb awoke after a short but sound sleep, and he awakened Greenberg. After Loeb and Greenberg showered and dressed, Loeb phoned Rabbi Sinai and Rabbi Katz to see if they were ready to leave for the day. Loeb and the Golem met the two rabbis in the hotel lobby. As usual, Loeb was carrying his bulging briefcase.

The four men walked a few blocks up the street, and then they turned down a side street towards Riverside Drive. Soon they came to a decrepit brownstone. Garbage cans and garbage bags littered the street, waiting for a pickup that seemed long overdue. Loeb descended the few steps that led to what seemed to be a basement apartment in the building. Without knocking, he opened the door, followed by his colleagues and the Golem. Inside, there was a small synagogue populated by a dozen or so men, all dressed in Hasidic garb. A religious service already had begun. No one seemed to notice the entrance of the four men.

The three rabbis donned their prayer shawls and phylacteries and joined in the seemingly chaotic and freestyle prayer service. Everyone seemed to be saying his own prayers at his own pace. Yet there was a sense of unity and coherency to the service. Loeb placed a skullcap on Greenberg's head and a prayer shawl around his broad shoulders. Loeb gave him a Hebrew prayer book, but the letters were not recognizable to Greenberg, and he looked confused. Greenberg was proud of himself for having learned how to read English, but now was dismayed at this unfamiliar alphabet.

At the front of the tiny synagogue, next to the Holy Ark where the Torah scrolls were housed, sat an ancient man on a large mahogany chair that was upholstered with blue velvet. Though absorbed in his prayers, he occasionally looked up, stared at Greenberg, smiled, and nodded to the other rabbis.

Once the service had ended, he arose with difficulty, and, supported by his cane, he stood next to his chair. Each man who had attended the service approached the old man, kissed his hand, bowed slightly waiting to receive his blessing, and left without a word to Greenberg or to the other rabbis. When they all had departed, the visitors approached. The old man looked the Golem over carefully, now at short range, touching his arm and his face. Turning to the rabbis, he said, in Yiddish, "For the first time in my long life, I watched the World Series on television. You did well, my friends."

Rabbi Sinai took the walking stick with which he had sketched out the Golem's form on the beach in Wilmette, and he handed it to the old man.

"It belonged to your ancestor, Rabbi Ya'akov Yitzhak Horowitz, The Seer of Lublin. Now, its rightful place is with you."

The old man diverted his attention from the Golem, and picked up the walking stick, kissed it, inspected it, caressed it, and placed in down next to his chair.

"Rabbi Loeb has informed you as to why we have come?" Rabbi Sinai asked, almost rhetorically.

"And, you believe it can be done?" Rabbi Katz interjected.

The old man ran his fingers through his enormous mane of stark gray hair, and then he contemplatively stroked his wild gray beard.

"I don't know," he said, "but we can try. At first, I didn't expect that you would even get this far." He took the Golem's massive hand in his tiny frail hands. "But, you *did* get this far, and maybe we'll get even farther together.

"As you know, only a few of our sages of blessed memory—may their merit protect us—believed that a Golem could become a human being in all respects. But, we shall try."

"If Pinocchio could become a real boy, then our Golem can become a real human being," said Loeb.

The old man, who was steeped exclusively in Jewish wisdom asked, "I don't remember ever hearing about that Golem. Which of our sages created him?"

"Never mind," said Loeb, blushing. "It's our Golem that is our concern right now."

"Yes," said the old man. "And we shall do our best."

Loeb stood next to Greenberg, his hands on the Golem's arms, his eyes looking deeply, almost fatherly, and with deep affection, into the eyes of his creation.

"You will stay here with Rabbi Sinai and Rabbi Katz," Loeb commanded his Golem. "The other man is a great sage and a saintly man, a descendant of saints and sages. His name is Rabbi Ya'akov Yitzhak Horowitz. I must leave soon, and while I'm gone, you must obey Rabbi Horowitz the way you obey me. These rabbis will teach you many things that you need to know. And, if they are successful, you will become like us—a human being, with the power of speech. You will be granted a human soul, a higher soul than the one you now have. None of your powers will be diminished, but you will be complete. No longer a Golem, but a human being in every way. You will not need to learn to communicate by sign language, because you will be able to speak like any one of us."

When Loeb mentioned that he would leave, a look of intense fear formed on the Golem's face. Loeb saw it, and he added, "I must return to Chicago to prepare for your future as a complete human being. But, for now, you must remain here. I will return at the proper time. In the meantime, you must obey Rabbi Horowitz's every command."

Greenberg still looked profoundly saddened, but there was a sparkle of hope in his eyes.

Before he left, Loeb went over to the old man and spoke to him in Yiddish so that Greenberg would not understand. Loeb said,

"The Golem is already more than half the way there. He learns quickly. His mind is sound. He wants to learn. He already has learned how to read English. He desperately wants to be fully human. He already has exhibited some of the essential human virtues, especially empathy and compassion."

Loeb went on to describe the Golem's interaction with the mute boy on the airplane. He offered other examples of the Golem's behavior as well.

The old man was pleased with what he heard. In fact, he seemed quite surprised. The old man said, "Our sages of blessed memory—may their merit protect us—taught that God—may his Holy Name be blessed—created Adam first as a Golem, and only later did The Holy One—blessed be He and blessed be His Name—make Adam into the first human being. Furthermore, in Hebrew, 'Golem' sometimes means 'embryo.' Hence, all human beings begin their lives as Adam began, as a Golem. Yet somehow we escape our golemic state and become human beings.

"All human beings were once Golems, but, regretfully, some revert back into the golemic state from which they emerged at birth. The challenge to all humans is *not* to revert back to being Golems— automatons, robots in human form, devoid of a human soul, a moral will, a developed intelligence, and the moral virtues. I pray that our Golem may become a human being in every respect. I do not fear that. What I fear are those human beings who allow themselves to become Golems once again—creatures with power but without prudence, beasts without compassion. Such individuals have already caused too much pain in our world. They make God cry."

The old man stroked his beard, thought for a moment, and continued, "Once a skeptic came to the Rabbi of Kotsk and said to him, 'I hear that you can perform miracles, that you can create a Golem.' The Rabbi of Kotsk replied, 'There is even a greater miracle than creating a Golem.' 'What's that?' the skeptic asked. 'It's when a human person becomes a *mensch,* a true human being, a morally and spiritually developed individual, a person who has become all he can be, a person who has crafted his soul into a work of art. When a person has worked hard to acquire wisdom, love, empathy, compassion and understanding—and has succeeded—that's the true miracle.'

"Now, my friend, go in peace. We have much work to do, and with God's help, the Lord God will, as Scripture says, 'establish the work of our hands.'"

Loeb bid his companions goodbye, and he climbed the stairs out of the basement, walked to Broadway, hailed a taxi, and went to the airport.

At first, Loeb could not identify the peculiar emotion that engulfed him as he left the small synagogue. But, on the way to the airport, his emotional memory reminded him of when he had felt it before. It was like the first day that Joshua had gone off to nursery school. In his heart and mind, the Golem was already human. He was his adopted son, Sandy Greenberg.

Loeb boarded the plane to Chicago, and a few hours later, he was in a taxi, a few blocks from his home. As the taxi approached his house, Loeb saw a couple of TV sound trucks parked nearby, and a crowd of reporters and Cubs fans that had gathered in front of his home. Either they were waiting for him to come out of the house, or someone had recognized him at the airport and had informed the press of his imminent arrival. Either way, he could guess what they would ask him, and he was prepared.

As Loeb approached the front steps to his house, the crowd gathered around him, with the reporters hurling a cacophony of questions at him. Loeb raised his hands, asking for quiet, and said, "Please let me just go into my house for a few minutes. Then, I'll come back to answer your questions. Five minutes, please."

Loeb fumbled with his house keys, and opened the door. His prostate was acting up, and he had an urgent need to get to the bathroom. As he was relieving himself, he heard Joshua yelling through the door, "Good work, Dad. It was awesome!"

Loeb exited the bathroom, recited the appropriate blessing, and kissed his son on the forehead.

"So, finally, you're proud of your old man?"

"Yeah, Dad. Where's Sandy?"

"Where's Mom?" Loeb responded.

"She's teaching today at DePaul Law School. But I think they're not talking about the First Amendment today, but about the last inning."

"How long have all those people been outside?" Loeb inquired.

"Some all night. Some only in the last hour."

"I have to talk to them. You stay in the house."

"Oh, Dad, do I have to?"

"Yes, you have to—for now," said Loeb, missing his more obedient Golem.

Loeb changed his shirt and tie, straightened his hair, combed his beard, and went outside. Like the teacher he was, Loeb quieted the group down, and asked for questions by a show of hands. The reporters, TV and radio sound crews, and the Cubs fans who accompanied them, almost all raised their hands.

Loeb sighted a news anchorwoman from WGN, the station that broadcast the Cubs, and he asked for her question.

"Where is Sandy Greenberg?" she asked.

Loeb had decided to respond truthfully to all questions asked, while still managing to protect the secret of Greenberg's origins. To do otherwise would subject the Golem to cruel medical experiments, ridicule, abuse—or worse.

"As you may know," said Loeb, "Sandy Greenberg came into this world without the ability to speak. Until now, the resources have not been available for us to seek a possible cure for his malady. All I can tell you now is that he's in the best of care at a private facility. When a prognosis is clear, you will be informed. In the meantime, I ask you to pray for his complete healing."

A forest of hands shot up as Loeb concluded his response. Loeb called on a female fan, wearing a tight, revealing tee shirt with the slogan, "I love Sandy" printed on its front and the number 18 on its back.

"Is Sandy married, engaged, seeing anyone? Is he gay?"

"No to all of the above," said Loeb, who then pointed to a reporter he knew from a small suburban newspaper, who asked, "Where did you first meet Greenberg?"

"I first met Sandy Greenberg," said Loeb, "on a beach in Wilmette, where I had gone to pray early one morning. He was very, very young at the time."

"You mean," one of the other reporters yelled out, "that he was an abandoned child?"

"I will respond to that question. But, please raise your hands to be recognized if you want me to answer any further questions," said Loeb, like an angry teacher trying to restore order in an unruly classroom. "Sandy Greenberg has no parents or family that I've been able to locate."

A few questions were called out, but Loeb ignored them. Instead, he called on a well-dressed reporter accompanied by a film crew, apparently from a major network,

"Rabbi Loeb, sir, we've heard in the media about your alleged magical abilities. Is Greenberg part of that?"

There was a sudden silence as Loeb contemplated a response. Loeb forced a smile and said, "As I think you saw, both in Yankee Stadium and in Wrigley Field, Sandy has a bit of magic of his own."

Some laughed, while others made notes. Some did both.

Seeing Nicklesen in the crowd, Loeb selected him for the next question, "Who named him?"

"I did," said Loeb. "When it became apparent that he came into this world to play baseball, I named him after the two greatest Jewish baseball players: Hank Greenberg and Sandy Koufax."

"And, when was that?" Nicklesen asked, as a follow-up question.

"Oh, when he was very young," said Loeb, moving on to a reporter wearing an ESPN logo.

"Will Greenberg play for the Cubs next year?"

"That's up to the Cubs GM, Roger Post. Only time will tell."

Loeb had learned that when one is unsure of an answer, one of two responses is usually appropriate: "Time will tell" or "What do you think?"

He used the second response for the next question, which was, "How much money will Greenberg ask for signing up for next season?"

Loeb knew that the marathon of questions and answers could keep going for the rest of the day. He raised his hands and said,

"I think that's enough for now, so let me conclude with three points."

As in class, Loeb always liked to summarize the major points he had made.

"One—please pray for the success of Sandy's treatment and for his full recovery. Two—don't try to find him until he wants to be found. In that way, he's like his namesake, Sandy Koufax. He values his privacy. Three—thank you for your interest."

Loeb took a deep breath, turned around and went into the house, followed by the shouts of additional questions. Loeb was sure that he had accomplished his goal: the generation of compassion, empathy and love for his protégé. The TV and radio news programs later that day and the next day newspapers confirmed his hopes. Yet, even to Tamara and to Joshua, despite their incessant interrogation, he refused to reveal the real origins of America's reigning sports hero.

THE WEEKS PASSED. LOEB CONTINUED
to give interviews, to answer correspondence, and to spend time in his
office in the Tribune Tower. He enjoyed having his own secretary, a
luxury he had never had before. Loeb had received the bonuses that
Kalinsky had negotiated with the Cubs, and was now a multimillionaire.
With the money, Loeb established a trust fund for Joshua's education
and a foundation to endow his new seminary. The school had its home
base in Chicago, with branches in London and Jerusalem that would
be directed by Rabbi Katz and Rabbi Sinai. Like him, they, too, would
be financially secure for the rest of their lives. Like Loeb, they would
now be free to devote themselves completely for the rest of their lives
to training generations of Talmudic and kabbalistic scholars.

Meanwhile, in New York, the Golem was engaged in an intensive
program of study. Each day, Rabbi Katz taught him the Hebrew blessings,
including what to say when rising from sleep, going to the bathroom,
eating different foods, and for other occasions. He taught the Golem
the Hebrew prayers for weekdays, for Sabbaths and for holydays. He

taught the Golem how to wear the prayer shawl, how to don the phylacteries, about the laws keeping kosher, observing the Sabbath and holydays. Rabbi Sinai taught him Bible and Talmud—the vast sea of Jewish law, lore and tradition composed during a thousand years from the time of the Maccabees to the time of Mohammed.

Rabbi Horowitz had given the Golem a Hebrew name—*Shalom*, meaning "peace," which he pronounced with a Yiddish accent as "*Showlem*." He called him, "Sholem, the Golem." From Horowitz, Shalom learned compassion, love, sincerity, and empathy. He learned how to manage his ego, control his anger, cultivate friendship, and practice humility and generosity. Horowitz also taught him how to handle the natural but sometimes dangerous physical urges; how to deal with daily temptations; how to control avarice, greed, lust, and other potentially dangerous human appetites. He told him of the good that dwells in human hearts, and about evils residing there—that when unleashed, can lead to damage, destruction and horror.

Horowitz taught the Golem how to think: how to evaluate a statement or a situation, to analyze an argument, to think for himself. And, when Horowitz began to see that the Golem was developing human qualities—both good and bad—he taught him about free will: how to make moral decisions, when to take the initiative and when not to do so, when to be silent and when to speak, when to act and when to have the self-restraint not to act. When Shalom made the wrong decisions, Rabbi Horowitz gently chastised him; after all, the ability to make choices, even the wrong ones, is, after all, a crucial feature of human life.

In the weeks after Thanksgiving, Rabbi Horowitz left Greenberg on his own to learn about life, especially from his solitary meanderings on the streets of New York City. There, Greenberg met tourists asking directions, prostitutes soliciting clients, businesspeople rushing from place to place with an air of self-appointed importance, teenagers enjoying the first rush of romance, old people sitting on park benches contemplating death, teenagers navigating their way through the crowds on skateboards while listening to music through earphones. He visited libraries, zoos and museums. He attended concerts and operas, trying to understand better the world into which he had been thrust. He visited churches and mosques to see how others prayed to God. He saw drug dealers trying to spread their poison. He read newspapers and magazines, listened to the radio and watched movies and television to find out what was going on in the world. Occasionally, he came across a news story about himself, usually titled, "Where's Sandy now?" And this amused him.

He learned to shop, and to cook. He helped disabled people cross the street, and wondered why more people did not help them. Once, late at night, while on the way back to Horowitz's, he stopped a mugging in process, and wondered why the young female victim had kissed him on the cheek.

By late December, Hanukah had begun. It was already bitterly cold in Chicago, and snow had accumulated on the ground in the parks and on some of the streets. In Manhattan, there had been only a dusting of snow. Greenberg discovered that he liked the snow, but not the cold.

One morning, during the eight-day holiday of Hanukah, The Festival of Lights, Greenberg came by himself to the synagogue in the morning, not waiting for Rabbi Sinai and Rabbi Katz to accompany him, as he usually did. Horowitz was alone in the synagogue studying the Talmud. Greenberg bowed to the old man, kissed his hand, and said, with his own voice, "I think I am no longer a Golem."

Tears came to Horowitz's wrinkled eyes, and a smile came to his lips. He embraced Greenberg and kissed his hand, not being tall enough to reach his cheek. Horowitz phoned the hotel to tell Sinai and Katz the news. He then phoned Loeb in Chicago. Sinai and Katz came to the synagogue as fast as their weary old feet could carry them. When they entered the room, Greenberg stood up, bowed to each of them and said, "Thank you for bringing me into this wonderful, terrible, and mysterious world." Each of the rabbis embraced him.

Meanwhile, Jay Loeb packed his briefcase, took a taxi to a downtown hotel where he entered a men's room, affixed a disguise, rushed into another taxi, and ordered the driver to take a circuitous route to the airport so as to escape anyone that might be following him. Loeb bought a ticket and headed for New York City. At LaGuardia, Loeb took a taxi directly to Horowitz's synagogue. When Greenberg saw him, a huge smile of relief and affection registered on his face. He ran toward Loeb, held him in a firm embrace, and greeted him with a name Loeb had heard only from one other person: "Father."

Horowitz invited Loeb, Sinai, Katz and Greenberg to his apartment, which was one flight above the small cellar synagogue. Loeb rode with Horowitz in an elevator that had been installed for the almost invalid Horowitz, who began to dance with joy when Loeb entered the room. The others ascended by way of the staircase.

In the book-lined living room upstairs, Horowitz's granddaughter served them a sumptuous meal, complete with plum brandy and vodka. The men ate, drank and sang. Sandy toasted each of the rabbis. When he was done, the rabbis toasted him. Over tea and cake, the rabbis made plans for the celebration that Sabbath of the Bar Mitzvah of Sandy Greenberg. They gave him the Hebrew name, Shalom son of Judah, after Rabbi Judah Loew of Prague, the common ancestor of the rabbis who had brought him into the world, and the legendary creator of the most famous Golem ever created—until now. However, while Loew's Golem had turned destructive and had to be destroyed, their Golem had become a real human being, as well as a famous athlete.

That Saturday, in the presence of the rabbis and the members of Horowitz's small congregation, Sandy Greenberg was called up to the Torah as the first Golem ever to celebrate his Bar Mitzvah. The following day, on Sunday, Loeb returned with Greenberg to Chicago. Leaving Horowitz, Katz and Sinai was a bittersweet departure, both for Loeb and for Greenberg.

A few days later, in the Grand Ballroom of The Chicago Hilton and Towers hotel, Greenberg met the press and a few hundred of his most fervent fans.

Roger Post welcomed those present and announced that Greenberg would be playing for the Cubs the following season. The crowd rose to their feet and applauded for a long time, until Greenberg motioned them to quiet down. With some trepidation, Sandy Greenberg approached the microphone. Everyone waited to hear his first words to them. His voice was a resonant baritone. His accent was strongly New York-esque, with a slight sing-song Yiddish inflection.

Greenberg thanked the Cubs, the press and his fans for their affection and support. He put a small skullcap on his head and recited the traditional Jewish blessing of thanksgiving both in Hebrew and in English translation. He then asked for questions.

The first question was, "Sandy, how ya doin'?"

Quoting Lou Gehrig, Greenberg said, "Today, I am the happiest man on the face of the earth."

 *Epilogue*

THE MEDIA SOON STOPPED TRYING TO discover how Sandy Greenberg had spent his early life. It was easier to accept the story of his life before the Cubs as Loeb had presented it: Greenberg was a foundling, probably delivered at home by his unwed teenage mother who had abandoned him on a beach in Wilmette one morning, hoping that he would be found and cared for by a wealthy suburban family. This explained why no birth certificate could be located. Loeb found him on that beach early one morning when he went there to pray. Because he was a mute, Loeb had to find a series of special caretakers for him. They educated him and cared for him. As he grew up, Loeb noticed that Greenberg showed an unusual aptitude for playing baseball. Loeb, therefore, made sure that his talents were cultivated as he grew up.

With the help of the *Chicago Tribune*, a birth certificate, passport, Social Security card, and other personal documents that Greenberg would need were obtained. No one in Chicago would refuse to help Sandy Greenberg, even if it meant bending a few rules.

Greenberg accepted the Cubs' offer of $15 million to play for the following season. He also signed contracts to do commercials for an additional $50 million. Much of the money he donated to the new seminary established by Rabbi Loeb. In addition, he established a fund to ensure that Rabbi Horowitz's family would always be financially secure. A large chunk of money was given to charities that helped speech-impaired people of all ages and to organizations that helped abandoned children.

ROGER POST got the job he always had really wanted. He was named Chief Operating Officer of the Tribune conglomerate.

WRIGGLES was named Manager of the Year, and he became the Cubs' new GM.

MINNIE SOTA became the Manager of the Chicago Cubs, to his and to Greenberg's delight.

JORGE MATALÓN was appointed head of security at Wrigley Field.

CHARLES FLAHERTY ran for Congress, but was defeated when the media revealed his long string of mistresses, and a long history of his sexual abuse of the firm's female employees. Soon afterward, the venerable Farnsworth firm collapsed. Hearing about it, Loeb quoted an old Polish proverb: "God is just—but slow."

RICK NICKLESEN became the Editor-in-Chief of the *Chicago Tribune*.

Rumors began to spread in Rome that PATRICK CARDINAL HOOD was on the "short list" to be the next Pope, the only American prelate under consideration.

JOSHUA LOEB was admitted to Princeton University, where his studies would focus on musical composition, and where he would play shortstop for the Princeton Tigers. He now considered Sandy Greenberg his adopted brother.

TAMARA LOEB'S textbook would be used by law schools and universities around the country, becoming the standard in its field. Rejecting offers from other firms, and turning down appointments to teach at a variety of law schools, she started her own law firm that specialized in representing professional athletes. Her first client was Sandy Greenberg. As April approached, Tamara Loeb enthusiastically awaited opening day at Wrigley Field. For the first time since she could remember, spring-time was not a season for the inevitable onset of impending despair, but a season for growth and renewal.

JAY LOEB established his school in Chicago, which accepted only the most promising young Jewish scholars, to whom it provided generous stipends. Rabbi Loeb and his colleagues, Rabbi Sinai and Rabbi Katz, could finally rest content that the immense learning that they had each acquired would be passed down to generations yet to come.

KATHLEEN WYNER, who had been confirmed as a federal district judge in Oklahoma by the U.S. Senate, was quickly promoted to the federal circuit court, headquartered in Chicago. Soon after her confirmation, she came to see Loeb to tell him that she had coverted to Judaism, and to ask him, once again, to father her child through artificial insemination—unless he preferred more conventional methods. But, that day, instead of finding Loeb in his office, she met Sandy Greenberg. It was love at first sight. It seemed that in Greenberg, Wyner saw many of the things she loved about Loeb. Besides, he was younger, stronger and much more attractive than his "father." It also seemed that Greenberg had somehow become ingrained with Loeb's attraction to her. Loeb was both pleased and relieved when he performed the marriage ceremony of his adopted son to his new daughter-in-law.

Wyner believed that her husband was about a dozen years younger than she, which seemed not to bother either of them. But, it never occurred to her that he was actually less than a year old when they were married.

On their honeymoon, the new couple attended to the ringing of her biological clock by conceiving a child. In the early months of her pregnancy, she sat in her courtroom, clad in her long, black robes, munching on Ritz crackers and sipping lemonade to deal with the pangs of nausea that constantly reminded her that her one remaining dream was about to come true. Greenberg was happy, too; not only because he would soon become a father and would make Loeb a grandfather, but also because he knew that Golems lack the capacity to reproduce. Now he knew for sure that he was no longer a Golem.

That February, SANDY GREENBERG reported for spring training with the Cubs in Mesa, Arizona. Awaiting him was a note that read:

"Good luck, kid—S.K."

 *About the Author*

Jay Loeb is the protagonist of *The Cubs and the Kabbalist*. Like its author, BYRON L. SHERWIN, he is a rabbi, scholar, author and professor, married to a Chicago attorney who suffers from a life-long obsession with the Chicago Cubs. Consequently, for her, as for her fellow Cubs fans, each spring is a season of hope, each summer brings acute anxiety, and each autumn inevitably becomes a time of abject despair. To address this situation, Jay Loeb successfully accomplishes a task that has eluded the author. He utilizes his extensive knowledge of Kabbalah—the Jewish mystical tradition—to heal his wife of her annual bout with disappointment and dismay by helping the Cubs win their first pennant since 1945 and their first World Series since 1908.

Educated in New York and Chicago, Rabbi Sherwin earned undergraduate and graduate degrees at Columbia University, New York University, The Jewish Theological Seminary of America, and the University of Chicago. Since 1970, Dr. Sherwin has served on the faculty of Chicago's Spertus Institute of Jewish Studies, where he currently is Distinguished Service Professor and Director of Doctoral Programs. From 1984-2001, he was Dean and Vice-President of the Institute. The author or editor of twenty-five books and over 150 articles and monographs, his writings have been translated into eight foreign languages, including Chinese and Polish. His most recent books include: *Golems Among Us*, and *Workers of Wonders*. This is his first novel.

The Cubs and the Kabbalist was written for the author's wife and for her fellow Cubs fans who hope to see a Cubs victory during their lifetime; for all lovers of baseball; for those curious about the mysterious magical teachings of Kabbalah; and, for those who live with avid sports fans, and who want to understand why happenings on a playing field evokes such ecstasy and agony in those they love.